*****

I am pleased to present *Night Watch*, the first novel in my new mystery/suspense series featuring Em Ridge, a female boat delivery captain. This book has been in my "to write" list for many, many years. Six books ago this story was there, wanting to be launched, to get on paper. I didn't have the chance then. I have now.

My husband and I spend most of our summers aboard our 34' sailboat, aptly named *Mystery*. We cruise the waters in New Brunswick in eastern Canada and we always head down to Maine. We've met so many wonderful people on our travels including a number of female boat delivery captains. Their stories over glasses of "sun downers" are fascinating.

I love boats and being out on the water, but my husband will tell you that I'm not especially brave when it comes to storms. I turn into a bit of a scaredy cat when the engine fails and we're heading toward rocks. Em, however, my alter-ego, is not. She's brave and competent and strong and can out sail anyone around. She can climb down and fix the engine, and she's well used to repairing heads, propane lines, ripped sails and anything else that comes her way. It's fun for me to "be her" as I write these books.

I've set Book One near Portland, Maine. It resembles Portland, but I've done what authors do when they need landmarks that Mother Nature hasn't quite provided - they make them up. The tidal island of Chalk Spit does not exist on any map. I needed a place for Em to live and nothing in and around Portland, Maine quite suited. If Chalk Spit resembles anything, it would be Minister's Island, St. Andrews, New Brunswick - but with a high tide ferry.

Book Two in the series, *The Bitter End* should be out in the spring.

I'd love to hear from you. If you have any questions or comments, my contact information is at the end of this book.

Linda

Dedicated to pirates gone

Bob, Ron and Ed

Since 1915, all U.S. Merchant vessels over 100 gross tons have, by law, divided the crew into three watches, working four hours on and eight hours off, and turning the dog watches into one evening watch. The Lore of Ships *by AB Nordbok, Gothenberg, Sweden, 1975*

Chapter 1

I was in the middle of a Jesse dream when Kricket disappeared. It was the best Jesse dream I'd had in a long time, and I wanted to stay in that place forever.

We were sailing. We always sail, the two of us, in Jesse dreams. We were out in the middle of the bay on my old wooden catboat, the one I had before I knew Jesse, before he was such a part of my life. I sold that boat years ago to someone who trailered it to Lake Ontario. But dreams are like that, full of curiosities and strange chronologies, yet somehow making full sense at the time.

The wind was a steady ten knots, the sun warm on our necks. We moved effortlessly on the tops of the waves as if across silk. I leaned back, held the tiller with both hands and pressed my sandaled feet down onto the leeward side. The creaking of the pintles, the whoosh of the water beneath us, and the wind filling the sail were the only sounds. We didn't talk.

We don't talk in Jesse dreams.

Down, almost at water level, Jesse was winching the sail in tighter, tighter, one beat-up boat shoe braced against the bulkhead. I looked with longing at the curve of his bare ankle. I wanted to reach out, trace my fingers along its bone, cradle it against my cheek. It had been so long. Too long. Almost two years gone. Yet, in some ways, it will always be yesterday.

I wanted to call out to him, but have learned not to in Jesse dreams. If he turned to look at me, would I see the face with the sun-ruddied grin? The mussed hair always in need of a cut? Or would he stare at me with cold, unseeing eyes, face streaked with blood? Would it be a stranger's face even, which turned to gaze up at me?

Jesse dreams always hold a sharp edge of terror that leaves me breathless and gasping when I finally claw my way up toward waking. Yet, despite this, I crave them, hunger for them. I will take the horror—all of it—for one moment more with Jesse.

Em?

He was calling to me? He never speaks to me in Jesse dreams. I held my breath and watched the muscles in his forearms as he gripped the lines tightly, barely moving as the boat made its way toward ever-deeper water. He moved his foot, and I saw it on the bottom of the boat, wrinkled, wet, lying there—the postcard. I looked away as fear rose in my throat like bile.

Em? He was tapping at my foot, touching it. Over and over. Tap. Tap. Louder.

I tried to speak, could not.

"EM!"

I blinked, opened my eyes wide, and in an instant came fully awake in the half-light. I scrambled out of my berth, knocking my glasses to the sole as I did so.

"Wha-what?" I bent down, grabbed for them. No, I wasn't on a catboat with my dead husband. I was the delivery captain of *Blue Peace*, a fifty-two-foot luxury sailboat, and we were somewhere out in the Atlantic Ocean en route to Bermuda. It was night, and I was being shaken awake by a crew member. No one wakes a captain unless it's a Mayday-Batten-Down-The-Hatches-All-Hands-On-Deck-9-1-1 emergency.

I put on my glasses, tried to focus. Rob Stikles, one of my three crew members, was standing in front of me, opening and closing his mouth, Adam's apple bobbing. The boat moved unnaturally in the sea swells, and I grasped for a handhold.

"You turned the engine on," I said.

"Yeah, um…"

"The winds die? If you're on watch, Rob, you don't need to wake me up every time you have to turn on the engine. I presume you know how to pull in the sails and turn on the engine—"

"It's—it's—not that…"

"What then?" At eye level, we were exactly the same height.

"It's Kricket."

I sighed. He woke me for Kricket? "What? She forget to take her seasick pills again? Is she puking over the side at"—I glanced at the brass clock affixed to the teak bulkhead—"two thirty in the morning?"

I pulled a gray sweatshirt, one of Jesse's, over the T-shirt and sweats I wear when I sleep on boats. "Let me go talk to her." I moved determinedly into the main salon. Kricket would be there, I was sure, lying on a settee in a fetal position, clutching at her stomach and demanding that we turn this boat around right now—*right now*—and take her home.

Behind the nav station, Joan, my chief navigator, was sleeping soundly, only the tiniest scruff of gray hair peeking out from under her thick woolen Hudson Bay blanket. I switched on one of the overhead lights, and the salon glowed eerie red. To maintain our night vision, we use only red LEDs down below after sunset. The light made Rob's face look ghostly, and it reminded me of tenting trips with my two younger sisters and holding the flashlight under my chin and growling at them, and them screaming and holding on to each other until our parents demanded that we all go back to sleep.

"Where is she, then?" I made my way toward the stern and to Kricket's aft stateroom.

Rob followed me. "She's not seasick. She's um, she's gone." He wailed this out, face flushed. His hands would not be still. His fingers kept crawling up the sides of his squall jacket like crabs. Joan stirred slightly.

Gone? What did he mean? Gone, as in dead? But, no one dies of being seasick. I pressed my palm into my forehead to get rid of the last remnants of Jesse. "Rob," I said, quietly now and trying to muster a certain amount of command to my voice. "Where is she? Where is Kricket?"

"That's just it. I don't know. Well, not for sure. She's…" He paused. "She's not on the boat." He stopped.

I raced up the companionway and out into the icy air which ripped at once through my sweatshirt. "Where is she?" I looked frantically around me but all I saw was black ocean. "She fell off the boat? Is that what you're saying? How did this happen?" I studied the chart plotter.

"Yes." He was behind me and shivering.

"Did you hit the Man Overboard button?"

"The what?"

"On the GPS." I turned and looked him straight in the eyes. "When you saw she went overboard, did you at least hit the Man Overboard button?" Even though I tried to keep my voice even, it was painfully strident at the end of all my words.

"I don't—No. I thought maybe she went down below. So, I didn't. No." His teeth were actually chattering.

The boat made a sideways lunge as we plunged through a sea swell. I grabbed the edge of the binnacle. Carefully studying our track on the chart plotter, I wrenched the wheel around. We would retrace our track. Maybe, just maybe we would be lucky. Once I had again engaged the autopilot, I raced down through the companionway. Rob followed.

"Joan! Peter!" I yelled. "Man overboard! We need you! We need everyone."

Rob slumped down onto a settee and put his head in his hands. I didn't have time to evaluate whether he was crying or not. I didn't know Rob. My other two crew members, Joan Bush and Peter Mauer, were almost family to me. Joan has always been like my wiser, older aunt. She and her husband, Art, were closer to me than my own family after Jesse died. Peter, cook extraordinaire, is like my hunky little brother. I'd known Peter forever. I first met him when I was in high school and taught sailing as a summer job. He was the brightest and smartest little kid in my class of ten-year-olds. I connected with him again when he was a cook on Windjammer cruises, where I crewed for two summers. He'd gone to chef school for a year, but then dropped out to work on boats. We'd been buddies ever since.

We hadn't needed a fourth crew member, yet Peter asked to have Rob come along. His friend was trying to build up his sailing résumé and needed more blue-water experience, he told me.

Yet, after less than a week on the water, I seriously doubted whether Rob had ever been on any kind of boat before. Something as easy as tying a bowline or a simple clove hitch had him fumbling all his fingers. And why had he not thought of hitting the MOB button? There was something else, too, something I couldn't quite put my finger on. He seemed very familiar to me, like I should know him from some place. And it wasn't a good memory.

On top of that, it was clear that there was no love lost between Peter and Rob.

Then there was Kricket. She was the owner's daughter and had come aboard her father's yacht with great reluctance. I'd been told that her father ruled his family like he ruled his corporations and felt his wild daughter needed a bit of an "outward bound" experience.

"And put her to work," Roy Patterson had told me on the phone. "I'm going to be asking you if she pulled her weight."

That little part of the equation had proved difficult, if not impossible.

"What's going on?" Joan sat up now and ran her fingers through her hair. A few strands of it were sticking up at the back. None of us looked our best this time in the morning.

"Kricket's missing," I said. "Possibly overboard."

"What! How? Was she wearing her PFD?" Joan quickly pulled a long-sleeved shirt over her slim frame. I frowned. We had not yet reached the Gulf Stream, where the water suddenly warmed. If Kricket had gone into the frigid Gulf of Maine water, it would be unlikely she would survive, personal flotation device notwithstanding.

"Yes." This came from Rob.

I turned to face him.

"She was wearing her PFD," he said.

"That's something, anyway," I said.

Peter was by now entering the main cabin in sweats and a Mount Gay Rum T-shirt that showed off his biceps. He ran a hand across his unshaven face.

"What's up?" he asked.

"It's Kricket," I said. "We think she's overboard."

A look passed between Peter and Rob, a look I didn't have time, at this point, to evaluate. I grabbed my yellow squall jacket from the hook at the bottom of the companionway and my PFD, stepped into my sea boots and headed topside. Too much time had passed with no one at the helm. Even on autopilot, a careful eye needed to be kept for stray containers from ships and other floating debris.

Joan followed. The wind on this night held a bitter edge and sliced into my face like a sea urchin's spines. In all directions, the ocean was a molten gray of constant movement. It wasn't white-capping, but the swells were high. It caught at me, as it always does, that here we are, a mere speck of flotsam on a huge indifferent sea. I tugged the hood of my jacket up over my head and pulled the elastic toggles tight under my chin, wishing I'd remembered my wool toque. Next time I went down below, I'd get it, along with my gloves.

I tried to collect my thoughts as I followed our jagged line backtracking on the chart plotter. I increased the RPMs and let out a bit of jib to steady us. I tried to remain calm, but I kept swallowing. My cold hands shook. The boat was pitching and yawing in the waves, and I fought back a flutter of nausea. Even in the calmest of weather, the sea is never still. It moves back and forth and sideways, a motion that experienced sailors get used to. It's called "getting your sea legs." But right now all I was feeling was sick.

"Em," Joan said behind me. "Why don't you and I give this boat a thorough going over? There are lots of places where she could be curled up sleeping, cubbyholes and things. Peter and Rob can watch."

Her idea gave me hope. It would be a good idea to exhaust all possibilities before I called a Mayday.

The opulent interior of this custom-built Morris sailboat included two staterooms with their own heads, plus a crew cabin consisting of two bunk-like berths. There were many places where Kricket could be even now. Joan and I went into her stateroom. Because Kricket was the owner's daughter, she got the best room, the aft cabin with its queen-size bed and private head. As captain on this trip, that room should have been mine, but I took the second-best bed, the one on the forward starboard side.

This was the first time I'd been in her room since we left Canada, and I stood in the doorway. If I didn't know better, I would have thought that someone had come in here and trashed the place. Shirts, jeans, sandals, bikini tops and bottoms, and bottles of this and that hair product and makeup looked as if they had been cast here and there in no particular order. Her phone lay across her unmade bed, its earbuds trailing across the mound of clothes like worms. Her Louis Vuitton suitcase was open and heaped with clothes—scarves, sundresses, tank tops, shorts and more.

I rooted through the pile of clothes on her bed. She wasn't underneath. I opened the door to her private head. This was a girl, I realized, who was not used to having to pick up after herself. A cylindrical bottle of designer shampoo rolled back and forth across the sole in rhythm with the sea. I picked it up and put it in the sink.

A feeling of raw fear began to gnaw at my insides. This was my first captaining job after getting my Coast Guard captain's license, and Kricket had to be okay. She had to be. I promised Roy Patterson that I'd take good care of his daughter. Back out in her stateroom, I opened the door to her hanging locker. This is where most sailors keep jackets, fleeces, woolies and foul-weather gear. Not Kricket. Her locker was hung up with pretty summer dresses. Clearly, she was looking forward to party time in the Caribbean. Without speaking, Joan and I went through all of her cupboards and cubbyholes before we left that room to search through the remainder of the boat.

After we had exhausted every locker, every cubbyhole, every closet, every closed and open space on the entire boat, I, Captain Emmeline Ridge had to concede that the absolute worst had happened. We were out in the middle of the ocean, a day from landfall and Katherine "Kricket" Patterson, the daughter of the very rich owner of this magnificent yacht, who'd given me my first-ever captaining job, had truly gone overboard.

I made my way to the nav station. With shaky fingers, I picked up the mic on the SSB radio.

I said clearly and distinctly and slowly, "Mayday, Mayday, Mayday. This is *Blue Peace*, *Blue Peace*, *Blue Peace*. We have a man overboard and missing. Repeat, we have a man overboard and missing. We are at latitude—"

Chapter 2

Morning was beginning to break over the sea above us, and shafts of pale gray gave an otherworldly quality to the light throughout the cabin. Down below at the nav table, I rested my forehead in one hand and held the satellite phone in the other. How do you tell a billionaire boat owner that his daughter is missing and feared overboard? How do you tell any parent that their child is probably dead?

The rest of the crew was up on deck. Peter and Rob were arguing in low tones, while Joan seemed to be trying to soothe frayed spirits. I couldn't catch specific words, and at this point I didn't care. Wispy smoke trails from Rob's cigarette wafted down toward me. I needed to make this phone call. That was first. Then I would go up and ream him out for smoking. Again.

I took a breath. Right now Roy Patterson would probably be asleep, his wife, Elaine, beside him in bed, neither realizing that they were about to receive the phone call that would forever change their lives. I exhaled and punched in the number. The phone was answered on the third ring by a tired-sounding female.

"Mrs. Patterson?"

"Yes?"

"This is Captain Emmeline Ridge aboard *Blue Peace*. May I speak with your husband, please?"

His first words were, "Something wrong with the boat?"

"No. It's your daughter, sir. I'm afraid she's gone missing. We fear she may have gone overboard. We're combing the area where this may have happened. She was wearing her PFD, so there's a good chance we may find her. I've contacted the Coast Guard, and they're sending a fast rescue boat. They promised aircraft at first light. We're still about a day away from the nearest landfall in Maine, which would be Portland."

There was a moment's silence. Then his measured words, "How on God's green earth did you let this happen?"

I swallowed. As captain, I knew all too well that the buck stopped with me. If I had doubted Rob's ability to stand watch, I shouldn't have let him. I said, "We're not sure, sir. She was talking with my crew member at the stern of the boat, and then in the next moment she was gone. He thought she had come down below—"

I knew how full of excuses and holes this story was. Patterson would demand answers. There would be an inquest.

When my husband's kayak was sawn in half in the middle of the night by two kids out on their uncle's lobster boat, who thought they'd merely "run over a log," I needed answers. I wanted to know exact timelines, precise moments. I needed to mark in my mind the instant he died. Later, I paddled to the location where it happened and threw flowers in the water, but it wasn't enough. I could know every detail, every breath taken, every last word spoken and it would never be enough. It wasn't for me. It would not be for them.

"Could she have met up with someone? I know she balked at going," Patterson suggested.

"There's always a chance," I said. We had certainly thought of this, even though it was extremely unlikely that a boat could have come alongside *Blue Peace* without one of us hearing something.

In the end he said that he would be dispatching one of his planes, as well.

"That would be good, sir."

"And Captain Ridge?"

"Yes, sir?"

"You better find her. You damn well better find her."

I clutched the edge of the nav table tightly with one hand. "I'll do my best, sir."

"You do more than your best."

Joan came down below while the phone was still in my hand. "I know it's a stupid question," she said. "But have we checked to see that the life raft is here?"

"I did," I said. "It's here."

"The inflatable?"

"Accounted for."

Joan blew out a breath. "I was just thinking—" She paused. "The girl seemed so interested in the nav instruments. Do you remember?"

I did. Yesterday morning I'd wandered out of my cabin after a nap and had come upon Joan and Kricket in deep conversation about the radios, the GPS, the charts. I'd leaned against the companionway with my mug of coffee and watched curiously as Joan patiently showed

Kricket how to plot a course on a paper chart using parallel rulers and the compass rose.

"Even though we have all this new electronic equipment," Joan quietly explained, "it's imperative that a good sailor know how to plot a course the old-fashioned way, with charts and the stars and a good sextant. Electronics have been known to fail at the worst possible moments."

Kricket had eagerly asked, "Can you show me?"

I thought about that now. Had the girl been planning some sort of escape? A fast, quiet boat with her aboard could already be in Maine. I poured coffee into my insulated mug.

"I'm going up," I said.

Soon we were all sitting outside in the cockpit and back to the approximate place where Rob thought she may have gone over. Carefully marking this out on the chart plotter, we began moving in ever-larger search circles. No one spoke. No one. Peter, Joan and I scanned the gray horizon with binoculars while Rob sat at the stern, staring down at his big, dirty, wet sneakers. The only sound was the steady drone of the engine and the rhythmic whoosh of water as it passed beneath us.

I said to Rob, "You sure you didn't hear or see any other boats?"

"I don't think so."

"Think again. This is important. You need to be absolutely sure."

"I keep going over it. I don't think so. I would have heard a boat, I think. But, maybe."

"Oh, you don't know, but maybe?" I tried to keep the snarkiness out of my voice.

"Let's just keep looking, shall we?" Joan said.

Crew overboard maneuvers are standard on all vessels, but they are as about as effective as life jackets on a 747, even though air passengers have to patiently listen to the instructions of the flight attendants. Most sailors concede that man overboard means a dead person.

"She could still be alive," Rob said after a while. His words came out pinched and strained. "I saw this thing on the Discovery Channel? There was this guy who fell off a cruise ship? He floated around for two days. They showed that on TV. Then they found him—"

"Rob," I snapped. I was going to add "shut up" to that sentence, but thought better of it. Instead, I said, "This isn't helping."

We needed to be a team. I needed to remain in control. I took a drink of my coffee. When it hit my stomach, it didn't feel right. I placed my thermos on the seat beside me. Despite my brand new winter sailing gloves purchased especially for this trip, my hands were cold. I held them between my knees for a minute.

Joan said, "If she's out there we should see the strobe."

All of the life jackets aboard *Blue Peace* were equipped with strobe lights that automatically activate when they hit the water. I was having doubts that we'd even be able to see any sort of strobe, though, with these swells.

The full morning sun was breaking on the horizon when Joan stood up, her binoculars to her eyes. "I see something," she said. "Up ahead. Twenty degrees port."

Peter scrambled to turn his own binoculars in that direction. "What? Where?"

She pointed. "Over there. Way out there. A light. No, it's gone now. Wait, there it is."

I saw it, too, a flash of light as the boat rose on a swell then disappearing as we settled into a hollow. I took the helm and aimed toward it. I prayed for a miracle.

As we neared the spot of light, there was no doubt that this was the strobe light from Kricket's life jacket. And as we got closer to the light, I knew that the orange mound was Kricket.

When I first saw her, I held out a moment's hope that she was alive. She appeared to be moving, her head up, her arms outstretched and floundering back and forth at her sides. My hopes were dashed when I realized that the hands were moving in rhythm to the waves. My stomach continued to clench as we got closer. The girl was face up, head back in the water, eyes open, mouth open. Her face was bloated and white, and it looked so unlike Kricket that at first I had this irrational thought that somehow we'd gotten the wrong person— as if random bodies float out here willy-nilly.

In all my years of sailing, I have never retrieved an unconscious body from the ocean. I've done more practice maneuvers than I can count, but nothing prepares you for the real thing.

"Okay," I said. "Let's get her on board. Let's do this."

Rob went and threw up over the side of the boat.

"Rob!" I commanded. "All of us. Damn it. It'll take all of us to do this!"

He nodded forlornly, wiped his mouth and said, "This whole thing was my fault. It was on my watch."

It's not your fault, I thought. This is something I will carry with me for the rest of my life.

"Harnesses everyone," I said. "Joan and I will bring her on board from the stern. Rob! Don't just stand there! We're going to need you on the winch. Peter, you take the helm and follow my every instruction."

I was freezing right through to my skin with the kind of damp, salty cold that you only get on the ocean. Yet an unexpected surge of adrenaline was making me suddenly warm. I found a length of strong line and tied a snap shackle to one end.

Kricket was about ten feet astern us. I didn't want to look at her, tried not to, but I couldn't keep myself from staring at her wet, white face. Pale strings of hair fanned out from her head and floated gracefully in the water beside her. She looked like some strange and curious goddess of the sea.

"Peter! Get the end of this line on a winch."

He did.

Joan and I climbed down onto the sugar scoop, which extended from the back. On a high swell, Kricket bobbed against the back of the boat. Joan held me as I bent over the ocean, trying to clasp the snap shackle into the rings in her PFD. I missed and nearly fell into the water. "Crap!" I yelled. "Double crap," I yelled louder.

Kricket drifted away from us. We caught our breath and waited. On the next swell, she came toward us, almost as if she were doing the backstroke. I reached for her. Again, the elusive Lorelei swam away. It was white-capping now, and the swells were just too strong, too high.

"Peter, keep the boat even," I called.

"I'm doing the best I can!"

I yelled, "Where is that bloody wind coming from all of a sudden? Peter, back up slowly, very slowly, dead slow, and when I say, flip it into neutral."

I thought I heard sobbing from Rob's corner.

I was trying to keep my teeth from chattering. Another sea swell, and Kricket again came within bobbing distance of us. I reached for her again. Missed.

Why was this so friggin' difficult? Peter flipped the engine into neutral, and the body floated toward us. Joan held tightly to the back of my PFD. I leaned into the water and snapped the shackle into Kricket's PFD. A cold wave washed over the swim platform, and seawater soaked us to our knees.

"Okay," I said. "We got her. Rob, get over here, and let's winch her up."

This is something else that looks relatively easy in training videos, but it's actually incredibly difficult to bring a lifeless person onto a boat, even someone as light as Kricket. As best I could, I grabbed her shoulders and the wet life jacket while Joan took hold of her ankles. Peter had wound the line on a port winch and was winding her up. Finally, she was level with the stern of the cockpit.

We winched, and hauled, winched and hauled, inch by inch. It was like lugging up a dead fish, something with all the parts of a human, yet not. I didn't want to look at the way her legs splayed out.

A few minutes later we had her lying on the floor of the cockpit, one leg skewed to the side, eyes open, head lolling. I took a few breaths and tried to calm the deep shivering that came from somewhere inside my very core.

Peter made a fist and punched the bulkhead. I sat down for a moment to catch my breath, while the accusing eyes of Kricket Patterson stared at me.

Joan went down below and came back up with a large towel, one of her own. She knelt down beside the girl and dried her face, closing the eyes with the towel as she did so. She arranged her hair around her face and smoothed away bits and pieces of debris. She removed the life jacket and wrapped her up in the large towel.

"What are we going to do with her?" Rob wailed. "We can't just leave her there!"

"Shut up, Rob." This came from Peter. "Just shut the hell up!"

"Peter!" I cautioned. As captain, I had to run a tight ship. On a small boat out in the middle of the ocean, tempers can't be allowed to flare. A person can't simply go for a hike up a mountain trail to let off a bit of steam.

Joan's voice was mothering and calm when she said, "We're going to take her down below and put her on her berth."

I nodded numbly. If I'd been thinking straight, I would have said no. Every time we touched her, we were fouling precious forensic evidence. When she was sufficiently wrapped up, Peter, Joan and I carried her down the steps of the companionway and into her cabin. We didn't even ask Rob to help. I stifled a sob as we moved the mounds of her clothing from the bed and laid her down on top of her bedding. Then, Joan placed a blanket over her. It was like we were tucking in a small child for the night. We didn't cover her face.

Then, shaking, shivering and drenched with salt cold, I went into the main salon and picked up the satellite phone.

"Mr. Patterson," I began. "I'm so sorry to have to tell you—"

Chapter 3

"Joan?" I stood curiously at the entrance to Kricket's stateroom, one hand on the doorframe. I didn't think anyone would want to go into the room where she lay, much less go through her things, but this is what Joan appeared to be doing. Her back was to me and she was humming. I watched her. She had taken one of Kricket's sundresses and was holding it up. She checked the pockets, folded it, smoothed it and placed it at the bottom of her suitcase.

It had been half an hour since I'd spoken with the angry and confused Pattersons. The Coast Guard boat was on its way. All we had to do now was wait. I'd come down to get out of my wet things and into some dry. That's when I'd seen Kricket's open door and Joan inside, humming away.

I kept watching. I should be in there with Joan. I should be looking for that postcard. Was that what Joan was doing? No. The postcard had nothing to do with Joan.

And everything to do with me. And Jesse.

The first inkling of my suspicion had hit me yesterday just after we'd motored out of Head Harbor at four in the morning. We'd left early to catch the high tide to head down the Grand Manan channel and then out and down toward Bermuda. I was at the helm because I know these waters like the back of my hand. Everyone else was asleep, but I didn't mind. I like the very early mornings and time alone. About an hour later I engaged the autopilot and went down to use the head and to maybe get myself a coffee. Peter made coffee all day long and transferred it to several thermoses. There was always hot coffee for crew on watch, no matter what time of day or night it was.

On my way out of the head, I saw that the door to Rob and Peter's cabin was ajar. Both of them were asleep, their backs to the door. In the corner, hidden from view of their berths, Kricket was going through Rob's backpack.

I stood in the doorway for several seconds, before I said, "Kricket, what are you doing?"

"Nothing." She quickly closed the backpack and stood to full height.

"Isn't that Rob's?" I asked. I was talking in a normal, conversational tone, hoping that Rob would wake up. He didn't.

She said, "I'm just getting something."

She shoved past me, and I could see that she was holding an ordinary postcard. "That card?" I asked.

"It's mine."

"And you got it from Rob's backpack?"

She nodded.

Without really thinking, I grabbed it from her. "I'm sure Rob will be very happy to get it back. Whatever this is."

I looked down at the thing in my hand. It was a postcard of a painting, like the kind of card you might purchase in an art museum gift store. It was of a farm, a barn and silo, the colors muted and indistinct. I turned it over.

When I saw what was on the other side, I gasped. A phone number was scrawled in pencil across the back of it, a number that I had called many, many times, texted numerous times per day, often simply to say, "I love you."

The phone number had belonged to Jesse, my dead husband.

She snatched the card from me so quickly that I wondered if I had really seen his number. I'd been having so many Jesse dreams lately that I could have been wrong. She raced into her stateroom. "I need to see that again," I called after her, but she was gone, her door locked.

I knocked. "Kricket, I need to see that."

She hadn't answered me.

All day I'd tried to find an excuse to go into her room to look for it. Never found one.

In the evening, she had come to me. "Em? Can I talk to you about something? It's really important."

She'd never called me Em. She had never spoken in that quiet, serious tone. So far it had been "Captain." Sometimes she would put her two fingers to her forehead in a mock salute and say, "Aye, aye, Captain."

"Yes," I said. "Certainly."

But then Rob had called her, and the two went outside.

"We'll talk later," I'd said to her.

"Aye, aye, Captain."

She'd died before "later" ever came. These thoughts made me

momentarily close my eyes and lean against the doorway to Kricket's room.

Joan picked up Kricket's phone, glanced at it briefly, then wound the earbuds around it and shoved it down the side of the suitcase.

Something about Joan's movements bothered me. She was stiff and determined, frowning into her task, wiping her eyes every so often. And there was that tuneless humming.

"Joan. Hey," I said, finally deciding to speak.

"Oh!" She jumped. "Em, I didn't see you." Her eyes were bright, wet and ringed with red. I thought back to the times when I had seen her and Kricket poring over charts. So close, they seemed.

"What are you doing?" I asked.

She looked at me and then at the girl on the bed. "I can't believe it." She shook her head. "I can't believe she's dead. I came in here because of the head smell, and then I just decided that maybe I should put some of her things away, you know, straighten up a bit. When the Coast Guard gets here, they're going to want to take her things. I just thought I should help. It's the least I can do for her parents."

But I was stuck on the first part of her sentence. *Head smell?* "What head smell?" I asked.

"You haven't noticed? Whenever I'm in the head, I get this faint whiff. I wanted to see if it was as strong in here. I'd asked Kricket if she'd noticed it in her head, and she said no."

"Really?"

Joan had lined up all of Kricket's sandals neatly on the floor in front of her suitcase. Old boats smell of teak and mold mixed with lemon oil and old holding tanks. By contrast, this luxury boat smelled clean and dry.

She folded up a T-shirt and put it in Kricket's suitcase. "It could be just me then." She paused, looked toward the girl and then at me. "How much time do we have before the Coast Guard gets here?"

"Couple hours, I think."

She nodded, went back to her task.

I paused before I said, "Have you, um, found anything?"

She gave me a quizzical look. "Like what?"

"Never mind," I said. "I'm not sure what I'm asking."

She went back to her task. "What's going to happen when the Coast Guard get here? Will you be going with them? Did they tell you?"

"I have no idea," I said.

At our present speed of seven knots, it would take us a good fourteen hours to deliver *Blue Peace* to Portland, Maine. The Coast Guard vessel was coming toward us at more than six times our speed.

I looked at the girl again and was suddenly anxious to be out of the room. "Joan? Why don't we go on up? Just leave all this."

She looked up at me. "I'm not done here. I really should clean up. I don't mind. It's the least I can do. You go on up. I'll be fine."

"I'll help you then," I said.

She looked at me for a long moment. I was getting the feeling that she didn't want me in there. Or was it my imagination? I went into the head to pack up her toiletries. I didn't smell anything. I yelled this out to Joan.

In time, we were finished. All of her clothes were put away, her dresses taken off the hangers and folded up. Her bathing suit tops and bottoms put away, her makeup in her makeup case.

I went up on deck in time to hear Rob say to Peter, "Yeah, well, maybe I *did* fall asleep."

I stood in the entrance to the companionway and stared at the two of them.

"So"—this came from Peter, who kept making fists in his lap—"you fell asleep. The big famous sailor falls asleep."

Rob was sitting under the dodger, his back scrunched against the bulkhead, hugging his knees, his head down.

I checked our heading and then sat next to him. "You fell asleep? Is that what I heard? While you were on watch? When Kricket went overboard? You were *asleep?*"

A pause.

"Rob? Answer me."

He looked up, "It's sort of a blur. It was so, um, so dark, and it was like five minutes later, and I sort of looked up and didn't know where the last five minutes went. I don't know for sure. And then she was, um, gone."

"So"—I felt my voice rising—"that whole story you told me before. You just made that all up?

He wiped his red nose on the sleeve of his jacket and stared at me. I blinked. There had been so many times during the past few days when he had looked at me like this, in a way that made me feel uncomfortable. It was almost as if he knew me from somewhere, and was taunting me. I shook off the feeling.

He said, "No. That really happened. We were talking. But then after. For a bit. Just for a second. But I never would've hurt Kricket. Never! We were friends." His voice broke, and he paused and looked down at his feet. "We were friends."

Peter got up, walked over and stood in front of Rob and glared down at him. "You idiot! I don't even know you!" He reached down, grabbed Rob by the collar, and pulled him roughly to his feet. "Go back to your friggin' farm!" Peter said.

I intervened, grabbing the back of Peter's jacket just before his fist made contact with Rob's face. "Stop it, Peter!" I yelled. "Stop this now! What do I have to do, separate you two? Put you in time-outs?"

Peter dropped his hands and stormed off down through the companionway. I could hear the rough slamming of doors, the noisy shutting of cupboards, the sounds of pots and dishes. I called down loudly, "We all need to be together in this, Peter, and that includes you. We will have no more blame, foul language or fistfights. All of us—I repeat, all of us, even if we won't admit it—know that we have fallen asleep one time or another. It's what happens. It was an accident. When the Coast Guard meets us out here, we all have to remain in control. You hear me? No more! It was an accident!"

"Get our stories straight, you mean?" Peter called up.

"No. There are no stories to get straight. There is the truth, and that's what we will tell."

"Yeah, yeah," grumbled Peter. "The truth. You tell 'em your truth then, Captain. I'm sure they'd like to hear *your* truth."

"Peter!" I wanted to go down, grab him by the shirt collar, demand that he tell me what the hell he was talking about. But I didn't. I sat down. No one said a word. Joan was looking down at her hands folded on her lap. Back underneath the dodger, Rob was breathing heavily, almost panting. What did Peter think he knew? Was this about Jesse? No. Jesse was not a part of this. I closed my eyes.

"Em," Joan said, quietly so that only I could hear. "It'll be okay."

This was not remotely true. Joan and I had been through hurricanes together, rogue waves, ripped sails and engines that conked out in the middle of the ocean, thunder and lightning, waterspouts out on the sea, broken bones, sprained ankles, cracked teeth and lots and lots and lots of seasickness, but nothing ever like this before. Ever.

Joan was still talking. "And when we get to Portland, after, well, after what happens, you are welcome to stay at my place, Em, and that includes all of us here. Peter," she called down through the companionway, "you and Rob, too. For as long as we all need to.

You're invited to stay at my house."

"Thank you, Joan," I breathed.

I live around a half hour from Portland on a spit of land called Chalk Spit Island, which is connected to the mainland by a tidal road. Only during low tide can you drive there. During high tide, you can take a private ramshackle ferry that sometimes runs and sometimes doesn't.

I would stay with Joan tonight, I decided. I often did. My little house at the end of the road would be too lonely and dark on a night like tonight. The place I lived was Jesse's family's summer cottage. Jesse and I had been in the process of winterizing it when he died. I lived there now, and I hadn't done anything to it since. It was pretty cold in the winter.

I thought about all of that. I thought about my aging golden lab, Rusty, Jesse's dog. I thought about my friends, my old gentleman neighbor, EJ, who tutored me through my ham-radio license and who was looking after Rusty. I thought about the loudmouthed elderly sisters, Isabelle and Dot, who lived two houses away on the other side, the "bickering sisters," EJ called them. I thought about my friends Jeff and Valerie and their fourteen-year-old son, Liam, who lived down the way and kept four hundred lobster traps. The seven of us were practically the only winter residents on that little bay which was dotted with summer cottages and cabins.

And then there were numerous sailing friends all over the world. What would they think of this accident? I was quite sure that to my face everyone would be helpful and supportive, but what would they say behind my back? I knew well how the sailing community, for all its appearance of friendliness and hardy work ethic, could sometimes be a back-stabbing place, full of its own brand of politics.

And my family, what would they say? I cringed a little when I thought about them. My sisters wouldn't say it, not in so many words, but their attitude would be, "I told you so."

"Rob?" Joan's voice was soothing. "I don't know where you live or too much about you, actually, but you can stay with my husband and me. We have three full floors of bedrooms. We have rooms we never even use. It's crazy for us to have such a big place, but we do, and you're welcome to stay."

Rob nodded miserably.

Two weeks ago I had gotten the call from billionaire Roy Patterson's assistant asking if I was available to deliver *Blue Peace*, a fifty-two-foot sailboat, from Fredericton, New Brunswick, Canada, to Hamilton, Bermuda, for a few days of provisioning and then on down to Nassau in the Bahamas. He had spent the summer on his boat in the St. John River system in the province of New Brunswick, and wanted to spend the winter in the Bahamas.

It took me about half a second to say yes, hoping that my salivating wasn't noticeable over the phone. A Morris 52! Under my command! My first-ever job as a boat captain, and I hit the big time!

"Yes, yes, YES!" I punched my fist into the air after I hung up. Then I texted my sailing buddies. I hugged Rusty. I went and told EJ. I jogged over to tell Dot and Isabelle. Finally, back on my front porch, I did the Snoopy Dance, and I didn't care who was watching.

A little while later, Patterson himself (himself!) had called to tell me that his daughter Kricket would be coming as well. He seemed nice enough on the phone, rather more down-to-earth than I'd expected. Being naturally curious, I'd looked up the reclusive Roy Patterson online and uncovered not a lot of information about him. The few pictures I found of his family were grainy and indistinct. Roy Patterson was certainly no flamboyant Donald Trump and Kricket no Paris Hilton. I learned that he was extremely protective of his wife, Elaine, and daughter. Katherine, or "Kricket," as she was called, was his only child.

His only child.

I learned that Patterson collected art and vintage cars. Apparently, he had rooms full of paintings and a barn-sized garage full of old cars. I learned that the Pattersons had homes in Boston, Miami and Las Cruces, New Mexico where he had an art museum.

A week ago I'd driven into Portland, left my car in Joan's driveway, then rented a car—all expenses paid—and drove up to Fredericton, where I met with Patterson's assistant. She turned out to be a no-nonsense woman with blunt-cut brown hair and black glasses so big and thick that they looked like the glasses you get when you go to 3-D movies. She escorted me to the Fredericton Yacht Club's work yard. *Blue Peace* was anchored just up river, and the inflatable was tied at the dock. We zipped out to the boat, where she gave me a tour of the most spectacular boat I'd ever been inside.

After I was settled by myself aboard *Blue Peace*, I did something rather undignified. I danced around the main salon singing *Margaritaville* at the top of my lungs. In two days, Peter, Rob, Joan and Kricket would be boarding, but for now, this whole little empire was mine, mine, mine.

In the evening, I sat down at the nav station in the comfortable leather chair (leather!) and took note of all the gizmos. There were two VHF radios, a single sideband radio, as well as a full ham radio outfit, satellite phone, TV and satellite Internet. Imagine! A boat with its own Wifi way out in the ocean!

Life jackets were equipped with strobe lights, the sails were all brand new, made of Kevlar and electronically controlled. The life raft had a week's worth of food and water. The wine glasses were made of crystal, and even the paintings on the bulkheads were originals. If I knew anything about art, which I didn't, I probably would've recognized them as being famous.

I had two days of provisioning and checking all the systems, not that they needed checking. I kept the rental car as per Patterson's instructions, because I made many trips in and around Fredericton for supplies.

My first night alone on the boat, I poured myself some wine, got out the paper charts, checked the GPS, and drew up a route that I easily transferred to the electronic chart plotter. We'd leave Fredericton in the morning and then overnight in Saint John while we waited for slack water at the Reversing Falls. We'd then catch the ebb tide, which would give us a boost through the Bay of Fundy for much of six hours before it came back at us.

The Bay of Fundy has the highest tides in the world, sometimes as high as thirty feet, and with that come some of the strongest tidal currents anywhere. I have sailed through all of them. I like to tell people that I have sailed right smack next to Old Sow, the largest whirlpool in the Western Hemisphere. My Canadian husband grew up near these waters. We met sailing here and we've sailed these waters together so many times I can't count them all.

Knowing *Blue Peace* would need a place to hole up until the change of tide, I decided on Head Harbor on Campobello Island instead of St. Andrews. St. Andrews has a certain appeal, and I wanted to make sure my crew stayed on the boat and sober. I promised Roy Patterson I would keep an eye on Kricket. We had no need to clear U.S. Customs at Eastport, Maine, because from New Brunswick, we would be making a straight shot to Bermuda.

I'd had two days in Fredericton, two days of lounging and watching a gazillion movies on satellite TV, TiVo-ing every program I would ever want to watch on the trip, surfing the Web, checking my email a gazillion times and texting my sailing buddies. "Hey, you'll never guess where I am right now—"

The day before we were to leave, Joan's husband, Art, drove Joan up from their home in Maine, and Peter and Rob came together by bus. Kricket was the last to come, and she arrived early on the morning of the day we were scheduled to leave.

I wasn't sure how I expected her to show up. In a chauffeur-driven limousine, perhaps? But, shortly after seven, a lone figure came traipsing toward us down the wharf in the cool dawn. An ordinary taxi had driven her in. She wore skinny jeans and a pair of high-heeled sandals that probably cost twice as much as my own little sailboat at home.

Her huge wheeled suitcase click-clacked behind her on the rough stones leading down to the wooden dock. Airline luggage is never a good idea on a boat. I looked at her and thought wryly that I would much rather be crewing in the Louis Vuitton Sailing Cup than tripping over a Louis Vuitton suitcase the entire trip.

And then there was Rob. From the moment he'd laid eyes on that girl, he couldn't keep them off her. Kricket handed her suitcase to Rob and said, "I have to tell you right off, Daddy's making me come. I don't want to be here."

Rob took her things and headed down to her stateroom as if he were her personal servant, which he mostly ended up being. According to her father, Kricket was supposed to "pull her weight," yet the first night in Saint John, I put Kricket on pot-washing duty. She turned up her nose, raised her manicured nails and said, "Eww." I had to look around to make sure there were no cameras filming an episode of some new reality spinoff of *The Simple Life*.

After that, she and I mostly butted heads. I would ask her to do something, and she'd get Rob to do it. It was always Rob who did her bidding. When she would ask Peter—and she did try—he would tell her to do it herself. He seemed inured to her charms, which both gratified and somewhat surprised me.

Then there was the seasickness. We were barely out on the river when she started complaining of a stomachache. If she was feeling queasy on the flat river, what would she be like out in the real sea swells?

She would close her eyes, double over, clutch at her stomach and then excuse herself and run to her stateroom. Within a few minutes, she'd be back in the main salon telling us that she'd just puked her guts out. The seasick pills I gave her didn't seem to help much.

Rule one of sailing: If you're going to throw up, do it over the side of the boat. Don't fill up the holding tank. I had told her this, but she didn't heed my advice, which led me to believe that she hadn't really been all that sick.

The approaching boat began as a distant buzz, like a bee, and got steadily louder as it neared us. The four of us grew silent while we waited.

Ten minutes later, the Coast Guard boat appeared out of the fog. I was horrified to see Roy Patterson and his wife standing on either side of the stern, bundled up and looking like two refugees in a storm. I had understood from the Coast Guard that they would be waiting in Portland. Their apartness bewildered me. I would expect them to be huddling together, not on either side of the stern and looking away from each other.

Joan, Peter and Rob secured the lines and fenders, while I stayed at the wheel and barked out orders like an automaton while the Coast Guard attempted to raft up alongside. Three members of the Coast Guard boarded *Blue Peace*, followed by a man in a nylon jacket and what looked like rather thin khaki pants for way out here on the ocean. I took an instant dislike to him when he climbed up onto the foredeck, stood in front of Peter and said, "You're Captain Ridge, I presume? I'm Detective Dunlinson from the Portland City Police."

Peter, who had just caught a spring line that had been thrown to him by a guy on the Coast Guard boat, simply stared at him. Finally, he said something I didn't hear and pointed to me. If I hadn't been so upset, I would have found the whole thing rather amusing.

Mr. Khaki Pants came down into the cockpit of the boat and faced me. I had never seen this man before, and I know a lot of the Portland police. He must be new, I decided.

"Captain Ridge," he said.

"Yes," I said. "Believe it or not, girls can be captains."

When he didn't smile, I felt instantly stupid for making a joke under these circumstances. I watched as he pulled out a small notebook from the inside of his nylon jacket. Any conversation we may have had was interrupted by the Pattersons, who were climbing aboard *Blue Peace*, helped on by Joan.

"Watch it there," she said, gently taking Mrs. Patterson's arm. "Boats are unsteady."

"Mr. Patterson—" I said.

He nodded curtly at me and went down through the companionway, his hollow-eyed wife following close behind. They didn't touch. Not once. They were followed by the police officer and then me. Their anger seemed barely contained as they made their way into Kricket's stateroom.

I stood outside and heard Elaine loudly sob out, "Oh, my God." And then more softly, "Oh, my God."

Wild-eyed, she emerged from Kricket's stateroom leaning one hand unsteadily against the door frame she stared at me. "Where's Katherine? That is not my daughter. What have you done with my daughter?"

Chapter 4

I opened my mouth to say something, but clamped it shut. What was she saying? "What do you mean?"

Mrs. Patterson spat her words at me and pointed. "What I mean is this—that girl in there is not our daughter."

"What?" I stared at her. How could this be?

"You heard me." Her face was haggard from lack of sleep, and wrinkles creased along the sides of her mouth. She ran a hand across her rather wild hair, the result no doubt of the fast ride on the Coast Guard boat.

It took me a moment, but I thought, if the girl lying on the bed in there wasn't Kricket, that meant their daughter was alive somewhere, didn't it? I wanted to ask her why she wasn't relieved. But I could say none of this to the woman who kept screaming at anyone within screaming distance, her husband, the police officer, the stunned Coast Guard members, "Who is that girl in there? Why didn't you check? How could you be so incompetent?"

"Elaine, calm down," said her husband.

I shook my head stupidly.

The khaki-panted police officer came over. "Captain Ridge." He regarded me, unblinking, with an expression I couldn't read. "Can I see you alone for a minute?"

"Of course." I had no idea where anyone would go to be "alone" on this boat. He moved determinedly near the front of the boat, stood against the door to the head, expression grim. I followed. He pulled a stubby pencil and notebook from inside his jacket pocket and regarded me intently.

"You're Emmeline Ridge," he said. "Captain Ridge." Did he put a bit too much emphasis on the word captain?

"Yes." No more jokes.

"My name is Ben Dunlinson. I'm with the Portland City Police. I just need to ask you a few questions."

I nodded. I breathed in and out, carefully. I guessed him to be about my age which is mid-thirties. He was a bit taller than me, and wore a brown cotton turtleneck under his thinnish jacket. He was clean-shaven and smooth-skinned. If it wasn't for a certain fierce intensity around his very blue eyes, he would have seemed almost boyish. The guys I hang with have lots of facial hair, sunburned cheeks and peeling noses. I'm used to guys who bathe in sea water and hardly ever wear shoes. Not this guy standing here in front of me.

"You looked at her passport when she came aboard?"

"Of course." I nodded. "As captain, I checked the passports of all my crew members."

"You compared her name with her photo?"

"Yes."

"And you're sure?" He looked at me. His eyes were very blue, a light blue, a blue you don't see much in eyes.

"Nothing seemed amiss." I swallowed back some nausea and tried to remember. Had I done these things? Of course I had. It was my first job. I had made doubly sure every "t" was crossed, every "i" dotted. "I'm sure," I said.

His expression didn't change.

I said quietly, "She really isn't Kricket Patterson?"

He didn't answer me. Instead, he wrote carefully in his notebook.

A few moments later we heard the Pattersons' raised voices.

"I told you. I told you, Roy—" Elaine Patterson's voice was a snarl. "I told you that man was bad news. Now, look what's happened."

"This has nothing to do with him, Elaine. Absolutely nothing."

"Oh, and you're the high-and-mighty one who knows everything about our daughter, is that it?"

I didn't know where to look, what to say. I stayed where I was, leaning against the forward bulkhead and left it to Detective Dunlinson to end their quarrel. He spoke quietly with the Pattersons. I didn't hear what they said to him.

Breaking up fights wasn't my responsibility here anymore. I was no longer the captain of this ship. I studied Elaine's profile. On better days, I could picture her filling in those hollow cheeks with blush, wiping away the dark eye circles with concealer, blow-drying the highlighted hair, and daubing up that slash of gray along her roots with hair color.

A sudden movement of the boat made me feel dizzy. I reached out and grabbed onto a handhold. Two boats floating in tandem on the waves, their hulls grinding against each other despite the fenders, was an unnatural rhythm, and all of us would be sick if this kept up.

For lack of anything better to do, I focused my concentration on one of the paintings on the wall, a lighthouse in hazy, muted colors. I kept looking at it. I had seen this framed print up here before, but had never studied it the way I was now. I clamped my hand to my mouth just then. Why hadn't I noticed this before? It was almost identical to the postcard Kricket had hidden. The same artist? It had to be. But—

Presently, the Pattersons, led by the police officer, entered Kricket's stateroom again. When they emerged a few moments later, Roy came over to me. "It's not her."

I stared, mouth open.

"How did this happen?" He asked.

I had no words.

Detective Dunlinson turned to me. "Captain Ridge, where is the girl's passport?"

"I assume it's in her stateroom. With her things," I said. "I haven't seen it since she came aboard."

He motioned toward the stateroom with his eyes. "Maybe you can help me look for it?"

Even though I didn't want to go in where she was, I had no choice but to follow him. In the room, he nodded toward the suitcase. "It appears her bags are packed. Perhaps she was planning to meet someone by boat?"

"Joan and I packed up her stuff," I said. "We thought it would be easier for her parents if all her things were ready to go."

He reached into his pocket, put on a pair of latex gloves and handed me a pair. While I put mine on, he moved her case onto a teak countertop. Systematically, he began removing items one by one and laying them on the shelf next to the suitcase. I stared. What if the postcard was in there? I should have searched more carefully when I was down here with Joan. Or I should have gotten rid of the thing when I had the chance. Yes, that's what I should have done. I should have ripped it up into a million pieces and thrown it far out into the ocean. I could only hope that Joan had found it, thought it was just a bit of trash and had thrown it out. Maybe it was, even now, in one of the garbage cans. I glanced nervously around the small room.

The detective ran his fingers through the various cloth pockets along the sides of the suitcase.

A few minutes later, he said, "Found it." He opened it up. "It belongs to Katherine Elaine Patterson." He looked again at the girl on the bed. "I can see why you would have made that mistake. It does look like her, doesn't it?"

I said, "Why did she come on board if she isn't Kricket Patterson? And how did she get this passport?"

"When we get to Portland, a thorough forensic exam will hopefully tell us who she is. We'll also work on figuring out why. Tell me,"—he put the passport in a plastic bag—"was there anything strange about this girl? Any red flags at all?" His gaze on me was too intense. I looked away.

I said, "Not really. Well, I don't know. Just that she was sick a lot."

"Sick?" He raised his eyebrows.

I regarded him intently. "Seasick."

He asked me to describe her symptoms and I did. I added that in my opinion it seemed a bit overdone.

"What do you mean by that?"

"Her dramatics seemed overdone. Like she was trying to get attention. That's how I saw it anyway. Her seasickness seemed like a theatrical performance."

He nodded and wrote it down. I wished I could tell what he was thinking. I could not.

"Detective?"

We looked up. A Coast Guard officer in a blue uniform stood in the doorway.

"Yes?" Detective Dunlinson said.

"What should we do? We're just floating. And the Pattersons are…um…"

Detective Dunlinson laid the item down that he was holding and said, "We need to get the body to Portland. We need to get the Pattersons back as soon as possible. I've got the passport." He turned to me. "How long will it take this boat to get to Portland?"

"Fourteen hours, give or take," I said.

He stared at me. "Really? That long? Can't you get this thing to go any faster?"

"No."

"Even if we tow you?" he asked, looking hopefully at the Coast Guard officer.

For several seconds, I didn't know what to say. Was he being serious? For a coastal police officer, his lack of basic marine knowledge seemed appalling. I didn't feel like giving him a crash course in planing hulls versus displacement hulls. "No, they can't tow us. There could be serious damage to the hull if we go any faster than our hull speed."

"Okay then," he said. "Let's move the body aboard the Coast Guard boat. Let's get her to shore. The Pattersons will go with you," he said to the Coast Guard officer. "I'll stay on this boat with the crew for the trip back. Captain Ridge will be in command."

Really?

He went out into the main salon and spoke quietly with the Pattersons, who were sitting as far away from each other on the settee as was physically possible.

I stood in the main salon while two of the Coast Guard personnel came down with a large black body bag.

All of us looked on silently, reverently, as the bag containing the unknown girl's body was transferred from *Blue Peace* to the Coast Guard boat.

Chapter 5

The five of us sat outside in the cold. We stayed that way, quiet, not speaking until the Coast Guard vessel disappeared into the fog. After we could no longer see or hear them, the detective said, "Since we're going to be with each other for the rest of the day, why don't you call me by my first name, Ben." He put his hands on his knees, leaned forward and continued, "Another thing—quick question—I obviously didn't wear the right kind of clothing for this journey. Is there something down below that I might be able to borrow? It's warmer than this on land."

"It's always warmer than this on land," Peter said in a monotone. "You should have thought of that."

I shot Peter a look. I wasn't sure what to think of this officer and with Peter's mood, I didn't want all of us to start off on a bad footing.

Ben smiled. "Guess I have lots to learn. I'm sort of new to all of this."

"That's obvious," Peter murmured, and Ben chuckled. I got the idea that Ben was trying to warm up to us. I wasn't sure it was working.

"Peter?" I said, "Can you get the officer a coat? Those *Blue Peace* ones are in the main hanging locker." One of the other things this boat came with was four monogramed foul-weather jackets, though we all wore our own gear.

Peter glared at me for a split second before he slid off his seat, motioned to Ben and said, "Come on then."

Then it was the three of us outside. "Okay, you guys," I said. "We need to cooperate with the police or it's going to be a long day."

Sunken-eyed, Rob stared at the ocean and said, "It's going to be a long day anyway."

"Yes it is," I said, "But, you're going to have to tell the detective everything you know about that girl. You can't leave anything out. You hear me? You tell the truth about what happened. Did you know her?" I hissed. "Do you know who she is? You two were awfully friendly. You better tell all of that to the police."

He said, "I thought she was Kricket. Same as everybody."

I looked at him and wondered for the dozenth time why he had been carrying around that postcard with my husband's number on it in his backpack. I wanted to ask him. Was it too late to ask him now? Probably.

A few moments later Peter and Ben were back outside. Ben wore a pair of flannel-lined sailing pants and a *Blue Peace* foul weather jacket with a hood. The jacket and pants were loose on him, and the suspenders hanging on him reminded me of a little boy dressed up in his daddy's lobstering overalls. If his expression hadn't been so serious, I would have laughed out loud.

He told us he wanted to interview us one at a time. "We can go downstairs for that," he said.

He indicated that I would be first and I followed him down the companionway. A sudden sea swell caught him off balance and had him reaching wildly for something to grab onto.

"One hand for the ship, one hand for yourself," I muttered.

"What?"

"Just something my uncle used to tell me." I looked at him. "Everywhere you walk on the boat, you should be holding on to something—handholds, railings, lifelines. Hence, the phrase 'one hand for the ship and one for yourself.'"

"Sounds like good advice." He stood for a second uncertainly in the main cabin before he said to me, "Let's go back to her room. I wanted to look through her things a bit more. You might be able to help there."

I followed him in.

"Tell me," he said once we were standing beside the bed that until moments ago held the body of the dead girl. "What do you know about the Pattersons?"

"Not much," I said. "I never met them before this morning. I only spoke on the phone once with Roy Patterson. All of the arrangements were made through his assistant."

"Is that normal procedure?"

"It often is."

"What is this assistant's name?"

"A Ruth somebody. I have it written down." I pulled my phone out of my pocket and read him off the pertinent information. He wrote it down.

He asked me more questions. I answered. We sat down on the

edge of the bed and for the next few minutes, I walked him through everything that happened while he carefully took notes. His gaze made me nervous and I'm sure it showed in my voice. I felt guilty and strange and wondered if I would be allowed to captain a vessel ever again.

I didn't say anything while he continued to write. He printed, I noticed, small, square, dark letters, precise, like he, himself seemed to be. He didn't talk much either and this added to my nervousness. The girl's cloth handbag was on the bed next to her suitcase and next to that a small makeup case. When he was satisfied with my answers, he donned another pair of latex gloves, opened up the handbag and began removing items one by one and laying them on her bed. "This might help us figure out who she is," he said.

In my pocket I still had the gloves I'd worn previously. I got them out and pulled them on.

"I'm interested in her phone," he said. "And her wallet. Did you and Joan find a wallet?"

"We put her phone in the purse and I don't remember a wallet."

Ben spread the contents of her handbag onto the bed—various tubes of this and that cream, a wand of mascara, a couple of pens, some coins, and a small notebook with a jeweled pen attached. Its pages were empty. The only thing like a wallet was a tiny change purse which held a few coins.

"So weird," I said. "It doesn't look like this stuff in here belongs to a real human being, especially not a girl. There's no personal stuff in here at all. Nothing. If you dump my bag out, you're going to find half a dozen crumpled Visa receipts, a wallet crammed full of credit cards and store points cards, and my driver's license. She doesn't even have a driver's license in here. She had that passport but no license. And the passport didn't even belong to her."

Ben picked up her iPhone and pressed buttons while I watched over his shoulder.

"Odd," he said. "All it has on it is some music. No games, no email account, no Facebook, that sort of thing. It doesn't look like it's connected to any sort of a phone plan."

"Let me see." I went into her settings and found nothing. I clicked on the photos tab, expecting it be empty. It wasn't.

One picture. A little ragamuffin girl. Maybe ten. Her hair was dark and stringy, and she was not smiling. He asked me if I knew her. I looked at the photo for a long time. I thought she might be the dead girl as a child, but the hair color and face shape were wrong.

He kept staring at the photo. "She ever talk about a little girl?"

"She didn't talk much to me about anything." I remembered that final request of hers to talk.

"I'll ask the others," he said. "I'll show them this when they come down."

He put the phone in a Ziploc bag and opened the small cosmetics bag, where Joan and I had packed away her shampoo and toiletries. He took them out one at a time and looked at them. He turned a shampoo bottle over and over in his fingers expecting it to speak to him.

"So sad and tragic," he said.

I took off my glasses and rubbed the bridge of my nose with my fingers. A headache was beginning somewhere behind it. I get them quite suddenly at times. I'll be walking along just fine and then they come out of nowhere and leave me scrambling for a place to rest my head. It's been this way since Jesse died.

What made me think I could do this, be a captain—a girl captain, no less—and make any kind of success of it? My sisters were right. I was nothing but a failure. My parents were right. I should have finished college and made something of my life. I just kept making mistakes.

Tears were beginning in the edges of my eyes, and I kept rubbing them away. I wouldn't cry now. Not in front of this police officer who was a stranger to me. I checked my pockets. No Kleenex for my leaky eyes. I got up and stumbled into the head to grab a handful of toilet paper. I pulled a bunch from the roll and leaned against the inner wall and shut my eyes. I needed to get back in control before I went out there and faced him again. Before I faced any of them again. What would happen when we got to shore?

When I opened my eyes, he was standing right beside me, too close, his hand on my arm. I was breathing heavily.

"Come, sit down," he said. I allowed myself to be led back into the room where he sat me down on the bed. I kept my head down. I couldn't look at him. I was pretty much crying now, one step away from outright sobbing.

"Detective Dunlinson, I—I'm not usually like this—I—this is not me." I had been trying so hard to be strong and brave, a captain to be feared and obeyed. I wanted to do this one normal, good thing and I manage to get a girl killed, a young, pretty girl who had friends and a family somewhere...

"Em...Em..." His voice was like a soft hypnotic murmur. The way he said my name did something to my insides.

"I'm so sorry, detective."

"Please—please call me Ben. And Em, it's going to be okay."

I was rapidly shaking my head. No, it was not okay. It would never be okay. This man could not know that my tears were as much for Jesse—for the loss of him in my life, for the aloneness that had become my life, for his ultimate betrayal of me, proved by his name on a card—as for anything that had happened on this trip.

The detective was being so gentle, this man who didn't know me at all. I was afraid to look at him, afraid that if I raised my head, looked into his eyes, I would weep and weep and weep and never stop. And, of course, I should tell him about Jesse's phone number. And the card being in Rob's pack. Of course I needed to do that. I couldn't. Don't ask me why. But I didn't.

Finally, I was able to force myself out of my stupor. I stood up, wrenched myself away from that gentle moment, and dried my eyes. He got up, too, and as quickly as it had occurred, it was over. I began to wonder if I had only imagined it, that moment of quiet tenderness with this hard-to-read detective.

Back topsides in the fog, I saw a plate of crackers and cheese on the small cockpit table. When had Peter fixed this plate? When I was in there crying? I didn't know why it was so important for me to remain in control in front of my crew, it just was.

Joan's turn was next. After she and Ben went down below, a bleary-eyed Rob said to me, "What's going to happen to us? Are we gonna go to jail?"

"I don't know, Rob." I didn't look at him, but my mind went back to the terrible time when reporters had called me after Jesse died. They had talked to my neighbors, my parents, and my younger twin sisters. Even though my sisters had nothing to do with me and mostly didn't even like Jesse, they had had plenty to say. People love reading about horror—other people's horror—and what is more horrific than a person and his little kayak being hacked right in half? What could be more graphic than the boys who did it saying over and over, "We just thought it was a log."

Trouble was, the truth was more tragic than anything their interviews could have uncovered. Jesse and I had been fighting about money. We always fought about money. Our argument that night was heated and loud. The last words I ever said to my husband were, "Get the hell out of my life and don't ever come back."

Whenever my husband was upset, he would climb into his kayak and go for a solitary paddle. Jesse and his boat-design partner had been on the cusp of a breakthrough—he'd tried to explain to me during our fight—for a revolutionary racing boat. They just needed a little bit more money.

At the inquest, they had asked me, "What was he doing on the water at two in the morning?"

My hands, their nails bitten to the quick had been flat on my lap. I had to consciously hold them there to keep them still. "He liked the peace and quiet of it."

"At two in the morning?"

"Jesse didn't care what time it was. Sometimes he would be up late working."

"He taught kayaking, correct?"

"Yes."

"So, he would be knowledgeable about the importance of lights and reflective gear? Especially at night?"

"Yes."

"Especially when there was no moon?"

"Yes."

I looked out at the waves now and brought my thoughts back to the present. The water mesmerized me. People, non-boaters, sometimes ask me what I "do" out here for such long stretches. I really don't have an answer to that other than to say that I could watch the water for hours and hours without boredom. I guess it's the closest thing that this non-meditator gets to meditating. I wished it would go on forever. Or that I could kick everyone off this boat and turn it right around and head out to the open sea and go wherever the winds took me. Like my Uncle Ferd, short for Ferdinand, but if anyone dares call him that, he'll walk away without answering. It was Uncle Ferd who taught me how to sail. When life got too full of questions, he simply climbed aboard his boat and left.

Soon, Ben had interviewed all of us and came up with Peter, both carrying mugs of coffee. I was momentarily irritated when I saw that he was using the insulated mug I always use, the one with a dolphin on it. It shouldn't have irked me, but it did. He was across from me, but looked just a bit uncertain.

"Well," he said. "I guess we're here for the duration."

"I guess we are," Peter said.

He looked out at the gray waves. "I've never liked the ocean much."

Peter said. "Funny you would get this gig, then."

I shot Peter a look.

"Yeah. Real funny…" Ben's voice trailed off. It was an uncomfortable moment, but then he brightened and said, "A lot of this is new for me. I have to admit that I haven't been on a lot of boats." He paused, then said, "I guess I should amend that. I haven't been around a lot of huge, saltwater boats like this one. I'm from Montana. I had a canoe there. With a small outboard."

"Wow," said Peter. I wanted to bop him.

Nonplussed, Ben went on, "I've been in Maine for three weeks. That's the extent of my nautical knowledge. I'm afraid I have a lot to learn."

"What brought you here?" Joan asked.

"Job."

Well, duh, I thought. "Is Maine someplace you wanted to come to?" I asked.

He didn't answer. Instead, he went on at some length about the little mountain stream where he fly-fished and how he hoped someday to go back there. He described a favorite fly and how he and his dad used to make them. I didn't quite trust all of his talking. In some ways, it seemed almost rehearsed, to put us at ease for what we might be waiting for us onshore. I knew that the police did this sometimes, pretended things so that those being questioned would be made to admit things. It seemed to be working with Joan. I, on the other hand, was more cynical. Or maybe more scared. I mostly kept quiet.

By early afternoon the fog lifted, which was a blessing because we could see more than a few feet ahead of us, except it brought choppy seas and a wind that caught us on the back quarter. We were steadily motoring on a straight course to Portland, while the following sea rolling in behind us and pushing us forward was getting worse by the minute. We still had hours ahead of us.

I could have raised a sail to head the boat a little away from the wind. Altering the motion of the boat would make it a bit less uncomfortable, but since that would have added a few hours to our trip, I didn't even suggest it.

With his back against the port side of the boat, Ben was becoming quieter and quieter.

"Are you okay?" Joan asked him.

"Maybe I'm not feeling so well," he said. "Was the boat moving like this before?"

I was feeling nauseated, too.

"It's just come up," Joan said.

Peter said, "Don't feel bad. Everybody gets sick on boats."

Well, almost everybody, I thought. Statistics indicate that, given the right set of circumstances, ninety-nine percent of all people could get seasick at one time or another. I've only ever known two people who never got seasick. My Jesse and Peter. Peter calls himself part of the one-percent.

The human species was made for land. Our inner ears, which control our balance, are finely tuned for solid earth, not the uncertain surface of a boat on water. When humans take to ships, it's an unnatural act.

"Stand at the stern and look at the horizon," Joan told him.

He got up. "This is supposed to help?"

A little while later, Peter brought up seasick bracelets, motion sickness pills, a plate of his homemade gingersnaps, ginger pills, candied ginger and a pot of ginger tea, all of which he placed on the serving table in front of the binnacle.

"Ginger," he said. "The old sailors' remedy for seasickness. *Bon appetit.*"

Ben took one look at the offerings and went and threw up over the side of the boat.

I felt sorry for him. Ordinary people are embarrassed when they vomit in public. Sailors, on the other hand, get used to it. After he was finished, he sheepishly sat down across from me, frowning. Joan handed him a bottle of water.

That's how the rest of the day went. All of us were sick at one time or another, except for Peter. Not a pleasant trip. Nobody wanted to go down into the cabin and lie down where the motion would be worse.

So we all sat topsides, feeling miserable, falling asleep here and there while we waited for this long and horrible day to be behind us.

Later, I pulled out a bit of the jib, and it helped a little. Even on a boat this big and this sea-kindly, there's not much that helps a following sea.

Hours later, I was watching the horizon with my binoculars.

"See anything?" Ben asked.

"Not yet. We should be in sight of land soon."

Next to me on the seat was a plate of leftover crackers, cheese and gingersnaps. The cheese was now dried, the edges curled up, and the crackers had become soft in the salt air. Nobody was eating anything.

It was dark when we saw lights in the distance. I smoothed a few wayward wisps of hair back under the yellow hood of my foul-weather jacket and headed for them.

Soon, the Portland Head Light on Cape Elizabeth came into view. I found myself counting the seconds between the red flashes. Four. The wind calmed somewhat as we neared the shoreline.

Ben asked, "How long till we're there?"

I looked down at the GPS. "Maybe an hour."

"It looks closer than that."

"Distances are deceiving on the water."

A few moments later, his cell phone rang. He faced away from us and talked in low tones. All I heard were a few "yeses," some "no's" and finally an "okay then."

After he hung up, I looked at him, wondering.

"She didn't drown or die of hypothermia," he said. "She was dead before she hit the water. This boat is now a crime scene."

Chapter 6

When we arrived at the dock, the police climbed all over the boat as soon as it got within jumping-on distance. When I barked out an order to Peter to hand the guy on the dock a bowline, an officer looked hard at me and said, "We got this."

Clearly, I was no longer the captain. I went quiet after that and did as I was told.

Ben stepped off the boat and conferred quietly with a female officer, someone I thought I recognized. I went down below and started packing up my duffle, but was told to leave it.

"But my laptop?" I argued.

"The boat's a crime scene," Ben said. "All that stuff has to be gone through."

"You're kidding me, right?"

Ben regarded me grimly and I left it where it was. My iPhone was buried deep within the folds of my pocket. I left it there, pleased that for now no one was frisking us. With deft fingers I managed to turn the volume off.

Without speaking, we followed them to two waiting police cars. I glanced up and saw Art across the street, his hands in his pockets. I always find Art a bit hard to read. He is a retired philosophy professor-turned-woodworker. He and Joan have been married five years, the first marriage for both of them. I wondered briefly how he knew. Joan must have called him on our way in. I wondered if Peter or Rob had contacted anyone. I hadn't. I probably should have tried to call EJ or maybe Dot or Isabelle. I just didn't think of it. Funny, I didn't call anyone when Jesse was killed either.

Joan and I were driven to the police station in the same car, Peter and Rob in the other. I leaned my head against the back of the seat and closed my eyes. I think I slept on the way there. I'd been awake for the entire boat trip without so much as a catnap. The others had leaned their heads against the bulkheads for quick naps. When I tried that, even for an instant, I saw the accusing face of the dead girl and I went over everything in my mind. Over and over. And then again.

At the police station, we were taken into four separate rooms. I was exhausted and so afraid. The room they put me in had one folding chair and a table. There were mismatched tiles on the floor and between them lines of black dirt. I know because I studied the floor while I waited.

Some time later, a man with a face like beef jerky came and took me to see Ben. He told me that he had to get my entire statement again for the recording. A red light blinked at regular intervals from a recording device and video camera.

I told Ben everything he asked.

"Captain Ridge," he said. "The victim didn't give you any indication that she wasn't Katherine Patterson?"

"No. I thought it was her. She never said the words, 'I'm Kricket Patterson,' but she talked about this being her 'daddy's boat' and she did have Kricket's passport."

He said, "I would like you to tell me about every single instance when she was seasick." He flipped through his pages. "Did she ever complain of being dizzy?"

"Do you think she was actually sick with something? Is that how she died? You said it was a crime scene, but is it a crime when someone just gets sick and dies?"

"We don't know anything for sure yet, Captain Ridge, not until after the autopsy. This was a suggestion from the medical examiner. And we have to take all suggestions seriously."

He asked more questions. I answered as best as I could. Point by point, he went over the notes he had taken on the boat. He was thorough. He was direct, cold even. Stern. And that part frightened me. He pulled no punches in his grilling of me. It was hard to believe that just a few hours ago, I'd almost fallen into his arms in the stateroom, overcome with tears. I was embarrassed when I thought about it now, humiliated. I didn't want this frowning man knowing anything more about me.

I told him that one minute the girl would complain of nausea, and the next she would be looking through the cupboards and cubbyholes. Wine, she told me when I'd come across her going through Roy Patterson's stash, was the perfect remedy for seasickness and did I know that?

"Wine is off-limits," I'd told her.

"But it's my daddy's," she always protested.

"It's still off-limits."

I told Detective Dunlinson that I'd held my ground with her in this.

To me, a tall glass of red wine or a good dark beer are two of the best things about sailing, but as captain, I decided that one of my rules was no alcohol on a delivery. None. My other rule was no sex. When I'd sat the crew down and told them that, Peter had rolled his eyes and Rob and Kricket—or the girl who wasn't Kricket—had acted amused.

"We're like the astronauts," I'd told them. "No sex. It just confuses things. Or smoking. Or drinking. And if you're going to throw up, do it over the side and not into the holding tank."

"Do we pee over the side, too?" Peter asked.

I glared at him.

Even so, the girl had persisted in going through the wine cabinet one bottle at a time, telling anyone who would listen (mostly Rob) that she should be allowed to drink since she wasn't technically a part of the crew. At times, she'd been the petulant child.

I told Ben now, "If she had some sort of medical condition, she didn't say anything."

I took off my glasses and rubbed my eyes. They felt gritty. I glanced at my glasses. No wonder everything was blurry—the lenses were filthy with salt spray. I tried cleaning them on the end of my shirt, but it only made it worse. I put them on anyway and looked at the detective through the haze.

At what I presumed to be the end of this interrogation, I said, "How soon before you know how she died?"

His voice was a monotone when he said, "We won't know anything for certain until the autopsy is complete. Because of the celebrity nature of this case, we hope that will be soon."

Celebrity nature? I blinked. Of course. The missing girl's father was a billionaire. I ran a hand through my limp, greasy hair. Everything about me felt saltwater itchy. Before the waves had gotten bad, I should have run down and grabbed a quick shower. I thought with longing to my shampoo and deodorant back on *Blue Peace.* I asked, "Do you have any idea when I'll be able to get my laptop back?"

He looked away from me and I thought I heard him say, "Don't hold your breath."

I walked out the door, then, with no clue as to what I was supposed to do now. Was I allowed to just leave? I walked down an empty hall, semi-looking for a ladies' room. Out of the corner of one eye, I watched Rob, his ball cap pulled down over his eyes follow an officer. He hugged his arms in front of him. This gesture reminded me of something, but I couldn't quite remember what it was.

I was glad to discover I was alone in the ladies' room. Given half a chance, I knew I could sit down in one of those stalls and either fall asleep or melt into a puddle of tears. I splashed water on my face and attempted to rub some water on my teeth to get rid of the sliminess. It didn't quite work. I poked through my deep pockets in case by a fluke I had a comb in there. No such luck. I put my glasses under the running faucet, rubbed some soap on them and got them passably clean.

My thin, straight hair, which I have to wash every day or it turns into a grease mop, hung in strands. I found a scrunchie in a pocket and finger-combed my mop into a sort of ponytail. My socks and shoes were still saltwater-damp, but there was nothing to be done about that.

Back out in the hallway, I saw no one, heard no one. The place seemed echoey and eerie this late at night. Should I walk on over to Joan's house? It wasn't far. Maybe Art was waiting for us somewhere. Outside, I zipped my jacket up as far as it would go, leaned against the building and breathed in the night air. It was early May, which meant the days might be warm, but the evenings were still cold.

The door opened. A round-faced, bespectacled man in a blue nylon jacket was pushing it open with his right shoulder while holding a sheaf of papers and file folders.

I recognized him and shrank against the building. This was the state medical examiner, Dr. Declan Meyer. Seeing him brought back all the memories of Jesse's death, and me hounding them all for answers that weren't there. It was an accident, nothing but a freak accident they kept telling me. The boys were remorseful minors. No drinking had been involved.

Too late, he saw me now, stopped, adjusted his glasses. "You," he said. It felt like an accusation.

I raised a limp hand.

He scratched his head. "You're the Captain Ridge in this case."

"Yep."

He looked confused. "Well, that's um—" He kept looking at me. "Emmeline Ridge, right?"

"Right."

He pointed across the street to a twenty-four-hour café. "I'm just heading over for a tea while I wait for Detective Dunlinson, who wants to be on hand for the autopsy. Would you like to join me?"

"Join you?" I was astonished. "I'm not sure I want to go to an autopsy."

"No." He pointed to the café. "For a cup of tea."

"I—I don't have my wallet. I had to leave everything."

"No matter. I'll do the buying."

At the corner, while we waited for the crosswalk light to change, he said, "For a number of months, I've been debating whether to call you or not."

"Me?"

"Yes. I have some information about your husband."

Chapter 7

"**W**hat about my husband?" It was the first question I asked after we'd gotten our sandwiches and tea and were sitting in the dark across from each other at a small café table outside in front.

"Little pitchers have big ears," he'd whispered to me when earlier I'd begun toward an inside table in a far corner. I'd looked around, wondering who he was referring to—the four police officers who were drinking coffee and eating pie at a center table or the three young people intent on their laptops way over in the far corner.

Outside, next to the front door were a few wrought iron café tables with chairs, placed there rather optimistically, I thought, for this early in the season. It was there that Dr. Meyer wanted to sit. I had no choice but to follow.

"It'll be quieter out here, too," he said. "It'll give us a better chance to talk."

But he didn't talk, not right away. Instead, he fussed with his sandwich, arranging it on his plate just so while I waited. I remembered him as being long on science but short on people skills.

It was quiet outside. There is a different atmosphere to the night. It's denser. I notice this when I'm out on a night sail. You feel the air around your face more acutely. Sounds are intensified but muffled. Cold seems colder, winds more pronounced. I was feeling this now. It was as if we were apart from the warmth inside, separated not only by windows, but by time and space.

He fiddled with his tea bag while I tried to be patient. What did he know about Jesse? I shivered and tightened the toggles on my jacket hood. Despite being hungry earlier, I wasn't the least bit interested in my sandwich. I think I ordered it just to be polite, or to have something on my plate to justify my sitting here. Plus, he had insisted on buying it for me. Dr. Meyer bobbed his tea bag up and down a few times, plucked it out, carefully squeezed it between his thumb and forefinger before discarding it neatly in a napkin, which he folded in careful squares before placing it on the table to his left.

"Dr. Meyer." I leaned toward him. "You wanted to talk to me about my husband?"

He held up a cautioning finger, and I followed his gaze. Across the street, two police officers deep in conversation were walking toward us. They looked at me curiously, nodded to Dr. Meyer and then went into the café. It wasn't until the door was closed that he said, "Okay. Now we can talk."

He arranged his sandwich pieces on his plate again, and then said, "At the time of your husband's accident, I remember promising you that if I ever found any new information, you would be the first one I would contact."

Eagerly, I leaned forward. "You have new information?"

"Certainly not enough to reopen the case, if that would even be a possibility, which it is not at this point, they tell me. This is merely an observation on my part, albeit an interesting one." He pursed his lips and continued, "There were a few things I questioned at the time, yet I was repeatedly assured that appropriate measures had been taken. I wondered why the Breathalyzer tests weren't administered right away. But that's in the report. You would have read that."

"I did. I didn't know what it meant."

"It meant that the Breathalyzer tests weren't administered until well after the effects of the alcohol would have worn off. That in itself began what I deem a comedy of errors. The Breathalyzer itself wasn't brought to the scene until well after. Everyone thought the other officer had it." He shook his head. "We were told repeatedly that the boys weren't joyriding, just doing some trap maintenance. At that hour? No one seemed to think that was strange."

"I did," I said. "No one listened to me."

When Jesse was killed, I expected the mantle of community support to fall on me. Jesse had been well known. We had friends. People knew us, liked us. Or so I thought. Yet, the full support of the city of Portland seemed to surround those boys. The locals on Chalk Spit Island supported me. But there were far fewer of us than people in Portland who apparently knew well these young, model students, who were leaders in their church and who'd never been in trouble a day in their lives. That's what people kept saying. "They've never been in trouble a day in their lives."

I ended up feeling like no one cared.

And, really, when you get right down to it, if it was anyone's fault, it was Jesse's. Jesse became the bad guy, the so-called expert kayaker who "should have known better." Out in the middle of the night. No reflective clothing. No lights. No life jacket. He'd been drinking. Drinking! The whole time we'd argued, he'd been working on his beer. His one beer.

Dr. Meyer went on, "I was assisting the local medical examiner at the time and yet felt stonewalled at every turn. Somehow it felt to be more—" He paused, ran his tongue over his bottom lip. "How shall I put it? It felt to be more of a political agenda, rather than anyone trying to find out what really happened. As you may be aware, the medical examiner who worked on that case has since retired."

I told him I didn't know that.

He sighed deeply and ran a hand across his rubbery face, a face pockmarked by ancient acne scars. His eyes drooped behind his smudged, rimless eyeglasses. He said, "I shouldn't have said this much, because these are largely feelings of mine rather than anything concrete."

I waited.

"Yet when I saw you, I knew I had to talk to you."

I nodded.

He picked at his sandwich and put it on his plate. "There is also something else you should know, something infinitely more important than what I have said thus far, the reason I knew I needed to contact you."

My hands became very still. The four pie-eating officers were exiting the diner now, and Dr. Meyer took the opportunity to take a few bites of his egg sandwich.

When the officers were safely across the street, he said, "Three months ago I decided to give the whole thing a second look. I simply wasn't satisfied with the original findings. I got out my notes and case files and went over everything from top to bottom, right to left and back again. I'm not even sure what I was looking for. I had to drive into Portland on hospital business and so got out the boys' addresses from the files and plugged them into my GPS. I'm not really sure what I hoped to find. I also had the name of their church, the one that supported them so thoroughly."

I clasped and unclasped my hands in my lap. "What did they say?"

He shook his head. "I couldn't locate them. That is what I found so alarming. I drove to the first address. A young family is living in the house now. They had recently moved in and had no knowledge of the previous inhabitants or where they now lived. I went to the other address. An older couple lives there. They've been there for forty years. No young man ever stayed there, roomed there, rented from them. They, frankly, didn't know what I was talking about."

I put a hand to my throat.

"I then looked up the church that gave them so much support. By this time I was not surprised that no such church exists."

I leaned forward, my throat tight. "But there were quotes in the paper from people from the church. I have the news clippings."

He shrugged. "I can't begin to explain it. All I know is that the boys don't live at the addresses on their files, and the church that supported them isn't there."

"What do the police say?"

He raised his eyebrows. "Not too much."

"What do you mean, 'not too much?'"

Some of the egg salad squished out of the side of his sandwich, which he remedied with the edge of a napkin. "They told me that the case is closed and if the families wanted to move away and start over, that was up to them. They had no answer about the church, yet it didn't seem too concerning to them."

I stared at him. To this day I have never met the boys who killed my husband, never even seen their faces. They were minors, and their names were kept from me and out of the news. Only once had I glimpsed one of them, head down and covered with a hoodie, walking out the back door of the courthouse and into a waiting vehicle. I wanted an apology from those boys. I never got that.

Across the street, Rob emerged from the police station alone. I followed his movements while I let all of what Dr. Meyer had told me sink in. I said, "They were protected so much because they were *minors*." I emphasized the word. "And yet my husband is dead." I looked up at him hopefully. "Now that you're the state medical examiner, can you, um, can you at least tell me who they were? Can I at least know that?"

He chewed on his bottom lip for a long time. Meanwhile, Rob sat down on the steps of the police station, an elbow on each knee, hunched forward and hugging his knees, his hoodie up and covering his head. I watched as he pulled out a cigarette, lit it. I watched the lit red end. I remembered the way he had come onto the boat that first day, the hood of his hoodie up on his head, pulled forward, his backpack, not hung over one shoulder and casually on his back, but held tightly in the front as if it contained gold. I thought it was odd, but I figured he was just shy.

Dr. Meyer said, "I will tell you this much. I'm going to go back up to Augusta and retrieve all of my notes on the case. I made lists of their friends, which includes addresses. If I find anything more of interest, I'll get in touch with you. I promise you that. As for their names—just trust me on this, Captain Ridge—I'll do what I can. Now, I have a question for you. Did your husband by any chance know those boys?

I stared at him. "How would I know if Jesse knew them if I don't even know who they are?"

"So your husband never mentioned a couple of boys, nor the boat?"

"I never knew the name of the boat, either, or where it was licensed. I knew nothing about any of it."

He looked at me steadily. "*Rosalena.*"

"What?"

"That's the name of the boat that the boys took out. It was destroyed in a freak explosion in a boatyard in Winter Harbor a few months after the accident."

I simply looked at him.

"A propane blast. An accident. A malfunction in one of the lines."

My thoughts were spinning. I hadn't told anyone that for months leading up to his death, Jesse had been acting strangely. There had been many nights when he had gone off in his kayak. He'd also talked with me less, shared with me less, especially if it concerned his work. When I would come upon him while he was intent on his laptop, he would immediately click into a different program or shut the top. When I would ask how the business was going, he would snap back with questions like, "Why? What have you heard?"

Back then, I thought we had time. I thought we'd sort through it all, that it'd get better in time. But we didn't have time. I knew his partner in the boat business, and I knew something was on his mind, but this had never been a part of the inquest. This had never been a part of anything.

My throat felt dry. I took a small sip of my tea. It didn't help.

There were three of them who had gotten together and formed Keel Concepts Boat Design—Jesse, and his friend Bryce and Bryce's wife, Amanda, helped out with the business. It was a kind of loose organization that had an office in an old boathouse out on Chalk Spit.

Very casual, very loose, and we all got along.

Until we didn't.

After Jesse died, Bryce came to the house and demanded Jesse's office keys. I looked everywhere and couldn't find them. I told Bryce that they were probably on Jesse at the time of the accident and were even now at the bottom of the bay. Bryce kept phoning me, showing up at the door, kept asking me to keep looking around the house. I was frankly upset that Bryce seemed more concerned about the keys to their office door than he was about Jesse being gone. Eventually, he quit hounding me.

I thought about all of that now as I took little bites of the sandwich I didn't want and watched Rob smoke across the street.

Dr. Meyer asked if I wanted him to continue to look for the boys and into the investigation.

"Thank you, and can you please let me know what you find out?"

He promised he would.

An officer came through the front door of the police station and talked to Rob. I watched as Rob followed him back inside, still hunched forward and crossing his arms in front of him.

Chapter 8

I could see the moon from where I stood, a perfectly round face, blemished only by drifting night clouds. I was outside on the widow's walk in Joan's centuries-old four-story home. The breeze had picked up slightly, dissipating the fog. Rather recklessly, I leaned my full weight against the railing. Joan was constantly telling me to be careful up here. Actually, she kept the door to the widow's walk closed and locked and told me not to go out there at all. "It's not safe," she always said. "I would hate to have something awful happen."

But I came out here anyway.

This was my special place to be after Jesse died. No one bothered me up here. I could lie on the floor of this square, postage stamp of a deck and keen out my tears for hours. Before that, it was Jesse and me up here, sitting cross-legged and looking out at the sea and making all of our plans. I placed my squat whiskey glass on the railing and kept my eye on the moon. I was up here because Peter, Rob and I had taken Joan up on her invitation to stay, "for as long as we needed to." By the time the four of us had met up with Art, it was after midnight, and by then none of us felt like talking much. We got to the house, chose our rooms, grabbed a quick tea, glass of water or in my case whiskey, and went our separate ways. What I really wanted was a heart-to-heart with Joan. That would come later, after we had all slept.

Peter chose a room on the second floor facing the back. Rob decided on a main-floor room near the kitchen, and I came up here. When I stay with Joan and Art, which is not infrequent, I always opt for this room, even though the nearest bathroom is down one level on the third floor. This house, built in the 1700s, has been in Joan's family for as long. A person can get lost wandering up and down its winding staircases, hallways, and into and out of its doorways and passageways. This was the house Joan and her five brothers grew up in when Portland was just a whistle-stop along the Eastern Seaboard.

A few generations before that, it was a true farmhouse, accessible only by buggy path or schooner. Now it stands, a sort of anachronism—a farmhouse whose surrounding lands have been carved into superhighways and chopped up into subdivisions, and strip malls with cafés and artisanal bakeries.

I liked that I was alone up here. I'm one of those people who needs a lot of alone time, and yet I sign up for long stretches on boats where you're rarely more than six feet away from the next person. Oddly, most sailors are solitary individuals. Because of that quirk, we know how to be quiet with each other. On long deliveries, no one feels they have to fill in the blanks with talk.

I gazed out at the sea, aware that in doing so I was part of a grand tradition. The topmost balconies on these old New England houses are called widow's walks because generations of women would stand up here and watch for their loved ones to return. I wondered if they felt as afraid and unsure as I felt now. I knew I needed to go inside and phone my parents. I needed to do this before they heard it all from someplace else, like the news.

I moved away from the railing and leaned against the wall of the house. Art's smoky, peaty single malt warmed me. I thought about my parents, my family. I thought about those boys. About *Rosalena*. I thought about Jesse, about Jesse's phone number on the postcard. Or had I misread it? Maybe, because I'm so crazy with grief, my mind had reversed a digit. Maybe the whole thing was something completely different than what it was.

I'd canceled Jesse's cell more than a year ago. When I received a bill anyway, I argued with the foreign-sounding guy for a long time. Yes, I was canceling the plan mid-plan. Yes, I knew that the plan had another two years to go. No, I was not going to pay. The reason? The owner of the plan died. He was dead. Dead. Dead. Yes, dead. I had to repeat it several times before it sank in. No, I did not want to transfer the plan to my name. I already had one, thank you very much and good-bye. Finally, he got it.

I pulled my cell phone out of my pocket, and before I could think too hard or too much about it, I called Ohio. I knew my parents, who watched TV news programs until late into the night from the comfort of their bed, would still be awake.

On the second ring, my father answered.

"Dad, it's Em."

"*What?*"

My father has trouble hearing on the phone, yet insists on answering it. I spoke louder. "Dad, it's me, Emmeline. From Maine."

"Emmeline! Everything okay?"

"No, Dad. It's not." I slid down the side of the house until I was sitting on the wooden deck.

"What? Em, just a minute. I'm going to put your mother on. We have the TV on. Here, let me turn it down." And then, "Where is that remote? I just had it." I waited.

When my mother got on, I told her what happened.

"A girl died?" she asked.

"Yes, a girl went overboard."

"Oh, Em, that's awful."

"One of my crew was on watch. He hadn't realized she'd gone over the side until it was too late. I came up then and—" My voice broke at the end of my words.

"Oh, Em! Oh, dear."

I told her I just got to Joan and Art's and before that we all had to give statements at the police station. I told her I hadn't had a chance to call her until now.

"Do you want me to come out there and be with you? I will, if you want. I can catch a flight first thing."

I told her it was okay. She didn't have to.

"Have you talked to your sisters?"

"Not yet," I said.

"Well, don't call them tonight. Let me call them. I'll take care of that for you."

"Thanks, Mom."

"I happen to know that Raymond has had many late nights working on a project. So has Marianna, and Katie's been down with the flu all week along with the kids."

My teeth began to hurt. I pressed my hand against my jaw. That my mother was giving me extended status updates on the lives of my sisters and their families was not unusual. She does this every time we talk. I know she wishes that the three of us were closer. I can't help it. We're just not. We lead different lives.

"And Em. We'll certainly be praying for you. I'll mention it to my ladies' group. Do you mind?"

This was her ladies' group at church. I wanted to tell her that I did mind, but I was sure this would not stop her from telling all her friends.

After we hung up, I squeezed my phone in my hand and forced myself to quit clenching my teeth. I was aware again of just how far I am from living up to the standard set by my younger twin sisters who live in the same Ohio town as my parents with their handsome church-attending, CEO husbands and their perfect, piano-lesson children.

I went inside and shut the door behind me. I sat down on the double bed with Joan's grandmother's quilt and kept staring at my phone while I tried to sort through everything that had happened.

I needed to know at least one thing for sure. I punched in the number I knew so well by heart.

Nothing except a message from the phone company that this number had been disconnected. What did I expect? Jesse's voice inviting me to leave a message after the beep? And, did this prove that it wasn't Jesse's number on the back of the postcard? Maybe. Maybe not.

Chapter 9

I'm mostly not a good sleeper. Not since Jesse died. I rarely get through a night without waking multiple times. I get up, wander through my small house, and run the ends of my fingers lightly over my things—the back of my couch, the lamps, the tops of the bookshelves. It's as if I need reassuring that these are solid and real parts of my world, and that in the morning they will all still be here. The only time I sleep well is when I'm on boats. But then I dream.

I don't know which is worse.

I hadn't expected to get any sleep. So when I woke up in the same fetal position I had curled myself into when I crawled under the quilt, I thought I had been down mere moments. My cell phone read 12:12. How could this be? When I had come in from the balcony, it had been closer to one in the morning.

I sat up, twisted in my sheets and damp with sweat as realization dawned. Was it the afternoon already? Had I really slept this long? I quickly climbed into a few of the clean clothes Joan had leant me and I made my way down the stairs to the bathroom. I splashed cold water on my face and basically tried to get my hair to do something other than lie flat on my head. Last night I'd soaked under a long, hot shower. This is what happens when I sleep on wet hair. It gets all cowlicky in places and flyaway in others.

The only comb I could find was a grubby one in the top drawer of the vanity, one of mine from a long time ago. I dampened it and slicked my hair back into a sort of ponytail. I brushed my teeth with a ratty toothbrush, also one of my own that I'd found in the same drawer last night. I looked at my wan face in the mirror and frowned.

On the main floor I heard voices and followed them down the hall and through the kitchen to the small sitting room just beyond. In another lifetime, this room was the pantry, a traditional scullery. Joan and Art had turned it into a sitting room by installing a wood stove in the corner, lining it with pine board bookshelves, adding a couple of comfy couches and a few rag rugs to the worn wood floor. This is the room Art retires to, to light his evening pipe and sit down with his boat-building magazines. It's the place Joan comes into with her chamomile tea and the latest mystery novel. I stood in the doorway now, a bit uncertain and, if truth be told, not entirely awake.

Joan saw me first. "Em, coffee's on the stove, and there's a loaf of fresh bread on the breadboard. Art was out to the market this morning. Help yourself."

"Thank you," I said. "Sorry I slept so long."

Across the room Art was leaning back, legs crossed, his pipe in his hand.

"We all did," she said. "Only Art was up at the crack of dawn, as per usual. Rob's still asleep."

Across the room Peter was hunched over his phone, texting, it looked like. He didn't look at me when I entered. That's when I noticed the two others. The guy in the white golf shirt and pressed pants was Captain Tom Mallen and next to him someone I'd seen on boats, but whose name I'd forgotten. I was stunned to see Tom. He was tanned, fit and healthy-looking. I was sure that a six-pack lay underneath the crisp white golf shirt monogramed with a fancy yacht club logo.

I crewed with him only once, a long time ago when I was young and crazy and would have hitchhiked all over the world on boats. There was a time when I owned nothing but sailing gloves, boating shoes and a variety of scrubby clothes that I wore under my foul-weather gear.

There are Boat Captains and there are boat captains, and in my line of work, class distinctions are alive and well. Tom is a Boat Captain with capital letters, who typically works for one or two private yachts belonging to the rich and famous. He's right at the top of the food chain. It's an old boys' network, always has been, and I'm neither old nor a boy. I had figured that most of my work, if I was able to get any at all would be for small boat brokers who needed used boats moved from one marina to the next.

The guy next to him, the one whose name eluded me, looked like a scaled down yet muscled-up version of Tom. He had one of those bodies that looked good on soldiers or police officers—compact, thick-necked, thighs like tree trunks. I looked from one to the other. What on earth were they doing here?

Tom must have seen my confusion, because he said, "We came to make sure you're okay and to offer our full support."

"Um—news travels fast," I said.

"News does travel fast," Tom gave me a bit of a smile. "You know Scott? Scott Uphill?"

"Hello," I said to him. "I think we might've met at one time or another."

"Could be," was all he said.

Since I desperately wanted caffeine before I attempted any more conversation on this headachy morning, I told everyone I would be right back.

In the kitchen, which I know like my own, I poured coffee from an ancient metal stove-top percolator into a mug that said *Maine: The Way Life Should Be*, cut a quick slice of bread, buttered it, put it on a white china plate, and made my way back into the sitting room.

The only empty chair was next to Tom. He patted it. I felt nervous, awkward and suddenly aware of my appearance—this old funny T-shirt of Joan's I was wearing and her pants that were too short for me. It came to me then, that this wouldn't have happened if a better captain—someone like Tom—had been in command of *Blue Peace*. What was I doing, thinking I could be a captain like one of the Big Boys? I sat down and placed my coffee on the pine table in front of me, balanced my plate on my lap and cast a sideways glance up at Tom. His presence seemed overwhelming in the room. It was almost like I couldn't breathe.

"Does anyone know who she is yet?" I said to no one in particular.

Joan shook her head. "The police haven't contacted us yet this morning. We're still waiting to hear anything."

"Oh." I studied the way the cream made patterns on the top of my coffee.

Tom said quietly, "You need to know, Em, that the entire sailing community is behind you. If there is anything we can do, just say the word."

I nodded.

"Accidents happen to every captain," he added.

I couldn't think of any sailor I'd ever known who'd had someone go overboard and die. Hurricanes, yes. Rough seas, sickness, broken boats, broken bones, sunken boats, knockdowns and broken teeth became the fodder for future stories over a round of beer. This would not. There would never be a time when I would raise my glass of Guinness and say, "I have a story that will top yours—"

I tore my bread into little pieces on my plate but couldn't eat any of it. Across from me, Peter's eyes were bloodshot.

"Peter?" I asked. "Are you okay?"

He looked away and didn't answer me. Art picked up his pipe and began tamping it down. My hands felt cold around my warm coffee mug.

Joan said, "Everyone's a little on edge this morning."

I took a sip of coffee and turned to Tom. "How, again, did you know I was here?"

"Scott called me," he said. "He saw *Blue Peace* down at the wharf and knew she wasn't supposed to be back in port until next year. Since I live here in Portland he called me. He and Kricket are close. What a shock to find out it wasn't really Kricket on the boat. That's when we knew we needed to come here. Offer support."

Scott said, "Kricket and I talked just about every day via satellite phone. She told me she was on *Blue Peace*. She talked about you. About the crew, about how much she hated being there." He looked me in the eye when he said, "Are you sure it wasn't her?"

I nodded. "That's what the Pattersons say anyway." I thought of something. "Do the police know this?"

"We have a call into them," Tom said. "We decided to come here, figuring they'd show up here soon enough anyway."

I nodded.

"And I talked with Roy," Tom said, "Just yesterday in fact. I asked how Kricket was, and he said he'd talked to her on the sat phone. She told him everything was fine, and she was getting along with everyone on *Blue Peace*."

I looked at Joan and said, "Patterson's satellite phone was in its own holder near the nav station. I never saw the girl use it or even go near it. Did you, Joan or Peter? Did you see her use that phone?"

Joan said no. Peter, who was still furiously texting on his phone didn't even answer the question. Scott reached into his pocket, took out his cell phone and flipped through it and showed me. "Is this the number of the sat phone?"

I looked down at it. "I'm not even sure I could remember, but no, this one doesn't look familiar. Does it to you, Joan?" I handed it to her and she shook her head.

When his phone was returned to him, Scott tried the number. After several seconds he said, "No answer today. Not even voice mail."

Peter suddenly stood up. "All this shit is my fault."

"Peter?" I said. We all looked at him.

"No, it is. I didn't even know him. He was just some guy. Some jerk-off guy."

Who?

"I met him. In a bar. Rob. Like a week before we were supposed to leave. When he found out who I was, he told me he *had* to get on *Blue Peace,* that he really, really, *really* wanted a chance to sail. He gave me some bullshit story that he needed to get on the boat—" He dug in his pants pocket and threw a bunch of bills on the table.

I looked up at him. "What?"

"It's what he paid me. A crappy two thousand bucks to help him come up with a phony sailing résumé. So I did. I wrote him up one that was totally bogus. For this lousy money. At the time I thought, what could it hurt? So I did it."

He stomped out of the room. I shot up and followed him. "Peter?" I followed him down the hall to Rob's room.

He was knocking on Rob's door. Hard. "Come out here, you little shit!" Peter called. "Or I'm coming in."

When there was no answer, he tried the handle. Locked.

"Stupid jerk," he said. "He's in there and he did this. He killed her. He pushed her off the boat. I *know* he did."

"Peter!"

A few moments later, Joan arrived with the master key.

She unlocked the door, and we all peered in. Empty. The room was clean. The bed was made and obviously unslept in.

Chapter 10

An hour later, the early afternoon grayness had turned into a sludgy, pouring down rain. There was even a sleety edge to it. My foul-weather jacket was zipped to my neck, the hood forward on either side so that my peripheral vision was seriously impeded. Tom, Scott and I were walking down to the wharf. Joan had suggested an umbrella, but I decided it was too windy. I could have taken my car—it was parked in Joan's driveway—but I was feeling antsy, panicky, like I needed to get outside for a walk. I've never been much of an indoor person.

When I'd tried calling Ben Dunlinson, I was told he was down at the wharf. Instead of waiting for him to come to me, I'd go to him, I decided. When I'd told the group I was going to walk down to the wharf to look for the police, Tom said, "I'll come."

"I will, too," Scott added.

I wasn't sure I wanted a party, but what could I say? Since finding out that the girl wasn't Kricket, Scott was redoubling his efforts to find his girlfriend and was calling every number he'd ever had for her. To no avail, apparently. He kept asking me questions about the girl on the boat. What did she look like? What did she say? What did they talk about?

I didn't know how to answer him. In the end, Joan decided to stay behind "in case the phone rings." She's just enough old school not to fully understand that people carry their phones with them. No one needs to stay at home anymore waiting for the phone to ring.

Rob was still missing, and now Peter was gone, too. He had stormed around, saying things like, "That idiot little shit!" Then he'd tromped upstairs, packed up his things and left. It took him less than five minutes. He didn't say good-bye. The money, all two thousand dollars of it, still sat on the coffee table where he'd thrown it. None of us, it seemed, wanted to touch it.

We couldn't walk three abreast on the wet sidewalk, and so it mostly ended up being Tom and me followed by Scott, who held his cell phone to his ear. Despite my early nervousness around Tom, I was finding him pretty easy to talk to. While we were waiting for a light at the corner, Tom's cell beeped. He turned slightly away from me when he answered it, but I caught the drift. "Don't worry. I'll take care of it," he said. "Look, I'm busy now. I'll get back to you."

When he turned back to me, he said, "Manure's already hitting the fan."

I looked up at him. "What?" The light changed.

"People are already calling. Newspapers—"

I eyed him as we walked. "And they're calling *you?*"

"Everybody knows me here."

"Apparently."

"They call me because they consider me the sort of local expert. I haven't told anyone anything yet." Then he smiled down at me. Not a huge smile, but a small one. It made me feel good to know that he was on my side. As we walked across the street he placed his hand on the small of my back to guide me. I found I didn't mind it there.

Tom doesn't know this, but much of what I am as a captain, I owe to him. I crewed with him only once, but that was enough. It was from him that I learned the whole no-drinking-at-all-on-delivery-not-even-a-light-beer rule. So many other captains are lax when it comes to this, especially when it's someone else's beer.

It was from Tom that I learned to use what some considered old-fashioned—four-hour watches. From him I learned the importance of maintaining a tight ship, being right there to intervene in arguments and always having the last word. Democracy may work on land, but at sea, the captain is The Captain.

As soon as we got to the other side of the street, it began to rain hard. It pinged on the sidewalk around us, sounding like rice flung onto tile. I should have brought Joan's umbrella. It's not like I'm not used to rain. I've helmed more boats than I care to think about in screeching, screaming, sideways rain. There comes a point when you're so wet that there's no point in even trying to remain dry anymore. You just sort of give in to the elements. Alone, and in warmer climes, I'm prone to removing every stitch of clothing and simply calling it taking a shower. When you've been at sea for a while, bathing mostly in saltwater to ration the fresh, a nice, soft rain shower is pure heaven.

We were on a street parallel to the water, and I caught the whiff of fresh coffee as we passed the little shop that roasts its own. I've been through those doors more times than I can count to fill up my thermos with the good stuff, before happy-as-a-larking it down to the yacht club. I wouldn't go in now. How far had the news spread? I couldn't be sure.

Ahead of us, down on the wharf, *Blue Peace* was tied up the way we'd left her. Was it just a week ago at this time that I'd been giddy with excitement at the prospect of captaining so marvelous a vessel?

Even though several police cars were parked at street level, from this distance the yacht looked almost deserted. I don't know what I was expecting, maybe something like on television—lots of lights and yellow crime scene tape and police in white coveralls, milling about and a whole city full of rubberneckers? Scott took off ahead of us and slid down the wet, grassy hill toward the boat.

Tom stopped and said, "I feel responsible for what's happening to you. You being mixed up in all of this is my fault."

I looked at him. "What are you talking about?"

He faced me. Rain dripped off his nose. I was having trouble focusing on his face through my rain-fogged glasses.

"How could any of this be *your* fault, Captain Mallen?"

"Please, call me Tom." He paused. "It was me who, ah, gave Roy Patterson your name. I recommended you for the job."

I stared at him, flabbergasted.

"I work for Patterson. Scott and I both crew for him. That's how, uh, how he and Kricket got to know each other so well. I was scheduled to deliver *Blue Peace* on this run. Scott was going to crew. It was just going to be the two of us. At the last minute Roy wanted his daughter to go. She can be a bit hard to, ah, handle." He looked away for a moment and frowned. "Roy was worried about Kricket with, um, Scott aboard and so decided he wanted a whole new crew with a female captain. Without hesitation, I gave him your name."

I was astonished. I had no idea this man even knew me. "You knew that I got my captain's license?"

"Word gets around. Your reputation precedes you. I knew you'd be the best captain out there for this particular assignment."

"Wow." I could think of nothing else to say.

He was still talking. "You're that good, Em. Don't forget it. And I do know you, you know." He grinned at me suddenly. "You remember that delivery to Florida?"

"I do," I said.

"More than ten years now."

"Yeah. Wow."

"I've never forgotten you," he said.

I stared at him, trying to keep my amazement from showing. *He hadn't forgotten me?*

"Em, this isn't the end of your career."

"I feel like it is," I said.

Down below us, Ben and Scott were standing on the wet dock talking. Scott was making wild hand gestures. Ben in true form, had out his little notebook and was writing. We headed down.

"Detective Dunlinson!" I called when we were closer. "I tried reaching you."

He said. "I should have given you my cell number. Thought I had. Would've saved you a trip."

"Rob's gone. Did Scott tell you?"

He nodded as Tom came forward. "Detective Dunlinson." Tom extended his hand. "Captain Tom Mallen. We've met before."

Ben nodded. "Yes."

Something, a look, passed between them. Something I couldn't identify. It lasted only an instant, and then it was gone.

Ben nodded and asked us questions and wrote things down while we told him about the money and Rob's and Peter's disappearance.

"Knowing what we now know about Rob," Dunlinson said, "that's not entirely surprising. We've been doing some of our own checking. Rob Stikles doesn't appear to be who he says he is. The home address he gave us in Vermont doesn't exist. The street doesn't exist. It was like he made up the whole thing. We can find no record of a Rob Stikles in that city at all."

"What about his passport? His name was on that."

Ben frowned. "We're checking into that. Tell me about Peter."

I told him that Peter was an old friend and totally trustworthy.

"Until he wrote up that phony résumé," Dunlinson reminded me.

I sighed. "Right. That's what I was getting to."

Ben said, "We have an address for him in Ellsworth. Does he actually live there?" He read out the street address to me, and I nodded. I'd been to his apartment many times.

Tom asked, "Do you know who the girl is yet?"

"No, we don't. We ran her prints but got no hits. We'll be releasing her picture to the media later today."

"Do you know how she died?" I asked.

"The ME has many guesses."

"So, it still could be something like a brain aneurysm or a heart attack." I didn't want to think about the alternative.

"We should know something definitively later today."

During this conversation, Scott wasn't with us. Instead, he stood at the end of the dock, talking loudly into his cell phone. I watched him from the corner of my eye.

Ben reached into an inside pocket and pulled out a few Ziploc bags. He said to me. "Something else. We found these items under the mattress in her stateroom. Do these mean anything to you?"

In one of the Ziplocs was a small black and white snapshot of a dark-haired child. "It looks like the girl whose photo was on her phone," I said.

Ben nodded. "We've determined it's the same girl."

"Who is that?" Tom asked, squeezing in and taking one of the Ziplocs.

Ben said, "That's what we don't know. We also found these postcards," he said pulling out another Ziploc.

When he said "postcards," I clenched my teeth together. There it was—the barn, the silo, the muted colors.

Tom leaned in over me and asked, "What are those?"

"We're not sure," Ben said. "These three postcards and the photo were under her mattress."

Why hadn't I been smart enough to check under the mattress? The second card he showed us was of a lighthouse, done in the same muted colors as the farm scene. This one was similar to the one on the wall of *Blue Peace*, but a different lighthouse. The third was a lithograph of a black cat. When I saw that final picture, I had to shove my hands deep into my pockets so that they wouldn't shake.

Ben turned the farmhouse postcard over and pointed at the number. I had not been mistaken. It was really Jesse's cell number. What should I do now? Tell him? Well, of course I must, because they would soon make the connection if they hadn't already. I was shaking, shivering now, and I wondered how much was cold and how much was fear.

Ben said, "Em?"

"The number." I pointed. I could barely speak.

Tom moved in closer to me and put his hand on my shoulder to steady me. "Are you okay?" I was grateful. I surely felt that I was going to fall.

I said, "That's my husband's cell phone number."

Ben peered at me. "Your husband's? You're married?"

"My late husband. He died eighteen months ago. That was his

number. What's it doing on that card?"

Ben said, "Do you have any idea why she would have your husband's cell number?"

I licked my lips, felt all shaky. "Maybe she thought it was mine? I don't know. That number was disconnected about a year ago. I'm sorry. I simply have no idea—" I felt near tears.

I was close to tears because the disconnected cell phone number was the least of my worries. It was the cat picture that I kept staring at. I knew this picture. I knew that cat.

This cat lithograph had been on Jesse's computer.

Chapter 11

Late one night four months before he died, Jesse had been sitting at the kitchen table with his computer. I thought I was rather noisy when I crept up behind him, put my hands around his eyes and said—"Boo!"—but I guess I wasn't.

He jumped a mile, but not before he slammed shut the top of his computer so hard that I thought he had broken it. But I had seen it—that black cat.

There had been pure rage in his voice when he got up, grabbed my hands and said, "Don't you ever come up behind me like that again!"

I tried to laugh it off. "Oh, Jesse, cats! Don't be embarrassed. How very cute! I never knew you were a cat guy. Next thing you'll be spending all your free time watching online cat videos. Or maybe that's what you are doing, hmm?"

"Em, Em." He held my hands so tightly that my fingers hurt. "Please—" That's the only word he said—please.

"Please, what, Jesse? You're scaring me—"

He loosened his grip on my hands. "Please, Em, promise me that you will never, ever tell anyone what you saw here. Not ever. Not anyone."

I pulled away. "Jesse, it's a *cat*!" I noticed then that all the curtains on every window were closed. We never did this. We lived so far out in the country that we hardly ever locked our doors, much less shut our curtains. We liked the view of the water, even at night. Especially at night. I didn't say anything about that, but I noticed. I noticed.

In the next moment, he was back to being himself and holding me and telling me he didn't mean to yell, I'd just startled him. He was tired. Things were out of control at work and he didn't know what he was going to do about Bryce, and when I looked into his eyes, I saw fear.

"What about Bryce?" I asked.

"He's interested in moving in a different direction with the designs."

"What kind of a direction?"

He hadn't answered me, just dropped my hands and sat down, wearily onto a kitchen chair. That night we held on to each other tightly and made furious love—one of the last times we ever did. Because after that, Jesse began to be different.

I should have told the detective about all of this. Standing out there in the rain, I should have, but I didn't. I couldn't. While Ben and Tom talked, I made a decision. I would keep this to myself. For now. I would go home and go through Jesse's computer first. I would find the cat picture. I would figure out what it meant. After I did that, and after I checked all through his files, there would be plenty of time to talk to the police. Wouldn't there? Because, what if I'd never seen the picture in the first place? I would have nothing to tell the police now.

All of this could have something to do with the fear that wouldn't leave me alone. Since Jesse's death, there had been one thought that kept coming to me over and over, one dreadful thought, one terrible, awful thought that would come to me in the middle of the night and make me sit up in bed, my hand on my throat.

Jesse had had an affair. My husband, my soul mate, my best sailing buddy in the whole world had betrayed me in the absolute worst way. It might sound stupid since he's been gone for almost two years, but it matters to me that Jesse was faithful. It matters to me that my parents weren't correct in their assessment of him. It matters to me that my sisters would never be able to say, "I told you so."

Stupid and selfish reasons to impede an investigation, but there they were.

I took off my glasses now, rubbed my eyes and said, "I think I'm just tired. Nothing is making sense. I don't even know what I'm thinking anymore." I swallowed. "I have no idea, none, why my husband's old phone number is on that postcard of the farm. I just— I don't understand that. And if I can figure it out, you'll be the first to know."

Ben asked me if Jesse knew the Pattersons.

"Not that I know of," I told him.

"Your husband had a business partner," Ben said. "Might he have known the Pattersons?"

"I have no idea. I haven't seen Bryce for more than a year."

I told Ben this while my throat was dry and my fingers trembled in my pockets, and while Tom watched me, a quizzical expression on his face. I opened up my phone and gave him what contact information I had for Bryce. He wrote it down.

I told Ben that as soon as I got home, I would look for a list of my husband's business contacts. I thought I might be able to find a few things at home. He wanted to know when I was heading home and I told him as soon as the police gave me back my laptop and my clothes and when was that going to be? He told me maybe soon. Good, I said, because I really wanted my toothbrush.

When Tom and I were alone again and walking back up to Joan's, he said to me, "When you saw that picture of the cat, I could see that you were visibly upset. Do you have a cat, Em? Is that why?"

"No. I have a dog."

In the distance, at the end of the block and leaning against a building in the rain, was Scott. He was still talking on his phone, stomping on the wet sidewalk and sending up little sprays with every step. He looked angry. Very angry.

Chapter 12

The first time the phone rang in my house after Jesse died, I thought it was my mother or one of my friends. I answered it. It was someone from the news wanting to write a story about kayak safety. Did I feel that kayaks ought to be equipped with more safety features, compulsory reflective stripes, for example, so that incidents like Jesse's could be avoided in the future? Did I feel that PFDs should be mandatory for any kind of small vessel?

Incidents? My husband's death was an incident? I hung up without answering any of their questions. Thus had begun the relentless pursuit by the media who seemed to find delight in turning my personal tragedy into their flavor of the month. The thing was, Jesse was an ordinary guy, not a billionaire like Roy Patterson, with a daughter who was MIA and a dead mystery girl who'd impersonated her.

Over the next day, the phone in Joan's house rang a lot. I ignored it. Most of the time Joan did, too. My own phone I could monitor, which I did. I was waiting for my stuff, didn't want to go home without my stuff. I really, really wanted my laptop. I felt naked without it. Tom left for his home after our meeting with Ben, touching my arm and promising me he would keep in touch. "You call me any time you need to talk," he said. "I'm just a phone call away."

I spent most of the rest of that day in the kitchen, drinking coffee and reading either the online news on my phone or the newspaper. The girl hadn't been identified, despite her picture being everywhere. I gazed at her face on my small phone screen. The photo had obviously been taken after she died, but some artist had made it look like she was alive. She barely resembled the girl who'd been on the boat. No wonder no one recognized this picture. No one knew where the real Katherine Patterson was, either.

When I tired of sitting at the kitchen table, I would take a cup of coffee up to the widow's walk and sit there, looking out at the boats on the horizon, hugging my knees to my chest and trying to figure it all out.

The next day at noon I got a short text from Tom:

Heads up—Patterson wants to me to take Blue Peace to Nassau when all this is over. I could use some crew. Actually, it might be good for you to get back on the horse.

Huh? I read it again just to make sure I'd seen the words right the first time. Another text came right away.

Haven't said yes yet to Patterson. Actually, I think just the two of us, you and me could handle the boat. We could split the captain duties and payment.

I stared at the words. This was confusing to me on so many levels. First, I found it a bit hard to believe that Patterson wanted to continue this trip with his daughter still missing. And second, Tom was asking me to go with him? Just the two of us? And third, were my feelings for this man growing? And what did I think about being alone with him on a boat, just the two of us?

If he was talking about a new relationship, I wasn't ready to "get back on the horse." If getting back on the horse was in reference to captaining, I wasn't sure about that, either.

Rather tentatively I wrote back, *Patterson still wants to go to the Bahamas?*

I ended it there.

He must've been right there on his phone, because a return message came immediately.

Man is strange. I've crewed for him for a long time. The stories I could tell.

When will you be leaving? I asked.

As soon as the police release the boat.

Do you know when that will be?

No clue.

What about his daughter? Any news?

He just hired a PI.

That's good, Maybe he'll find her. I'm still waiting for my laptop. I want to go home, but I want it more.

Don't blame you. Think about my offer, will ya? The two of us, we could have fun.

I put my phone in my pocket and went over to the kitchen window. Joan was tugging at weeds in her garden. I watched for a while, absently scratching my arm. In the sitting room, Art was smoking his pipe and reading the paper. It was quiet in here today. There could be worse places, I thought, to be stranded. This large home of Art's and Joan's was like a fortress to me, a place where I could hide out and be safe. I still hadn't had that heart-to-heart with

Joan, and every time I approached her, she seemed busy with other things. Back at the kitchen table I opened up my phone again, wishing for the bigger screen of my laptop. I did an online image search for lithographed black cats and was rewarded with hundreds of sites to look at, but nothing vaguely close. I also tried looking for lighthouses and silos, but the choices were too vast. I kept giving up and then going back. I decided there had to be a way to do this, and so I began a methodical search. I described as much as I could remember about the lighthouse picture on the postcard. This led me to more sites. I described more. More links. I drank more coffee.

Half an hour later, I was finally rewarded. There was the picture of the lighthouse—the exact one—and an accompanying note that this was one of several paintings that had been reported stolen. This led me to the farmhouse picture, the one with Jesse's number scrawled on the back. Both stolen. I stared at the paintings. There was no other information. Stolen from where? It didn't say.

I thought about the similar painting that currently hung on a wall on *Blue Peace*. I took note of all the sites. Should I call the police with this? I took off my glasses and ran a hand over my face. They must have whole departments tasked with online searches. They'd probably already seen this. I probably wouldn't be telling them anything they didn't already know.

My vibrating phone shook me out of my reverie. Tom? The caller ID read Declan Meyer, MD, ME. I answered it.

"Captain Ridge," he said. "I was wondering, would you perhaps have a moment to meet with me?"

"Yes." Did he have more news about Jesse? "I can meet with you at any time."

"This afternoon?"

"When and where? I'll be there."

He gave me an office number at the hospital, and I wrote down his careful directions. When the time came I drove in my own car and parked in the rear.

At the front door of the hospital, I followed his instructions. Down to the lower level, and then down again to the lower-lower level. Afraid that people might recognize me, I'd tucked my hair under a Boston Red Sox ball cap that partially hid my face. In this busy place, though, people for the most part tended to ignore me.

It didn't dawn on me until I was down here that I was meeting him in the morgue. Maybe this was where the girl's body was. I slowed my steps.

It even smelled different down here, harsher, more medicinal, as if the odors from every level and layer of the hospital eventually drifted and settled down here at the bottom like so much toxic dust. I passed someone plugged into earbuds and pushing a cart full of cleaning supplies. He didn't look at me as our footsteps clacked past each other. A group of nurses walked by chattering loudly, their voices echoing down the windowless hall. I kept my head down. As medical examiner for the state of Maine, Dr. Declan Meyer told me he mostly worked out of Augusta. He traveled throughout the state when needed, usually holing up in makeshift offices in the bowels of hospitals. Like this one.

I pushed opened the correctly numbered door. The room was empty and silent, the walls covered with institutional white paint. A couple of scratched metal desks were shoved up against one wall.

Several closed doors were at the rear of the oblong room.

"Dr. Meyer?" I called. "Hello?"

I heard humming behind one of the doors and ventured toward it. Dr. Meyer emerged, wearing a white lab coat, blue latex gloves and a little magnifying mirror on his forehead like a jeweler's third eye. He grinned when he saw me. "I can say with certainty, *Amanita phalloides*. Definitely *Amanita phalloides*."

I looked at him, uncomprehending.

"Follow me," he said. "I'll explain it all." Dr. Meyer had quite a protuberant stomach, and his rather smudgy lab coat didn't quite meet in the middle.

I entered the room, only partly concerned that he was leading me into the place where the body was laid out. He wasn't. The room was large and square. The walls sported a few old and torn-edged anti-smoking posters and one very outdated drug company calendar.

"Welcome," he said, "to my home away from home. Such as it is."

A square table piled with folders and books seemed to serve as his desk. "Have a seat," he said. "I'm sure the good detective has filled you in on all of this, so I doubt I'm telling you anything new. *Amanita phalloides*."

The good detective hadn't filled me in on anything.

"Death cap," he said.

What was death cap? I took a breath and waited.

"It was definitely a death cap mushroom that killed that girl," he said, tapping the paper with his mechanical pencil.

"The girl was poisoned by mushrooms?"

He nodded. "I'm certain of that."

"Peter's my cook. I don't remember eating anything with mushrooms. I don't care for them, so he wouldn't have even brought them onboard."

Even as I said it, the words dried on my tongue. I remembered the money that was still on the coffee table at Joan's. Was Peter involved in all of this?

"No cook worth his salt would mistake the death cap for a butter or other edible mushroom," said Dr. Meyer. "After ingestion, symptoms can take up to twenty-four hours to manifest, which gives credence to my theory that she ate this particular mushroom prior to getting on the boat."

"Something she ate in a restaurant?"

"As I said, no cook worth his salt would ever make that mistake. However, I think the RCMP are checking restaurants in New Brunswick, Canada as we speak. But again, I think that is a useless venture. I have more here—" More page turning. "It appears she fell overboard but she could have died in her sleep just as easily." He looked up at me. "The police are pursuing the idea that this may have been deliberate."

I looked at him without saying anything.

"The likelihood that she may have gone out mushroom picking isn't too probable," he said, "given that the Amanita phalloides are not native to this continent. This kind of mushroom is fairly common in certain places in Europe. There are many tragic incidences where people have picked them in their own backyards and eaten them in error and died."

All I kept thinking about was Peter. The money he'd taken, his obvious dislike of the girl, his disappearance. From underneath a pile of files, Dr. Meyer pulled out a thick botanical volume, which he opened to a plate of colored photographs. I read the accompanying descriptions and symptoms. Yes, the girl had had all of these complaints, which horrifyingly mimicked the symptoms of seasickness. I ran my fingers along the outer edge of the pictures. The death cap looked like all the mushrooms I'd ever seen in the grocery store. I decided then and there never to go mushroom picking on my own. Ever. And never to eat mushrooms again. Ever. Not that I ever had in the first place.

"That information will be released to the public soon," he told me. "Maybe someone out there will help us. Sometimes that helps. Sometimes that hurts."

I blinked, took off my baseball cap and ran the brim through my fingers. Jesse loved mushrooms, but when we cooked anything with mushrooms, we left them cut really, really big so I could pick them out and put them on his plate. He loved them in everything—casseroles, gravies, omelets, salads. A girl murdered by mushrooms had been walking around with my mushroom-loving dead husband's canceled cell phone number in her pocket.

"Captain Ridge?" Dr. Meyer asked.

"Yes." I snapped back to reality. "Sorry, Dr. Meyer."

He looked at me for a moment. "Why don't you call me Declan?"

"And please," I said, "you can call me Em." I didn't think I wanted anyone to call me Captain Ridge ever again. "So somebody gave her mushrooms and she died."

"It might look that way. There is still more testing to be done. More investigation. The boat is being scrubbed for fibers and mushroom particles as we speak. But I have told the police that I believe that is a waste of time. We need to be looking at places she was before she boarded."

I nodded.

"But my advice, well, sometimes it goes unheeded."

I nodded.

"It certainly did with your husband."

I looked at him expectantly. "Um, did you happen to find any more information about my husband?"

He closed the file. "The boys are gone. Their families are gone. My notes are gone. It's inexplicable."

I stared. "What?"

He tented his hands on the table and said thoughtfully, "Recently, my office was moved. I had carefully packed up my personal notes and files, but someone else, I guess, took it upon him or herself to reorganize my papers. As it stands, the notes for that particular case seem to be missing."

There was a silence in the room, and I didn't know how to respond. "I'm going to be looking into this more," he continued. "I can promise you that. I'm going to be asking some questions. That girl's death was not an accident. And I don't think your husband's death was an accident, either."

Chapter 13

What was Declan Meyer suggesting? Someone had murdered Jesse? I could barely breathe, barely contain my thoughts, as I drove back. Yes, the idea had crossed my mind. I had certainly broached the subject at the inquest. But the police kept insisting, over and over. Accident. Accident. Accident. Tragic. Accident. That's. All. It. Was.

When I got back to Joan's, I decided I wanted to look through the paper Art had been reading when I left. Neither Art nor Joan would tell me where it was, though.

"Probably the recycle," Joan said from over the top of her book. She seemed distracted.

"Already?" I huffed out to the blue box on the back porch. It was overflowing. I leafed through the papers at the top. It wasn't there. "I can't find it!" I called.

"Just news," Joan said from her chair. "All so bad. Nothing good."

I came back into the sitting room. "I just wanted to have a look through it," I said.

She shrugged.

"Joan?"

She looked at me, and then beyond me to a space somewhere behind my back and said, "I think we all need a break from this."

She left me standing there and made her way into the hallway and presumably to her room. Art sat there without saying anything.

A break from me, she means. It was time for me to leave. I knew this. I needed to get home. I was probably overstaying my welcome as it was. Even good and wise and patient people like Joan have their limits. She had reached hers. I was close to reaching mine. I needed to get home and get on with my life—whatever that was going to be now. But, I needed my things, my own clothes and most of all my laptop. I also needed to get home and into Jesse's computer. I needed to straighten that all out. Ben wanted a list of Jesse's business contacts, and I certainly wasn't doing anything about that sitting here, was I? I made a decision then. I would go home, even without my computer. I went upstairs to my room to pull the sheets from the bed, and half an hour later I figured out why Joan didn't want me to read the paper. It began with a terse text from Tom, which read,

Don't believe what you read in the news. If I find out who this so-called anonymous source is, I'll personally kill him. I'm not kidding. I'm making inquiries.

So of course I had to immediately click into the online version of the newspaper. What I read stunned me. A Portland newspaper had quoted an "anonymous source in the sailing community," who described me as "inexperienced." Much was made of the fact that this was my first captaining job. The source went on to say that he or she had crewed with me "on several occasions" and that I appeared, "feisty, indecisive and moody."

What? If this had been an actual newspaper, I would have flung it across the room. Instead, I paced muttering and pressing down keys on my phone. I have *never* been indecisive, and when was I feisty? I pride myself on never being feisty. And moody? I'm always in control. I'm so calm I could teach yoga. I fisted both my hands.

Plus, Jesse's death was making for a convenient sidebar. Did everyone know that I was the wife of the man who stumbled out drunk in the middle of the night and had gotten himself chopped in half by a power boat? The paper hadn't been quite that graphic, but I knew that's what they were thinking. Drunk! He hadn't even finished one beer. I know, because I drank the half he left on the kitchen table.

I don't know where they dug up *that* picture of me. I was standing at the wheel of a boat, looking distracted and fierce. I was wearing my yellow jacket with the toggles done up. Is that how I look in it? It looked too big on me. My hair was all flying back and out of control. I looked stern and, well—old. "Feisty? Indecisive? Moody?" was written under my picture. Not my name, just those three words.

When I got my breath back, I sat down on the edge of the bed and tried to quell my furious shaking. I texted Tom.

Even though the police haven't returned my things, I'm driving home in a few minutes. I have things to do there. The police need a list of Jesse's business contacts from his computer.

I wanted to check out the cat picture.

Right away he texted back.

Don't leave. Not right now. Have dinner with me tonight. Hope you're still thinking about my offer.

I leaned against the wall and in a few minutes texted him back. *Sure. Dinner would be nice. Where can I meet you?*

An hour later I was sitting on the wooden bench outside of Ben Dunlinson's office, waiting for him to be finished with whatever it was that was keeping him in there. I felt much like an errant student waiting outside the principal's office. It just so happens I've had experience with that, too.

When I'd called and asked him if I could finally pick up my things, he'd said, "Can you come in then and see me for a minute? I'll bring you up to date on what's happening. I also have something I'd like to talk to you about."

I shut my eyes briefly and was a little afraid.

I checked the time on my phone. I'd been here twelve minutes. How long was I just going to sit here? At the thirteen-minute mark, he came out and saw me. His eyes widened.

"Em? How long have you been here?"

"Twenty minutes." I stood.

"I told Miriam to take you to the coffee room so you wouldn't have to be out here and be subjected to the wolves."

"The wolves?" He led me into his office.

"The news. Paparazzi. They've been here night and day. The missing daughter of a billionaire generates interest."

"There's a news van parked outside Joan and Art's. I've managed to avoid talking to anyone." I sat down, wondering how long it would take some enterprising journalist to figure out how to get to my house out at the end of Chalk Spit Island. I guessed five minutes. Did I really want to go home to that? Yes. I wanted to go home. Not to that, but I wanted to go home.

Ben sat down, and I took the same seat I'd been in a few nights before. "So you're heading home." It was a statement not a question.

"Yep. I've been at Joan and Art's long enough. I'm not that far from Portland. Forty-five minutes, tops. Longer if I have to take the ferry. Is it possible for me to have my computer and my backpack back? Do you still need them?"

He smiled. "It just so happens," he said reaching under his desk. "I've got your things right here." He brought them out and put them on his desk. I pulled my laptop toward me, wondering how much snooping they had done.

His desk phone rang and he answered it. I waited, privy only to his side of the conversation.

"Just keep me up to date on that," he said. "And make sure we find places for those children to go."

Children? I couldn't help myself. I raised my eyebrows.

After he hung up he said, "Another matter. I've been up to my ears and then this gets thrown into the stew. Sorry I haven't gotten back to you sooner." There were lines around his eyes.

"You do look busy." I put my computer on my lap and backpack close to me on the floor.

"Just before that girl went overboard, I was dealing with a weird case of illegals. Still got that on my plate."

"Illegal whats?"

"Undocumented people. Coming in by boat. Children. Well, we don't know how they're getting in. We're assuming by boat."

"And they're coming to *Maine*?" I said, trying to lighten the mood. "I've been to Canada lots. There are not a whole lot of Canadians sneaking over the border to live in Maine—"

"They're not from Canada." The way he frowned bespoke the seriousness of whatever the situation was.

"Where are they from then?"

"Our best guess is eastern Europe."

"Where are they now?" I asked.

"We've got them housed in a safe place, but none of them are talking. Well"—he shook his head and frowned—"none of them can really speak the language."

"Children?"

He nodded.

I was remembering TV documentaries of wide-eyed, scared and ragged people sitting in the backs of trucks or railroad containers. But that usually occurred in places like Texas or New Mexico. Not Maine.

"I've got my best officer working on that while I concentrate on this. I never thought Maine would be such a hotbed of crime."

"It usually isn't."

He told me then what I already knew—about the mushrooms and that they still didn't know who the girl was, but they were going on the assumption that she'd been deliberately poisoned. I asked if they'd found Kricket Patterson yet, and he shook his head.

"What about Rob?" I asked.

"No to that one, too. Plus, we still can't locate Peter."

"I haven't been able to, either," I said. "I've been texting him nonstop."

He said, "According to neighbors, he hasn't been to his apartment. No one has seen him. Do you have a list of friends or family where he may have gone?"

I clicked into my phone and gave him a list of some of our mutual sailing friends. He wrote everything down.

"And your husband," he said. "You still have no idea why his number was on the back of the postcard that was found in her effects?"

I swallowed and told him what I'd found online that morning, that the paintings depicted on the postcards had been stolen.

"We probably found that information here same time you did. You must be a crack computer hacker. But," and he eyed me. "Any idea why your husband seems to be linked to it?"

"No." His gaze made me feel uncomfortable. I shifted in the chair.

He said, "We tried the contact information you had for the fellow that your husband worked with. His email bounced back."

"I'm not surprised."

He paused before continuing. "It appears Patterson bought a number of paintings a few years ago. He reported them stolen a year ago."

"They were Patterson's?"

"It appears so. He was collecting art by that particular artist."

We talked for a few more minutes, and this time I felt at ease. He was a strange man, this detective, one minute stern and standoffish and the next buddy-buddy. I didn't quite trust people like that.

Finally, he said, "Em, I have a favor I'd like to ask of you." He paused and looked down at his desk before continuing. "You may have noticed that I don't have a lot of experience when it comes to boats. Actually, life in Maine in general."

That was an understatement.

He went on. "What I'm looking for is someone I can trust, someone from outside the department who has expertise on all manner of sailing, boats, the ocean, life in Maine. Fishing. Lobsters. All of it."

"You want me to suggest someone?" I thought immediately of Tom. Or even Joan. Art would be a good choice, too. I mentioned their names.

"No." He looked at me again with those eyes. "I was thinking of you."

"Me?" You could have knocked me over with a piece of fishing line.

"I've got lots of guys here on the force who grew up on boats and come from a long line of lobstering families. But what I'm looking for is a more personal touch. Maybe a woman's point of view." He paused. "I was very impressed with you when we were on the boat coming home. You were capable and in control."

I simply stared at him.

He gave me a bit of a smile. "It may come as a surprise, but when I was out there on the water with you, that's the farthest I've been from land on any sort of boat. I've never been out on a boat where I couldn't see land. I was scared to death. I hope it didn't show too much."

"It didn't show at all," I lied.

He sort of gave me a half smile when he said, "I'm trying to greatly redeem myself for thinking Peter Mauer was the captain."

"I assure you, girls can be captains, too."

"I know that now. You handled yourself well out there."

"Thank you," I said. "That means a lot." I paused before continuing. "What kind of stuff would you want?"

"The police liaise with local citizens, use expert witnesses all the time. In your case, I'd just like someone from the outside who can answer my stupid questions every once in a while."

"Okay. Sure. I can do that."

He wrote something on the back of a business card and handed it to me. "My private number. Please call me if you have any questions, and can I call you? That's why I was so free in telling you about the children. We think they came in by boat, but we haven't been able to find it. Keep that under your hat, would you? I may need your help on that at some point."

I promised him I would. I also assured him I would have lots of time to do what he wanted. "It's not like I'm going to be getting any sort of job any time soon."

He looked at me sadly. "It wasn't your fault, Em."

I looked down. "Here's your first lesson, detective. When something, anything, happens on a boat, it is always the captain's fault. Period."

Chapter 14

"**I**'m surprised you want to be associated with somebody who's so feisty, indecisive and moody."

Those were my first words to Tom after I sat down across from him at the restaurant that evening. Since it wasn't far, and a nice night, I walked instead of drove. Given the choice, I always prefer walking or biking over driving, and tonight I had an even better reason. A news van had pulled up outside the front of Joan and Art's and was sitting there at the end of the driveway. Blocking it, actually. I could, though, walk out the back door, climb over the short fence to the alleyway and escape to town that way.

The place Tom had chosen was a small café down a flight of stairs below street level that featured cutely retro-red candles on checkered tablecloths. I thought I knew Portland pretty well, but this spot, tucked away in the corner of a backstreet, was new to me. I'd thought long and hard about what to wear from the stash of boating clothes I had with me. I didn't have a lot in my backpack, but I did manage to find clean jeans and a green button-down shirt that wasn't too wrinkled. I washed my hair and went at it with a blow dryer. I even put on makeup. And earrings. Tom wore a crisp white golf shirt with the Nassau Yacht Club embroidered on the upper left. I had an idea that this guy couldn't look bad if he tried.

He did not smile when I said those words. "Don't, Em. You demean yourself. It's not funny. No one should have said that. You're one of the finest sailors I've been privileged to crew with. That's why I had no trouble recommending you to Patterson. And that's why I'd love for you to accompany me on the *Blue Peace* trip even now."

"But you don't even know me. We were only on that one delivery so long ago."

He gazed at me intently when he said, "And as I have told you before, I haven't forgotten you."

Really? I looked down at the top of the table, hoping the dimness of the place hid my blush. I said, "Patterson might not want me on his boat."

"If I ever find out who that anonymous source is, they'll hear it from me. We sailors don't treat each other like that."

"Thank you," I said. Maybe this meant I was really accepted into the fraternity of captains.

He reached across the table and covered my hand with his. The move was unexpected. He didn't move his hand away, and neither did I until the waitress came and set down two glasses of Guinness.

He winked at me. "Guinness, right? Your beer of choice?"

"How'd you know?"

"I know a lot about you."

My face was becoming too warm. "I hope all good." Stupid. Stupid. What a stupid thing to say.

"Always," he said.

He picked up his menu. So did I, but my emotions were such a jumble I was having trouble making sense of the words on the page. "What's good?" I managed to mutter. "This place is new to me."

"Everything. Homemade pasta is their specialty." His voice was softer now.

"Comfort food," I said. "I need comfort food."

He put the menu down and looked straight into my eyes. "How are you coping with all of this, Em, really?"

I shrugged. "It'll be nice to be home. I miss Rusty."

He raised his eyebrows. "Rusty?"

"My elderly dog."

"Ah, your dog. Tell me about your dog."

"You really want to hear about my dog?"

"Sure," he said. "I like dogs. I want to know everything there is to know about what's important to you."

Was he laying it on just a bit too thick? I told him that Rusty was Jesse's dog and how at first Rusty hadn't accepted me, but then finally he had, and now the two of us were best buds. Rusty was getting old and arthritic and couldn't run very fast anymore. "So, mostly we go for slow walks. He likes it outside, but he doesn't go much past the front porch."

"Sounds like a nice dog."

"That he is."

The waitress came. Tom ordered stuffed ravioli appetizers for us. I ordered a chicken dish, and Tom decided on the veal. After she left, I took a long drink of my creamy beer.

Tom asked, "What will you do when you get home?"

I put my beer down. "You mean now that no boat owner will ever hire me ever again? I don't know. Maybe try to get some work at the boatyard out on Chalk Spit. I've worked there before. Maybe teach in the sailing school. That is, if the parents will trust me with their children. I've sort of even been thinking about going back to school. In Portland. Or online."

"Really?"

"I never finished college. After one semester, I turned myself into a sailing bum."

"You're no bum." He leaned forward, and I thought he was going to put his hand on mine again, so I kept it within reach. I was starting to realize that I liked the feel of his touch. "You're about the hardest working person I know."

"Thanks but, Tom, you don't really know me."

"I'm hoping that will change."

I couldn't explain it, but I was feeling a bit uncomfortable. Was all of this moving too fast?

He looked at me sadly. "And you're heading home?"

"I am. Tonight. After we eat. I'm at the end of Chalk Spit Island. I'm not that far."

"Why do you live way out there?"

"I just do."

He raised his eyebrows.

"Actually, it was a summer cottage that had been in Jesse's family forever. No one else in the family wanted it, so it ended up where Jesse and I lived year round."

"Really? Nobody in his family wanted it?"

"Jesse has one sister, in western Canada. She didn't want it. His parents didn't want it, either. So it's mine with the proviso that if his family wants to visit, they can."

"You okay with that?"

"Of course. If anyone ever comes, I'll go live on my boat. But no one has."

"Tell me about your neighbors."

Was he really interested? Nevertheless I did. I told him about EJ and his ham radio. The bickering, gossipy sisters on the other side. Over appetizers, I asked him how he got into sailing. Well into the main course, Tom told me about every single boat he had ever owned, one by one. We laughed. We compared notes. Despite myself, I felt comfortable being with him. He told me he had recently bought an old forty-foot wooden schooner that he was taking apart and putting together again from scratch, "scratch" being the operative word, he told me with a laugh.

"What's the name of your boat? In case I see it around."

"You won't," he said. "Engine's shot, and she's got more leaks than a colander. She's not going anywhere. The name on it now is *Second Time Around*, but that ridiculous name will be changed. I haven't come up with a new one yet."

"Why'd you buy it?" I asked.

He laughed. "I love a challenge?" Then he got real serious and shook his head. "Weirdest thing, though."

"What?"

"I went down to my boat yesterday, and it was like—" He paused before continuing. "It was like someone had come aboard and methodically gone through all the cupboards."

"Really? Was anything taken?"

"There's nothing on it to steal." He looked into the middle distance when he said, "It was just like someone had come into my boat, gone through everything and then put everything back, but not quite back the way it was in the first place."

"What did the police say?"

"Didn't call them."

"Why not?"

"Because I can't be sure. It was just a feeling, a very funny feeling. Nothing was missing, so what I've decided to do is to keep my boat locked up, even though I'm in a locked dock area."

"Where do you live?"

When he told me, I said, "That's a pretty nice place if it's the condos I'm thinking of."

"It's been a dream of mine for a long time. On the water, all the amenities. When they were constructing that new place, I got my name in there first."

Over dessert and coffee, I told Tom about the stolen artwork. But, following Ben's urging, I didn't tell him about the children.

"Does Ben know this?" he asked.

"Ben was the one who told me."

"Really?"

He speared his cheesecake with his fork and, looking down at his plate, seemed to be searching for words. "I happen to know something about that."

He looked from left to right as if to satisfy himself that no one was within earshot. He put the forkful of cheesecake back on his plate. "I wasn't going to unload all of this onto you, but you probably should know something about the Pattersons."

I waited.

"Roy Patterson is a difficult and demanding person. I also—" He stopped, as if thinking how to formulate his next sentence. "I also happen to know that his businesses are in serious financial trouble. He said his art was stolen? That's not entirely true. He's been selling off his art collection piece by piece. But—" From another table, there came laughter. "There is a right way and a wrong way to sell art. I don't think he's entirely doing this the right way. I fear for him. I think Patterson is in over his head."

"Does Ben know this?"

"Detective Dunlinson?"

I nodded.

"Let me ask you something. What is your impression of Ben Dunlinson?"

I shrugged. "I don't know him. He's new to Portland. He seems efficient enough."

Tom nodded soberly.

I said, "We were on *Blue Peace* for fourteen hours. You get to know a person when you're on a boat that long together. He certainly seems to be working hard on this."

He looked thoughtful. "I just wonder…" His voice trailed off and he frowned.

"What do you wonder?"

His lips were a thin line. "He seems qualified, and certainly he's a nice enough guy, but—" He paused. "I know some of the other officers. I guess it's because I live here, you know. You hear the stories. Do you know Dunlinson's story at all?"

"He told me a little while we were on the boat together, about how he misses Montana. But that's about all he said."

"That's all he would say, I'm sure."

I looked at him.

"His entire story is online," Tom said. "Every sad little piece of it. And it's not a pretty tale."

I waited.

Tom said, "He shot and killed an innocent person. A bystander.

Back in Montana."

I still didn't say anything.

"That much is online. That's why he came here, I guess. I don't want to be disparaging of him. I'm just concerned, is all. I like the guy well enough. I do worry, though. This is a pretty high-profile case."

I decided that now was not the time to tell Tom that Ben had asked me to be a sort of expert on local culture.

I looked up in time to see Scott weaving his way through the tables toward us, grimacing.

I leaned forward and said quietly, "We have company and he looks upset."

Tom turned. "Oh, his Speedo's always in a knot over something. I think it's because he wants to come on the *Blue Peace* trip, and I don't want him to."

"Why not?"

"Because I'd rather have you. Look at him. He's a hothead. Hotheads and long-distance sailing don't mix."

Scott now stood above us. Tom said, "Scott, Scott, my friend, what are you doing here?"

"I could ask you the same thing," Scott said. "Wasn't this the evening we were supposed to get your *engine* worked on?"

Tom said, "Scott, I'm out with a lady. She's heading home. The engine can wait." He smiled widely at him, but it was a weird, almost malevolent smile. "And I did send you a text."

Scott roughly pulled over a chair from a neighboring table and sat down between us. He said, "I feel like I'm doing all the work here. On your boat." He pointed his finger at Tom. "Your boat. And you're running off having dinner. I can't be expected to do it all. I could use some help here."

Tom put his hand on Scott's shoulder. "Chill, Scott. It'll get done. It'll all get done."

"Yeah. Right." He got up and roughly shoved the chair back across the floor to the other table. "I'm heading *home*." He stretched out the word home, the same way he had elongated the word engine. He leaned down toward Tom and said something that I couldn't hear. I could see the top of his shaved head. Tom scowled. Scott slapped his hand on the table. "I'll talk to you later." On the way out, he looked back and cocked his forefinger at us like a gun.

"Wow," I said after he was out the door. "What was that all about?"

"He's working on my boat."

"Well, yeah, I got that much, but why was he so upset?"

"Guy's crazy. I hired him because he's one of the best diesel mechanics around, if a bit high-strung."

"Ya think?"

Tom sighed, "And it doesn't help that we're neighbors now."

"He's in one of those condos, too?"

"No. He's sleeping on his boat, an old lobster boat. It's docked in the slip next to mine while he works on mine."

When the waitress came, Tom took the check, and over my protests, he paid for the whole thing, which I guess, turned this officially into a date. He insisted on driving me back to Joan's even though I said I was well able to walk and really didn't want to run into the people from the news van. Nevertheless, at his insistence, I climbed up into his Jeep. "Nice wheels," I said.

"I like 'em."

On the road, he said, "You want to come over to my place? For a coffee or something?"

I looked over at him sharply and said, "I need to get home. Tonight."

"Think you can avoid the news people?"

"I'll do my best."

"Well, some other time then," he said. He looked disappointed.

"Some other time."

At Joan's door, I quickly climbed down from the passenger seat, but Tom was around the front of the Jeep before I could even get the door fully opened.

"You're not allowing me to be chivalrous."

"Guess I haven't had that in a while."

His voice was gentle and his face very close to mine when he said, "I'd like to change all of that."

He reached out and touched my cheek. I thought for a moment that he was going to kiss me, but in the last second I moved back and away and went inside.

But I had seen clear into his eyes, through them and into his heart, and I had sensed some deep sadness. Like me, both of us were flawed.

Chapter 15

I plugged my phone into my car stereo and tuned into a music playlist for my drive. It was dark by now, but low tide, so I'd be able to get home quickly and with no problem.

I was barely out onto the highway when a favorite song was interrupted by what sounded like a chicken being slaughtered. I jumped in my seat, nearly drove off the road, until I realized this was the particular ring tone I'd chosen for family members. I hit the hands-free operation and answered. My sister Katie.

"Emmeline! Are you okay? I haven't spoken to you since all of this happened. It's just horrible! It's all over the news—"

"Yeah, it is. I guess."

"Even on CNN."

"I'm famous." I pulled off the highway into a rest area to continue the conversation.

"We're all so worried," she said. "Everyone is."

"I'm okay," I said.

"Do the police have you?" she asked. "Are you in custody?"

What! "What?" I asked.

"Just wondering."

I sighed. "No, Katie. I'm not in jail."

"She ate mushrooms? That was on the news."

"That's what they're saying."

"Like the psychedelic ones?"

"No. Like the poisonous ones."

"Oh. You didn't eat any of them, did you?"

"No. Because, as you can tell, I'm alive and talking to you."

Stop it, I chided myself. *Stop being so sarcastic.* But I couldn't help it.

"Did they find the real girl yet?"

"No."

"We're so worried. I've been worried. You're my sister."

"I'm going home."

"Will you still get paid then for the delivery?"

I blinked, looked into the darkness of the rest area around me. Trees stood like armed guards. I was the only one parked in here. "Actually, Katie, that was the last thing on my mind. But thank you for your concern."

"Emmeline?" She paused.

"Yeah?"

"I want to tell you something, well, ask you something, and I don't want you to immediately say no. It's why I asked you about being paid. I want you to consider something. I want you to promise to think about it. We've all talked about this. Mom, Dad, all of us. Jack and I have lots of room. Mom must've told you about our new house. We have a whole spare loft that we're turning into a guest suite, and you're welcome to come and stay here. It's not quite finished yet, but if we know you're coming, we'll make getting it done a priority. And you can stay here for as long as you need to. Jack would love it. In fact, he was the one who suggested it, and Mom and Dad and Marianna and Raymond would love it, too. We all would. Including the kids. They don't see enough of you, you know. None of us do. We'd love to have you here for a while. Don't immediately say no."

"I'm on my way home now."

"Emmeline, this is your home. We are your home. We want to be here for you. We're family. We're all each other has. Even if you don't realize it. You can't live in that cabin for the rest of your life."

"It's not a cabin. It's my home."

"Still…"

"I'm okay, Katie. Really I am."

"But what will you do for work? Do you have a job?"

"I'll manage. I always manage."

"Oh, Emmeline! We were talking about this, too. Jack and I were talking about it. He would gladly take you on in the company."

I was still for a while. Living in my sister's loft, working for her husband appealed to me about as much as performing my own root canal. A car pulled into the rest area and parked. A family. I watched them. A mother held the hands of two daughters, one on each side of her as they made their way up to the restroom. It made me inexplicably sad.

She went on. "I don't even think you've seen the baby—"

She was referring to my sister Marianna's baby, who was born just after Jesse died, and no, I hadn't seen him. What was wrong with me? Was I really so estranged from my family? Had I done this? Yes, I had.

"Really. I'm fine. I'll be okay."

"We want to be here for you."

"I know. I'm sorry if I sound ungrateful, but this is just one of those times when I'm better off by myself. I would be horrible company."

"We don't mind horrible company. We've gone through things here that you know nothing about. It's not all been roses for us either, you know. We want you to come back. Come back home."

Very slowly and quietly, I said, "I can't. My life is in Maine. My life is here. My home is here."

When we finally said good-bye, my music was back to something soft and mournful. It fit. I know I'm an ungrateful daughter, an awful sister, a crappy aunt. It's not all my fault, though. My perfect family—they all have each other. They always have. Even when we were kids, I was a fifth wheel. There was my Mom and Dad, and then Marianna and Katie in their little twin world. And then there was me. The older daughter, the awkward one, the not-pretty one. The one who had-so-much-promise-but-didn't-finish-college one. When I married Jesse, I thought they would finally accept me. They didn't. It only got worse.

I pulled out onto the highway again as the music moved into the next song on my playlist, something bluesy with a lot of saxophones.

So, yes, I'm horrid. I've never gone back to Ohio to visit any of them. I sent a gift for the baby, though. At least I remembered to do that. A little sleeper with a sailboat on it.

Then again, my sisters have never come to my home here. Not once. I doubt they could even point on a map to where I live. They have no right to refer to it as a "cabin." It's waterfront property, for goodness' sake. Worth a fortune, maybe, if I were to sell it. Which I wouldn't.

Their major problem was that Jesse and I had lived together before we were married. That got me "the big lecture" from Marianna and Katie. Rather than actually coming and visiting me at my house, they had attempted this weird "intervention" thing over Skype. Jesse, like me, was nothing but a boat bum, never mind that he had a master's degree in marine engineering. He was a boat bum. I was a boat bum. And neither of us would ever amount to anything. We would be boat bums until we died and floated away in our sad little boat-bum boats.

I know that what gets them is that I'm too much like my mother's brother, my Uncle Ferd. Uncle Ferd is a name that's always bandied about as the worst possible example of a family member to emulate, ever. He lives all over the world on an old hulk of a schooner. Still does. I don't know where he is currently, but in a week or a month, I'll get an email from him, and he'll be in the Mediterranean or Thailand or New Zealand.

It makes me sad that I'm not the kind of aunt who has a favorite niece or nephew who thinks their aunt is cool and who comes out sailing with me. I would love that. That's what I had with Uncle Ferd. He was the one who taught me to sail. I spent lots of time on his boat and loved every minute of it. The few times I met my nieces and nephews, they stood in the background, eyeing me uncertainly and saying polite thank-yous when prompted by a parent.

My mother and father came to Jesse's funeral, but my sisters did not. My parents stayed with me for two days. They had to get back to Marianna, who was "having complications" with her third pregnancy and who was "due any day." Non-pregnant Katie could have come. She didn't. My sisters didn't send flowers, nothing. They didn't even phone until two weeks after Jesse was gone. Unlike my sisters, my Uncle Ferd came to Jesse's funeral. He anchored his boat down in front of my house and stayed there for a month sitting with me, just sitting with me while I cried.

I turned off the highway and onto the road that would eventually wind down into the tidal flats before it emerged onto Chalk Spit Island and the gravel road which led to my home.

My music stopped, taking me out of my reverie. A text from Tom.

Let me know when you're home. I want to make sure you're safe. Scott and I are leaving day after tomorrow for Bermuda. You sure you won't reconsider? I'd gladly trade Scott for you, and he knows it.

Chapter 16

As much as I love traveling—and I'm usually on the water a good six months out of every calendar year—by the time I'm home, I'm ready to dump my duffle bag onto the floor and bundle up my salt-saturated clothes and throw them into the washer with a good shaking of detergent. I'm ready to stand under a hot shower for a full hour and wash every vestige of salt and sweat off my body and out of my addled brain. I'm ready to stand there and stand there and stand there until the room stops swaying and I get my land-legs again.

The closer I got to my home, the more I found myself looking forward to seeing the two irascible old "bickering sisters." I wanted to eat some of Isabelle's potato chip covered tuna casserole and, over glasses of sweet sherry, listen to every bit of island gossip there was.

I longed to hug my big old dog and feel his coat against my face. I wanted to go next door and drink strong black tea with my elderly neighbor EJ and hear all about who he had raised on his ham radio and to see his newest collection of QSL cards. Even though I tell him that with today's technology, you can Skype people more easily and quickly, EJ is an old soul. He grew up in a time when ham radio was the coolest social media out there. He still does code, even.

I also wanted to admire his latest boxes. EJ makes handcrafted wooden boxes, big ones, like cedar chests, down to tiny, exquisite ones with miniature hinges small enough to cradle a diamond ring. I wanted to ooh and ahh over all his latest designs and creations.

I wanted to see my friends Jeff and Valerie and their son Liam, who live on the other side of Dot and Isabelle and keep three hundred lobster traps and let me tie my boat to their dock. I couldn't wait to head over to the boatyard on the other side of the island and talk boats and weather and fishing and politics with Harvey, who manages the place.

Right now, the road just couldn't get me there fast enough.

There's a funny contrast to that, though. I'm home maybe a week tops before my feet start itching for the water, and I ache to be out on the salt again.

The closer I got to home, however, the more nervous I became. I swallowed back the lump in my throat. What would people say? Would Harvey want me to work for him or would my name and infamy be a hindrance? Would Mavis allow me to pick up a few shifts at the diner next to the boatyard? Or, would I scare away the customers? Thinking about my current bank account made me want to crawl into a corner and chew on the ends of my sweater sleeves.

Dot and Isabelle must have seen the lights of my car, because when I pulled beside my house, they were outside to greet me. Isabelle wore clean, white Keds, and her hair was tucked under a silk scarf a la Audrey Hepburn. This was in contrast to Dot's frizzy red head, loose trousers and orange gardening clogs. As I got out of my car, my two eccentric friends rushed toward me, arms flung out.

Then I was with them, and they were hugging me and cooing, and I was trying to stifle the sobs welling inside me.

"It's okay," Isabelle crooned. "It's okay. You're home now."

"Come over for a nightcap," Dot said. "We bought a new bottle of sherry."

"Leave her be, Dot. She doesn't want a nightcap," Isabelle said. She was holding a square foil-wrapped container. "Goodness, give the girl some air. She doesn't want to come over now. She wants to go in and unpack, don't you, dear? I took this out of the freezer for you. I thought you might want something to eat."

"Thank you," I said.

"Your hands are full. I'll just take it in and put it in your fridge for you. It's tuna casserole. And if you want to come over later, we'd love to have you. But don't feel obligated, no matter what Dot says."

"Let her make up her own mind. If she doesn't want to come for sherry, she doesn't have to."

I put my hand up and grinned. "I'll come over tomorrow. Right now, I'm just bushed."

"We understand. We've been following this in the news. Terrible thing."

"Awful thing."

"Such a terrible thing."

"We're here for you."

"If you want to talk."

I smiled and said thank you.

"Oh, we should tell you something."

"There's been some action on the house next to yours," Dot said.

"Action?" The house next to mine, smaller than my own yet with a better view of the water, had been for sale from before Jesse died.

I dragged my duffle bag to my front door. Later, I would go over to EJ's and pick up Rusty.

"And he's very handsome," Isabelle was saying.

"Who?" I asked.

"The young man who's been over there looking at that house. Very handsome. He would be a nice addition to the neighborhood."

"Such a handsome young man."

"Well," said Isabelle, "provided he wants to live here year-round. Not many people do, you know."

"Oh, he looked like the type who would. And he looked about your age, Em."

"Oh, you guys," I said. For almost a year, Dot and Isabelle have been trying to fix me up with any single man who happened along. "The guy's probably married with a bunch of kids."

As it turned out, I didn't have to go over to EJ's. Rusty came down the steps from EJ's house like a crotchety old man. Following was EJ in his slippers and old man's gray sweater.

"Hey, hey, Rusty. Hey, boy." I bent down and nuzzled at the dog's neck, warmed by his hot, panting breaths and slobbery kisses. In the next instant, I lost it. I began to cry. All of the sobs I'd been holding back finally surfaced. Above me, the sisters could have bickered all they wanted about who was handsome and who wasn't, I barely heard. It was like something in me that had only been cracked before was now broken and spilling out all over the place, and I couldn't stop it. I hugged my old dog, and I cried and wiped my wet eyes into the shaggy doggy-smell fur of his neck.

"Em, it's okay," Dot said. "It's going to be okay. You'll see. We're here for you. Everyone is."

"You guys," I said.

When I got to my feet, EJ gave me a handshake and said, "Captain Ridge, you're the finest sailor woman I know."

This coming from a man who lives at the water's edge but never goes out in boats. I managed a smile.

"Can you all…" I started rather timidly. "Would you all like to come in for a glass of wine or something?"

EJ made a dismissive gesture. "You ladies visit. I have quite a lot to do back at the house. I have a pot of meat on the stove and a couple of boxes in the tender gluing stages."

"A roast cooking at this time of night?" Dot asked.

"Just let him be," Isabelle said. "If he wants to cook roast at ten at night, that's his prerogative."

"It's mostly bones," he said. "They'll be simmering all night." Good old fussy EJ never trusted anyone else's cooking. The man eats only meat and potatoes. Literally. But at eighty-eight, he is healthy as a horse. Either he has a good constitution or is doing something right.

I looked from Isabelle to Dot to Isabelle again.

"No," Isabelle said. "You're busy, and we all need to get out of your hair."

"We just want to offer moral support."

"And, Em, just so you know, we're heading into Portland tomorrow for a few days."

"Syb's getting a hip replacement," Dot said.

Syb was their sister. There were five sisters in their family, so plenty of nieces and nephews, and they were all close. I envied that.

"We just wanted to let you know."

"Leaving first thing in the morning."

"So, when you don't see us, that's where we'll be."

"Give her my best," I said. "I hope it goes well."

After they all left, I went inside. I walked around and switched on every light in my too dark house. I was jumpy and antsy. I made sure every window was locked. I pulled down every blind and shut every curtain that would close.

My one-level home has a big room in the front that runs the entire length of it. The floor of my house is made of wide, old barn boards that have been worn to a sheen. Large windows all across the front overlook my little corner of the bay. Several large trees out front impede my view slightly, but it's still pretty spectacular.

On one side of the front room is a sitting area with a fireplace that uses real wood, which I chop and split myself. My couch and easy chairs are old, covered with throws, but lumpy and comfortable. I keep thinking I should get new stuff. On the other end is my kitchen of sorts with its deep, stained porcelain sink, a bit of a wobbly gas stove, and open cupboards, which look lovely in magazines when everything is lined up so neatly, but not so much when things are jammed in every which way, like in mine.

My pride and joy is my ginormous, heavy, dark wood table which has been in Jesse's family for generations. It looks faintly medieval, is a bear to move, and I love it. It even has narrow drawers in it where I keep the silverware. Too bad there are no chairs to go along with it. If I was a better garage-saler, I would be able to find something a little more suitable than these old metal church basement chairs.

Another beautiful thing I own is a wooden coat tree beside my door. EJ made it, along with the cedar chest in my bedroom. Actually, EJ and Jesse made the chest. When Jesse was a boy, this is the place his family came to every summer. Through the years, he and EJ developed a strong bond. Jesse used to tell me that he spent more time over at EJ's when he was little, learning how to work with wood, than here at the cottage with his family.

The back of my home is divided into three rooms, well, four, if you count the mudroom/laundry room. Next to that is the bathroom, which has an actual claw-foot tub. Actually, one of the claws is missing and I've got a brick on that side holding it up.

In the middle is my office, and my bedroom is at the far end, which faces the house for sale. My bedroom has two windows, one that faces the back and one on the side that overlooks the woods. I sleep on a queen-sized bed, one of our new purchases.

I dumped my duffle bag into the washer in the mudroom. A movement outside the sliver of window where the curtains didn't quite meet, caught my eye. Someone was there? A reporter? Had they found me so quickly? A shudder ran through me. I felt shivery and nervous. I switched off the light and stood in the dark and watched through the gap in the curtains.

With relief I finally saw what the "strange apparition" was. A couple of deer were making their way up the gravel road to the highway. All this jumpiness for a couple of deer. I turned the light back on, dumped soap into the machine and got her going.

Em, get ahold of yourself.

I went into the living room and opened my closed drapes an inch. I stood there and looked out and across towards the lights of Portland. I felt antsy and vulnerable. I turned and stared at my wooden coffee table, another treasured possession. Wait a minute. Things were off. Something misplaced and out of order. Something missing.

In the center of this coffee table I keep a wooden bowl filled with carved wooden apples. The bowl was something that EJ had turned for me on his lathe. Jesse had made the fruit pieces when he was a teenager. Both were precious to me. Both were missing. Huh?

I looked around. Had I moved it before I left for Canada? I was confused. And down deep, I was a bit uncertain, frightened. No. I never touched this thing. Maybe there was a simple explanation. EJ must have it, I thought. He must've come over here and taken it for some reason. It was too late to call him. I'd see him tomorrow.

I went into my office. My desk is a huge piece of plywood set to the right height by a series of cinder blocks. Nothing fancy, but I'm not a home-office type of person anyway. Mostly this room is a catchall for junk.

I pulled the curtains a little closer together before I headed to the closet. Time to have a look at Jesse's computer. I dug his now dusty computer case from the floor of the closet and brought it over to the desk. I would spend whatever time it took to get answers from his laptop. I would stay up all night if necessary. I would find that cat picture that so intrigued him. I would try to figure out why his number had been scrawled across a postcard of a stolen painting.

I unzipped the case.

The computer wasn't there.

I gasped and gaped at the empty space where the computer was supposed to be. I rifled through all the pockets and compartments in the computer case, as if a computer could hide in small side pockets. *How can this be?* Oddly, the power cord was still there. I opened the front pocket. Jesse's wedding ring was there.

I stared at the case, trying to make sense of this, trying to think, trying to breathe normally, trying to remember. I went back to the closet and stood there. Just after his death I had gotten into his computer and checked his emails to see if there were things I needed to take care of, people who needed contacting. No problem for me, because I knew his password. At the time, the cat picture had just been some silly picture that embarrassed Jesse. At the time, I hadn't connected the picture with the mysterious person he was having an affair with. At the time, I hadn't wanted to know who "she" was. So, I hadn't looked. At the time, I had kept all of these awful thoughts tucked away deep inside me.

After dealing with a few emails after his death, I had simply packed the computer away. In here. I climbed up onto a chair and tore the boxes down from the top shelves of my closet—old tax returns, canceled checks, receipts, books, magazines that were due to be recycled, newspapers, sailing logs and journals—a waterfall of old paper, sailing gloves, baseball caps, blankets, tarps, magazines, books.

But his computer was gone.

Chapter 17

What do I do? Call the police? Was this a robbery? Had someone come into my house and stolen this? Had someone come in here, rifled through the closet until they found the computer, and then as an afterthought taken the wooden bowl and apples? Or, were the apples and bowl at EJ's house and in my confusion and grief had I merely misplaced the computer? I have to admit that my mind was a bit hazy after Jesse died. Maybe I hadn't put his laptop back here at all, but only thought I did. In that case, calling the police would be entirely premature. I thought about Tom not wanting to call the police after "feeling" that someone had been on his boat.

Since Jesse died, I haven't had the greatest relationship with the local police here on the Spit anyway. They would probably just give me looks and then tell me that I must have forgotten where I put it. Because, wouldn't it make sense that the person who'd stolen the computer would take his wedding ring, too? But that was still there. I pulled it out of the case and stared at it in my hand. I exhaled, unaware until then that I'd been holding my breath. His ring had been on his dresser after he died. No, he hadn't taken it off in a rage. He often removed it when he worked, especially if he was working on boats with chemicals. Caustic paints and fiberglass are hard on jewelry.

After he died, his ring lay on the dresser for months, and every time I walked past, I'd simply looked at it. Finally, in a rare bout of housecleaning fury, I'd plopped it into his computer case. And that was that. Was the computer there then? I couldn't remember.

I pulled more things out of the closet. I piled up old clothes and shoes and boots that I no longer wore. The computer was still not there. I tore the rest of the house apart, bit by bit, every closet, even under the sink, and in the bathroom, under my bed, behind random oars and old life jackets in the mudroom, on top shelves in the kitchen.

Could it be down on *Wanderer*, my sailboat? I hadn't taken it there, had I? Why would I? Had my mind really been that crazy with grief?

But during those early months after he died I found random possessions of his all over the place. I would pick up his shirts to take to the Goodwill, and then not being able to bear the thought of them not being in the house, I'd hang them in a different closet, or put them in a box, or store them folded, under a settee on my sailboat. I'd check for it tomorrow. No way was I walking over to Jeff and Valerie's dock in the middle of this black night.

I knew I wouldn't be able to sleep, so I plugged in Jesse's espresso machine and ground some beans. I still call it Jesse's espresso machine because Jesse was the coffee snob in the family. When we were married, his sister gave us this fancy coffee maker from Italy. I barely knew how to use it. In the months since his death, I've learned. It's amazing the helpful videos you can find online.

I made myself a double espresso and then cleared a place on the corner of the couch. From the rug in front of the unlit fireplace, Rusty opened up one eye and looked at me as if to say, "Go to bed already."

I had things to do, though.

Even without Jesse's computer, all was not lost. I knew I could get into Jesse's webmail from my own computer. I'd done it before. I found his webmail site, but when I attempted to get into his email account, I got the "incorrect password and/or username" message. *What?* I tried again and again, until I was locked out.

My head was hurting. I rubbed my temples. His was an email account that was attached to the domain name of his business. If the business was no more, then the email would be no more. Obviously. So, all of his past correspondence was lost? Is this what they do when people die?

I could barely even remember what happened to his business after he died. The lawyers took care of it, sent me a bit of a check and then everything folded. There was a time when the four of us were very close. Amanda and I shared a love of sailing and dark beer. When Jesse died, they grieved with me. Amanda even came and stayed with me and slept on the couch and made food for me and coffee and held me when I cried and cried. Bryce and Amanda stood by and told me how sorry, sorry, sorry they were, and if there was anything they could do—

They did this for two weeks, and then they went back to their lives. I was especially saddened to lose Amanda. I had grown to appreciate, even love, her brusque, blunt way of dealing with life. In those early months, I emailed her numerous times, but my emails, while not bouncing, were never answered. I had read that when a spouse dies, you lose all your "couple" friends. So, I chalked it up to that. It hurt. It still does. I thought about her now.

I sent emails to Amanda and Bryce, asking if they knew of a way I could get into Jesse's old work email from my computer. The email to Bryce came back immediately as undeliverable.

Despite the espresso, I must have dozed on the couch, because when I awoke, slashes of morning light were knifing into my front room around the sides of the drawn curtains. I felt the loss of my husband all over again and the sadness of waking up in a house alone.

In those early months of grief, I read a lot of articles, thinking they would help. They mostly didn't. Once, I read a magazine story about a young widow's grief. On the day her husband was killed in a car accident, they had held on to each other for a longer time than usual the morning before he left for work.

"It was as if we knew this was our last morning together and we were saying our good-byes. I'll always remember that kiss on the morning of the day he died," she'd written.

When Jesse walked out that night, I expected to see him an hour later. The longer he stayed away, the angrier I got at him. Even when the police knocked on my door at three thirty in the morning, I didn't believe them. This was Jesse, and he was playing a joke on me, getting his cop buddies to come and say he was dead so that I'd feel bad and forgive him.

I wasn't about to.

When they finally convinced me that it wasn't a joke, I fell onto the floor of my porch. I was his wife, the closest person on earth to him. I should have felt it, should have sensed the precise moment when he died.

I got up now and rubbed my eyes. My mouth felt stale from all the coffee. Rusty was whimpering impatiently at the door. I let him out. I knew he'd be back sitting on the porch in a matter of minutes. No need to even leash him anymore.

I spent twenty minutes shoving all of my stuff haphazardly back into my closets and then headed outside. As predicted, Rusty was on the porch waiting. It was a warm morning, and the sun on the water out on the bay looked like crinkled gold paper. In the far distance were tiny dark clouds the size of fists, but for now the sun shone.

It wasn't too early to head over to EJ's. He usually rose with the sun and went to bed shortly after it set. He was sitting on his porch in the sunlight, drinking his tea out of a china cup.

"Hey," I called.

"Good morning, Emmie. Tea?" He raised his cup. EJ is the only person on the entire planet who is allowed to call me Emmie.

"No, thanks. I've got to head down to my boat. Um, did you by any chance come and get the plate from my house?"

"Plate?" he asked.

"The one you and Jesse made. The wooden one with the apples Jesse made. It seems to be missing. I thought maybe you had it?"

He shook his head, but his eyes brightened. "No, I don't, but I'm so pleased you mentioned that." He got up from his chair. "I've been cleaning out my back room and came upon a bunch of little boxes and trinkets that Jesse carved when he was little. Do you want to come in and have a look at them? I can spare a moment even now. I'd forgotten what a talented young chap he was."

The mention of his name gave me an unexpected pang. I wasn't sure I wanted to see those things. The mood I was in I would probably just dissolve into weeping. "Right now I've got to get down to *Wanderer*," I told him.

"Okay then. You have yourself a nice day."

There are several ways I can get to my boat. I can take the gravel road behind the houses until I come to Jeff and Valerie's house and then hike through their yard until I get down to the dock. Or at low tide I can pick my way along the rocky shoreline in front of my place. It was low tide. I decided to take the beach route. It was quicker.

I walked down in front of the house for sale and then past Dot and Isabelle's. Jeff and Valerie were at a commercial fishing trade show up in Bangor so their place was empty.

Even with the sun, it was chillier than I expected and near the water I pulled the sleeves of my sweatshirt down over my hands. My dog panted beside me, his breath in the morning mist like smoke. Ahead of me was my boat, and in front of it, Jeff and Valerie's big lobster boat, all closed up and silent. I stopped and looked curiously at *Wanderer*. The top hatch board was lying on the coach roof. *What?* Jeff and Valerie were back? Or Liam? It had to be their son, Liam. He often took *Wanderer* out on his own, but he usually asked first. I glanced up at their place, but neither their truck nor car were there.

Quickly, I ran down the rocky beach toward the dock, nearly falling, my runners slipping on the slick rocks. I could see the side of the hull of *Wanderer* moving unnaturally against the wharf. Someone was definitely on my boat. "Hey! Liam! You there?"

With one movement, I pulled in the aft dock line and climbed into the cockpit of *Wanderer*. I peered down into my the cabin.

The first thing I saw was the mess. All of the cupboards had been opened, their contents strewn over the sole and settees. Even the bilge boards had been pulled up, revealing the dark and nasty water underneath. All of my stuff—dishes, coffee cups, charts, pens, pencils—was strewn everywhere. "What the—"

Then, I saw her.

She was all in black—skinny pants, black boots and a black hoodie with the hood up over her head. I knew in an instant that I was looking at the real Kricket Patterson.

The gun she was pointing at me was also very real.

Chapter 18

Staring down into the barrel of a gun is truly an amazing and frightening experience. I couldn't move. My legs, my arms would not obey the commands of my brain, which was to turn and get the hell off this boat and back up to my house and lock the door behind me. I managed to scrabble in my pocket for my cell phone, but drat, where was it? Not with me. On my kitchen table. Of course it was there. I was forever putting my phone down and then forgetting where I left it. Without my phone I would have no way to call 911. Stupid. Stupid.

The only bright spot—if there could be a bright spot about being on the wrong side of a gun—was that the little girl who held the big gun with both hands, looked to be about as afraid as I was. There was something about her unsteady stance, the way her hands trembled as she held the gun high, the way her eyes darted from me to Rusty to her gun and back at me again. My dog had taken up a post at my side and was growling softly.

When I found my voice, I said, "You're her. You're Kricket Patterson."

Her nod was barely perceptible.

"What do you want?"

"Information," was her curt reply.

"What kind of information?" I looked around me at the wreck of my boat, everything emptied and strewn everywhere. What was she looking for? Her eyes flickered. My dog growled.

"Did you kill her?" There was a frail, whispery quality to her voice when she asked me that question. I had to strain to hear. "Did you push her off that boat?"

One step at a time, she was moving closer to me. Maybe my initial assessment of her as someone scared and hesitant was off. She seemed every bit in control now. Her nostrils flared. "You did kill her," she said.

The hood of her jacket fell to her shoulders revealing hair so gossamer as to be see-through. It went past her shoulders, and with one hand she reached up and grabbed a hunk of it and tucked it up and behind one ear. Her other hand held the gun steady.

"She was poisoned," I said. "It was on the news."

Kricket peered at me, eyes like slits. "What? Poisoned? How?" Her gun hand shook wildly.

"I don't know how she was poisoned," I said. Beside me, Rusty growled louder. "She just was—"

"You did it." It was a statement.

"I did not poison her," I said. "I didn't kill her. I don't even know who she was. The whole time, I thought she was you."

She regarded me with narrowed eyes. "Don't lie to me."

I had been standing in the companionway. I now took a tentative step down into my boat. "I'm not lying to you. Why would I kill her? Or you?"

She paused before she quietly said, "Because of Jesse Ridge."

It was like a punch, like someone had literally taken their fist and slammed it into my stomach. I struggled for breath, dizzy. Afraid I would fall, I thrust out a hand and grabbed hold of the bulkhead.

When I did speak, my voice broke. "Kricket, I— What—" Slowly, I moved toward her. "What do you mean, 'because of Jesse Ridge?'"

"Get that dog to stop growling," she yelled. "Or I'll shoot him! I swear to God I'll shoot him right now. And you, too! Get back. Get away from me! Don't come any closer or I'll shoot."

"Okay, Rusty," I said, carefully bending down, but keeping my back straight, my eyes on her. "It's okay boy." I scruffed him under the chin and used soothing words. He could sense my uncertainty, my fear, but thankfully, his growling turned to whimpering.

I kept my eyes on Kricket and the gun. I had wanted to scour through my husband's computer for clues, right? Did this girl in front of me know something about my husband?

"Kricket." I was hesitant. "Did my husband know that girl? If you have any information, you have to tell me." My voice broke, and I coughed to cover it up.

She didn't say anything. A couple of times she opened her mouth as if to, then shut it firmly again.

Finally, finally, very quietly, I asked her, "Was it the girl? Was the girl on the boat having an affair with my husband? Is that why you think I killed her?"

She stared hard at me, and I immediately wanted to gather those words up and shove them back inside of my soul. I closed my eyes briefly, felt myself swaying, opened them and saw her shaking her head.

"Are you crazy?" she asked. "I never even laid eyes on Jesse Ridge. And I, um…" She paused. "I don't know who the girl is."

"Then, why would I kill the girl because of Jesse Ridge?"

She shrugged. Her long hair fell into her face, and she gathered it up again.

I said, "I asked you a question. What does Jesse Ridge have to do with you being here?"

"His name came up. That's all."

"Came up in what connection?"

"His name was on a card."

The postcard. I struggled to inhale and exhale like a normal person. "I saw that card," I said. "It had an art painting on it. The girl who died had it. It was in another crew member's backpack. What do you know about that?"

"Nothing. Not much." She looked away from me, bit her lip and said, "The card was, um, it was in my father's office. I don't know much, um. That's why when I saw you were the captain, I totally freaked. I thought they sent you to kill me, like you and Jesse Ridge were going to kill me. And then when I went back, the card was gone."

"Kricket, my husband has been gone for almost two years."

She clamped her thin lips together, seemed to consider something before she said, "Where did he go?"

I stared at her. "He died."

Her eyes widened. "Jesse Ridge is *dead?*"

I nodded.

Her eyes became saucers. "I thought Jesse Ridge wanted to kill me! I thought—It was just a card. I swear. I saw his name. That was all."

I had a feeling we were talking at cross purposes, but I continued, "His name wasn't on the card."

"Then…why?" She seemed genuinely confused. For some inexplicable reason, for which I was grateful, she lowered the gun. I could sense that she was wavering. I looked at her hand and the gun and thought about grabbing it away from her. I'm strong. I've been known to scramble up to the bow in thirty-knot winds, hanging on with one hand and pulling down a jib with the other. I've been known to shimmy halfway up a mast to free a sail and then back down again in record time. This girl in front of me was no match. Her legs encased in tight black jeans were like two sticks, and I outmuscled her by fifty pounds, at least. If I hadn't known she was the daughter of a billionaire, I would have thought she was some skinny street druggie.

And yet, a gun is nothing to get into a fight over, especially on a boat. I had this awful fear that she would end up shooting right through the bottom of my boat. Even a hole the size of a half-dollar could sink a boat like mine in a matter of minutes. My knowledge of guns is limited to seeing them in movies. The fact that I could have reached the grand old age of thirty-six without ever having even fired a gun in this land of the free and the brave is truly momentous.

Jesse had no use for guns, and often told me so. Even though many of our cruising friends wouldn't be without a gun or two taped in the bilge for "pirating emergencies," this was a practice my husband thought dangerous and unnecessary. We just chose to stay out of waters where pirates might lurk.

She said, "Jesse's name wasn't on the card, but I saw his name. And your name and then when my parents ordered me on that boat with you, I thought, 'No way am I getting on that boat. No way in hell. Not with the wife of Jesse Ridge. No way.'"

I was still very much confused.

She continued. "Someone—um—people are trying to kill me. They thought it was me on the boat, that's why I'm hiding, why I have to hide."

A wind was beginning to come up. I felt its cold edges on my neck as I stood in the companionway. Those fist-shaped clouds were now overhead and I thought of something. Perhaps I could persuade her to come up to my house. Once there, I could get my cell phone from the kitchen table—where I was sure I had left it—and surreptitiously call Tom or the police. Or, if I was lucky, EJ would see this girl with a gun and call 911 on his own. Then maybe we could straighten this whole thing out. There could be lots of reasons why Roy Patterson had Jesse's phone number scrawled on a postcard. Jesse was a designer, after all. Maybe Jesse had known Patterson somehow. I had another thought. Maybe Jesse had gone to the billionaire for help in financing his project. The more I thought about that, the more I realized that this could be true. Maybe in an odd and convoluted way, this was what everything was about. I thought of the postcard. I thought about his missing computer. But, then—major hole in my theory—why hadn't Roy Patterson mentioned to me that he knew my husband when he hired me?

And why had I blared out the fact about his affair to this stranger?

"Kricket," I said. "I have an idea. Why don't we go up to my house? We can sort all of this out there. I'm not going to hurt you. I can promise you that. We can warm up and get some coffee."

The first raindrops, fat and heavy, began to splat on the coach roof. The boat fenders creaked against the dock as the breeze picked up. I finally asked, "Was she a friend of yours, the girl who died?"

She looked at me, her lip trembled, she looked away. "I don't know who she even was."

"How did she get your passport?"

In a voice so quiet I could barely hear, she said, "Maybe she stole it."

I thought about the wad of money that was probably still on the coffee table at Joan's house and had another idea. "How much did she pay you to trade places?"

One tear managed to escape her left eye. Angrily, she brushed it away with a free hand. "I told you. I don't know who she is."

She looked away from me when she said. "That's the funny part. I don't know. I had decided I wasn't going on the boat. I was going to skip town, not show up. And then the next thing I hear is that I died from going overboard. That's why I'm here. To find out what's going on and who wants to kill me. I don't even know how she got there!"

Something about her story rang true, but you could drive a freighter through other parts of it. I looked around at the shambles of my boat.

"Kricket, What were you looking for here?"

"What?"

"Why did you open every cupboard and dump everything out? What are you looking for? The computer?"

Her mouth continued to gape open. The rain increased.

"Well?" I said.

"It was like this when I got here. I swear. That's the part that has me so scared. That's why I don't know what to do. Whoever it was got here before me. Maybe they found it."

I stopped. "Found what?" Jesse's computer? Is that what this is all about?

"The key. The one he stole."

I stared at her. "What key?"

"I heard them talking about needing to find the key that Jesse Ridge stole. That's all I know. I swear! I've told you everything now. Absolutely everything."

I looked at her, and for some reason, I believed her. I believed her this time.

Chapter 19

Above the settees on *Wanderer*, on either side and against the hull, are shelves. On the starboard side is where I keep my safety gear—flares, first aid, PFD, sailing gloves, hats, lantern. On the port side is where I have my stash of reading—novels, chart books, the latest boat magazines. It looked as if someone had swept their hand across the works and knocked these things to wherever they happened to fall. My settee cushions pull forward to reveal more cupboards where I keep dried and canned food, pots and pans, cutlery and dishes. All of these had been emptied and thrown out onto the settees or sole. Underneath the seats are my holding tank and water and diesel and more storage for towels and fishing rods and blankets and tarps. These had been fished out too, unfolded, and thrown out onto the floor. Behind my galley I have a small built-in shelf where I have more food items—salt, pepper, sugar, etc. Whoever had come aboard had even dumped out the sugar and run their fingers through it. I could see the marks.

"I swear to you. I swear to God," she said again. "It was like this." She put the gun into the pocket of her hoodie.

I looked over at my make-shift nav table. I don't have a lot of electronics. This is a small boat, and I use a handheld GPS, not like the bigger boats with their chart plotters, radar and banks of radios. The only thing I have is a VHF radio, an old one, but I could see that whoever had done this had torn the cover off and wires lay everywhere.

"It's a mess," I said. "And you didn't do this?"

"I swear to God," she said, flinging a chunk of hair back over her ears. "I'm telling the truth."

I walked forward into the boat. "When did you get here?" I asked her.

"As soon as I heard about the dead girl, that's when I came. I had to talk to you. To figure out things."

"You've been here since then? You slept here?" I asked.

She nodded. The v-berth contained similar wreckage. Pillows had been strewn about, and part of the mattress had been upended. The little door to the forepeak was open, and even the skuzzy stuff I keep up there—old anchors, lengths of rope—had been thrown out on top of the berth. One side of the berth held a sleeping bag—mine, I saw—and this, obviously, was where Kricket had slept. On the berth was an unfamiliar duffle bag. "Yours?" I said.

"Yes."

Outside, the rain was beginning in earnest. "Kricket, I have an idea. Why don't we go up to my house, and we can sort all this through. Are you hungry? I might even have something we can eat. I'm not going to hurt you. You have to believe that."

She put her hand into her pocket where the gun was and said, "I'm not hungry."

"A nice shower, then. Some tea." I tried to smile. "I have lots of hot water and it's warm up there. I've also got a comfy couch."

She looked at me for several seconds before she said, "Okay. I'm not going to give you the gun, though."

"Fine with me."

The rain, sounding like falling knives, almost drowned out her last words, but I think she said, "Don't try anything."

"This boat leaks. Come on, if we run hard, we won't get too wet."

She looked up at me, then at Rusty. Very quietly, she said, "I've been too scared to think about eating. But maybe that would be nice." She swept another wayward white-yellow strand of hair behind one ear. The section of hair nearest her face had measured indentations in it, as if it had at one time been braided. I tried to imagine her painstakingly braiding her hair.

"I make the best coffee. Everyone says so. Grab your bag."

She did. Outside, I put the hatch boards in. I'd deal with the mess later. I was not without a plan: First, I'd win her trust. Second, no girl could refuse a shower when she hadn't had one in a few days. While she was showering, I'd text Ben or Tom. Third, I'd get that darn gun away from her any way I could.

I looked up at Jeff and Valerie's house. All dark. No lights at Dot and Isabelle's, either.

I said, "Okay, let's make a run for it."

We stayed very close together as we dashed along the waterfront up to my house through the rain. The tide was coming in, and she fell once on the slick, sea-weedy rocks. I took her arm, helped her up. She looked like she was crying.

Rusty bounded on ahead, pretty fast for an old dog, old man that he is, but he doesn't like the rain. He was waiting by the door when we got there. Once inside, I pulled off my wet jacket and hung it on a hook next to my car keys and a few other jackets.

I said, "I'll make coffee. You want coffee? I want coffee." Drat, where was my phone? I thought I had left it on the corner of the kitchen table next to my laptop. Maybe the end table in my bedroom? "Just a minute. Let me get you a towel." Darn thing could be anywhere.

My phone wasn't on my bedroom end table, on my dresser, in my backpack. Of all the times to lay it down and not remember where. In the bathroom, I grabbed a towel then got Kricket set up with a shower. I explained my finicky shower head to her and showed her how to use it.

While she was showering, I got the coffee going and then looked everywhere for my stupid cell phone. I never go anywhere without it. Had it fallen out of my pocket? I looked all around my kitchen, on the counters, under the table, all through my bedroom, living room. I could not find it. My car? That was certainly a possibility. I tried to remember the last time I had called or texted someone. Couldn't.

By the time she came out, her hair wrapped up in one of my towels, I was thoroughly confused about my phone.

"Thanks for the shower," she said.

"No problem."

I told her I had coffee, but no milk, and sugar might be doubtful. I did have tea bags. Did she want tea? She shook her head and merely asked for a glass of water.

While I was running the tap water to get it cold enough, I tried to come up with Plan B. Maybe Kricket had a cell phone. I said, "Do you have a cell phone, Kricket? You should at least call Scott."

"Scott?"

"He's really worried about you."

"Who?"

"Scott. Your boyfriend Scott."

"I don't have a boyfriend named Scott."

"Scott Uphill."

She looked away from me when she said, "I don't know that person. Not anymore."

I sighed. Okay. A lover's quarrel. She pulled the towel off her head and began finger-combing her hair. She had put on stretch black yoga pants and a pink tank top over a long-sleeved black tee.

I went on. "Well, that's funny. He said that you two were together. He said he talked to you the whole time you were supposedly on the boat."

"He's a liar and a jerk. A class-A jerk." Then she looked at me curiously. "Where did you see him?"

"He and Captain Tom Mallen showed up the morning after we brought *Blue Peace* in. Do you know Tom Mallen?"

Her whole body became absolutely still. It was like a switch had been flipped. Outside, torrents of rain beat against the window.

"What's the matter?" I asked.

"Tom? You saw Tom?"

"He crews for your father, right?"

A nearly imperceptible nod.

"Kricket?"

She went over to one of the front windows. "He's been my father's captain forever. He hates me. He would do anything to destroy me."

She pulled the gun out of her pocket, aimed the gun at the window and said, "Kapow."

"Kricket!"

She came back and laid the gun on the kitchen table. "Don't worry. I'm not going to shoot anything. I don't even think it's loaded. I might as well give it back to you," she said.

Back to me? "Thank you," I said, without touching it.

She said, "I'm surprised you didn't recognize it right off."

"Why would I recognize it?"

"Because it's Jesse's."

Chapter 20

Even though I knew she was at the very least misinformed—or at the most, blatantly lying—it was another gut punch.

I said. "My husband has never owned a gun."

She laid the gun across her palm. "Boy, there's a lot about your husband you don't know, isn't there? He was having an affair, you say?"

"That's none of your business."

"Well, you asked me—"

"I know, but forget I said that."

"Maybe the gun was for that," she said.

She put the gun on the table, walked calmly over to her bag and pulled out a small, pink leather wallet. She said, "If you don't believe me, I have the registration. I brought along his permit to carry a concealed weapon. His name is on it. Jesse Robert Ridge. Even a picture. That's his middle name, right? Robert? I can show it to you."

I said, "If this document exists, it's a forgery."

"You want to see it?" She pulled it out of her wallet. "Here, I'll show you."

She set a laminated card on the table and pushed it toward me with the flat of her hand. Her fingernails were polished a bright pink.

"Here he is, in person. Jesse Ridge. Jesse Robert Ridge."

I looked down at the plastic card but didn't touch it. State of Maine. Resident permit to carry concealed firearms. His name. His picture. Our address. *This* address. All official looking. I picked it up, turned it over. Read everything that was on it, all the fine print, every bit of it.

A trembling began somewhere deep inside me. Jesse—my sailing partner, my best friend, my soul mate, my lover, my husband—he knew everything there was to know about me. He knew all about my dysfunctional family, my sisters, the guy I lived with and thought I was in love with before him, all my fears, all my dreams. Did I really know so little about him?

"Where did you get this?" My voice was small, unrecognizable even to myself.

"That's him though, right?"

When I looked at his picture, it was a physical pain in my chest. It was him. It wasn't a picture I recognized, but it was him. It wasn't the photo on his driver's license, nor the one on his passport. His hair was cut short in this one, military-style almost. For as long as I'd known Jesse, which had only been five years—not a very long time, really—his hair was always a bit too scruffy around the ears and always on the longish, messy side. Yet, this was Jesse. There was no doubt about it. His face, his ruddy cheeks, his pouty lips, his downturned eyes. Jesse. And yet not Jesse. A younger Jesse. Had Jesse owned a gun in some lifetime before I knew him? Was Kricket right? Was there so much about my husband I didn't know? He grew up in Canada, but spent the summers in Maine. Some time before we met, he was living in Maine pretty much full time. I tried to think back to the things he had told me, but it wasn't much. He didn't share a lot about his early years. There were great chunks I knew nothing about. I always figured we had a lifetime to learn about each other.

Jesse and I had been married for a little over three years when he died, and we lived together for two years prior. What had he done before we met, back when he was in his twenties? Did he have a gun then? Was he involved then, in something that would explain his total aversion to guns when we met?

I looked at the date the permit was issued, fully expecting it to be a decade old. I received my second shock. It was issued four months before he died, which was around the same time I'd seen the cat picture on the computer, which was around the same time he'd begun to be distant.

I studied the gun, afraid to pick it up.

"Kricket," I said finally. "I will ask you one more time. Where did you get this gun and this phony registration?"

She rubbed a sleeve end to her eyes. "I told you. I found them in, um, in my father's desk. It was there with the postcard, the one with his name on it. That's why when I heard you were going to be captain, I freaked. The gun was in the same box with the card, so I took it and ran. I knew they were after me. I thought a gun might come in handy."

I forced myself to pick up the gun. I took it into my mud room where I put it on a high shelf. I'd deal with it later.

Back in the kitchen I said, "Do you know Rob Stikles?"

"Who?"

"He was one of the crew on *Blue Peace*. He and the girl who died seemed to know each other."

She walked over to my fireplace. Her back was stiff and to me when she said, "Well, I don't know her, so why would I know him?" On the mantel was a framed picture of Jesse and me and Rusty. She picked it up. "He looks different here than in the gun permit picture," she said.

"That's because he *is* different."

She put the picture back.

I said, "You're sure you never heard the name Rob Stikles?"

"Maybe they did that on purpose, the two of them, the girl and him. Maybe they were going away together on the boat. And then she just—" She made a sweeping motion of her hands—"died."

"She didn't just die. She was poisoned. Kricket, you need to phone your parents. Your parents are worried about you."

"No." Her eyes were wide. "They can't know I'm here."

"Will you at least phone them and tell them you're safe? You don't have to tell them where you are."

She sighed and sat down on the edge of my couch and said, "I forgot my phone. When I ran, I just didn't think of it. I was in so much of a hurry. That's why I didn't know anything. About the poison and stuff."

I found that a bit hard to swallow. What young girl goes anywhere without a phone these days?

Rusty, who is a pretty good judge of character, wagged his way over and sat beside her. She ran her hands over his head and said to me, "Do you have a phone? I could use your phone. I could phone my parents on your phone."

"If I could find my phone, you'd be welcome to it," I said. "It appears to be missing. I might check my car, if I can trust you to stay put here."

"You can trust me." She scuffed Rusty under the chin. He seemed to enjoy it. Then, "Where would I go?" She paused. "I don't have any place else to go but here. Wait a minute. I remember something."

"What?" I said.

"I saw a cell phone on the dock."

"What? When?"

"When we got off the boat. It was raining so hard, but I think it was there. On the dock. Just beside your boat."

"Why didn't you say anything? Why didn't you pick it up?"

"How was I supposed to know it was yours?"

"It must have dropped out of my pocket."

She looked out the window. "You want me to go get it for you? I remember where it was."

"No." I sighed. "You better stay here." I had another plan. If I got down there and got my phone, I could call Tom or the police before I came back. "Just tell me where you saw it."

She gave me precise directions.

I grabbed my jacket from the hook beside my door. I almost grabbed my car keys, thinking it might be quicker just to drive over to Jeff and Valerie's. No, the tide, although coming in, was still low enough for me to scramble along the shore. It's always quicker to take the route down by the water.

When I left Kricket, she was on my couch, feet up, one of my throws around her, Rusty beside her, the bulk of his weight on her. I like to tell people I have a fifty-pound lap dog.

When I got down to my boat, there was no cell phone on the dock. It must have fallen into the water. *Just great.* I looked all around my boat, tried to see under the water, but of course the water around here is too murky and the day was too gray. If it had fallen through the boards and was now in the water under the dock, it would be ruined anyway! Rats, rats, rats, which was my religious father's favorite expression. And then shit, shit, shit, which was more my own vernacular.

So, okay, my cell phone was gone, and I had a missing person staying in my cottage, a celebrity missing person. What more could go wrong today? I made my way back up to my cottage, where I quickly discovered the answer to that question—plenty more.

I called her name as I went in through the back door. I glanced over at the couch and all I saw was my whimpering dog.

"Rusty?"

He flattened his ears, sat down on the ground and put his head between his paws.

"Kricket?" I made my way through the rooms of my small house. She wasn't there.

I ran to the mudroom window. My car was not there. I glanced over at the hook where I hang my keys. Gone! Kricket had stolen my car! I checked for the gun on the top shelf. Gone, too. When I looked down at Rusty, he merely looked up at me and whimpered.

Chapter 21

"Un-freaking-believable!" I raced out of my back door and partway down the lane. I wanted to pound my head against a fence post. I stopped and backtracked over to EJ's. What kind of an idiot leaves her car keys in full view of a girl who'd already proved once that she's a flight risk? Yeah. Only someone like me. Stupid beyond belief. Ben Dunlinson will have a fit when I phone him. Oh yeah. I can't phone him. Don't have a phone. Not even a landline. Haven't had a landline for years. Nice.

It was raining. Again. Of course it was raining. What else could go wrong? I slammed the side of my hand on to a tree so hard that it hurt. I rubbed it with my other one, sailor curses knocking around in my head. *That stupid little*—I inhaled. Tried to breathe. This is why God never gave me kids. I'd believe every little frickin' word they told me.

Not only had the twerp stolen my car, but I was sure she'd made up the whole thing about my phone. Thinking about it again, I knew she had my phone. I know I left it on the corner of my table. I remember that now. Probably, she was the one who stole the wooden apple bowl, although for what reason, I had absolutely no idea. I began hyperventilating. Okay. Calm down. Paper bag time. I thought about my last view of her—so small, teary-eyed, so "scared" huddled under the throw on my couch, shivering with fear, Rusty beside her. On her lap. Even Rusty had been taken in by her little-girl charms. Was she even the real Kricket Patterson? Had I been totally one hundred percent duped? And the gun registration? How had she managed to fake that?

If I borrowed EJ's truck, maybe I could catch up with her. The tide was coming in. Maybe she wouldn't get across to the mainland. One could hope.

"EJ! Hey!" I called. "Can I use your phone? Can I borrow your truck? Did you see a girl take my car?"

EJ came out onto the porch. In one hand, he held a glue gun

trailing the electrical cord and in the other, a small hammer.

"What? Emmie, slow down."

"A girl—my car—" I was breathless. "She stole my car!"

Behind him, his stereo was on, something loud and vaguely opera-ish.

"What girl?"

"I need to use your phone."

"Be my guest." I raced past him and inside. Drat! I didn't even know Ben's private number. That too was nicely listed on my cell phone. I dialed 911. But in my haste, I couldn't get my message out. "She stole my phone! And my car! Can you call Detective Dunlinson and tell him?"

"Are you in any danger now, Miss?"

"Sorry, sorry, sorry. I need to go. Just tell Ben that Em called."

I hung up realizing that that would go down as one of the stupidest 911 calls ever.

"EJ, can I borrow your truck, like immediately? Like right *now*?"

"Well, certainly, my dear. But the battery is dead. I've been meaning to come over for a jump."

Great.

"What about Dot and Isabelle's car?"

"They're in Portland," I said.

"Jeff and Valerie?"

"Still in Bangor." Thinking about Jeff and Valerie gave me a fragment of an idea. "Thanks, EJ!" I ran toward their house.

There is only one road from the main highway down to the houses out here on the point. It's a winding one, and part of it is always under construction. I live at the very end of it. Where Chalk Spit Road meets the highway, there's a small fisherman's dock. I'd tied up there before. If I could get there in a fast boat, I could climb the bank and stand in the road and wave her down. Even on the worst of days, it's always much speedier getting to Portland by fast boat than it ever is by car.

I don't own a fast boat, but Jeff and Valerie do, and they wouldn't mind. I've used their boat before. I know where the keys are.

I ran along the shoreline, getting my sneakers wet and trying to outrun the fast and sloshy incoming tide. I slipped once and grabbed

for a handhold on the wet, kelpy rocks. I was a mess, but Kricket would not get away with this. I would catch up with her. I would get my car back, and my phone and she would explain to me what was going on.

On the dock, I jumped aboard the *Valerie J* and found the keys hanging on a hook behind the rub rail. All I had on was my light windbreaker, so I threw on a stained yellow lobstering jacket that hung by the door. It smelled like fish. I didn't care. I started the diesel and felt it roar underneath me. Quickly, I undid the dock lines and stowed them on the deck. I had the thing up to full throttle in no time and was speeding through the rough water up the outside of Chalk Spit, leaving a huge and noisy wake behind me. With the wide engine cage underneath, I didn't even have to worry about getting the prop tangled in lobster floats. They would just glide under the boat and disappear.

I had wasted precious time up at EJ's. Had Kricket already made it across the tidal bridge? I hoped not. I didn't want her driving my car through the water on an incoming tide. Seven minutes later, I was throwing lines to Pete and Warren, the lobstermen who owned this dock and who happened to be down here. "Hope you don't mind," I called. "Emergency!"

"Fine," Pete said.

"Whatever you say," Warren said.

They looked at me curiously as I scrambled up the slick, wet bank. I was breathless and panting by the time I reached the road, but I didn't have time for explanations.

There was my car! Kricket had pulled off the road and was parked there as if she were simply waiting for me. "Kricket!" I yelled loudly as I grabbed a tree root and heaved myself up the last of the embankment. "You better have a good explanation. I trusted you. I let you stay in my house and take a shower and pet my dog—"

My car was unlocked, key in the ignition.

But Kricket was not there.

"Kricket?" I looked around me wildly and ran through the trees, first down to the water's edge and then up to the road. "Kricket!" I didn't see her. "Kricket!" I cupped my hands around my mouth and called as loudly as I could.

I went back to my car. I would take the ferry and try to find her, or I'd go in and see Ben. I started the car and then something on the floor of the passenger side caught my eye.

A handwritten note.

Chapter 22

I'm sorry. I didn't want to borrow your car. I had to. I needed a head start. If I could tell you the whole story, you would understand. Please don't look for me. You were very kind to me.

K.

I looked down at the tide road, already swirling with water. Had Kricket walked across it? Or was she still on the island somewhere? Was I being tricked once again? I didn't see her in the distance, but it was rainy and it was quite possible that she had made it across in time.

At least twice a year, some idiot tourist tries to get across, either by foot or by car, when the road is half-covered. Just as often, the Coast Guard has to come in the big inflatable rescue boat and navigate the treacherous currents that swirl around during high tide.

I drove as quickly as I could over to the ferry ramp. I felt at sea without my cell phone, detached from the world and from the police, from Tom and Joan. From everyone! It occurred to me that if I had my laptop I could probably get my phone texts, or at least I think I could, but I wasn't sure. I decided not to drive back to my house, but to head right into Portland. If I didn't see Kricket on the way—and who knows where she went—I would go straight to the police station.

Our little island ferry doesn't really run on any kind of a schedule. It just goes back and forth when there are cars or people waiting. It had obviously just left the mainland and was returning. I got out of my car, put my hand up to shade my eyes from the rain and tried to see across, but the day was too gloomy. Nothing to do here but wait. I got back in my car.

I know Gerry, the guy who runs the ferry, pretty well. He lives on the mainland and has two little kids and a wife who's a nurse. When the boat finally returned, I drove up onto the ferry. I set the brake, got out and climbed the steps up to the bridge.

"Hey, Em," he said when he saw me.

"Gerry." I was out of breath. "I need to know something. Was there a foot passenger just now? Girl? Skinny? Black hoodie, black pants?

He shook his head. "Nope, just two cars. The Blatchfords and the young Ryan fellow. No one on foot."

I blew out a breath and said, "She must've walked across, then."

"With the tide this high? She'd be crazy."

"Yeah," I conceded. "She sort of is."

Twenty-seven minutes later, I was standing at the police station and asking for Ben Dunlinson. Early afternoon and the place was buzzing, people on phones, officers rushing past me importantly, people in huddled groups who looked in my direction and then away when they saw it was me. I went to the front desk, and in no time at all, Ben was there, his face ashen, his expression grim. "Em—" he said. He used my first name.

"Ben, I—" I fingered the note which was deep in the pocket of the lobstering coat which I still wore.

"Come with me." He put his hand on my shoulder. "I've been trying to get ahold of you. Been calling and leaving messages."

He led me into a bare, utilitarian room with two chairs and a table and motioned for me to sit down. I did. He pulled a chair close to me, not across the desk like before, but right up next to me, close, close.

"Ben?"

"Em, I have some very bad news."

I looked at him.

"It's about Peter. He's dead."

Chapter 23

There wasn't enough air in the room. I opened my mouth several times to say something, but nothing came out. It felt like I was drowning, like my lungs were collapsing inside my chest. "No," I finally said. "Not Peter."

"His body was found early this morning, Em."

I shook my head rapidly. "How—"

"Em," he said softly. "Peter was shot. He was found on *Blue Peace*."

I was rapidly shaking my head "That can't be."

His blue eyes were soft on mine. He reached over and covered my hand with his. The gesture was at once intimate and startling. I didn't pull away. My breath caught. My eyes filled.

He looked me straight in the eye. "Tom Mallen and Scott were getting ready to take *Blue Peace* to Bermuda. This morning Tom returned to the boat with some provisions and found Peter there."

I was trying very hard to breathe normally, kept clutching at my neck, my chest. "What was he doing there?" I asked. "Where was he all this time? You said he was shot? Who did this? Someone killed him?" My words came out in incoherent spurts. "Who?"

"We don't have any answers, Em. All we know is that to the best of our knowledge, he never went home. We don't know where he went after he left Joan and Art's home that morning."

"But—"

"Em, we have the bullet. We know the make of the gun. If we find a gun, we can get a match."

The gun! My fingers fluttered. Ben's hand tightened on mine. Kricket's gun. Jesse's gun. No, not Jesse's gun. It couldn't be Jesse's gun. Did Kricket kill Peter? She couldn't have. She was with me this morning. She was on *Wanderer* last night. Or was she? I kept swallowing, kept trying to put things together in my head.

"I know he was a special friend of yours."

"He was one of my sailing kids," I blurted out. "He was such a sweet and nice person. Who—who would do this?"

"We're looking for Rob Stikles, or whatever name he happens to be going by now. We're thinking this whole thing might be related to Rob and the money he paid Peter. We're hoping this might ultimately lead us to the unidentified girl on *Blue Peace*."

"You still don't know who she is?"

He shook his head. "Despite pleas on the news, complete with her picture, she remains unidentified. Also, the picture of the girl on her phone? We found that little girl. She was one of the refugees." He removed his hand from mine and got out his notebook.

"What refugees?" I asked, my thoughts twirling.

"Remember I told you about that other thing I was working on?"

"Oh. Right."

"We think there might be a link between them and what happened to Peter. The little girl and some other children and a few babies are with social services now."

I didn't understand any of this. This did not make sense. I kept saying that over and over.

"We know, Em. We haven't found any parents, just a couple of nannies who seem very frightened and speak no English. We're getting an interpreter in ASAP, but I'm not sure we'll even get much from them. I think they're as much victims as the children are."

I was stunned.

He went on, "Did the girl on the boat say anything about children or babies when you were with her? Did she talk about adoption? Like couples wanting kids? Anything along those lines?"

"No. Nothing like that, but she didn't talk to me a lot. We sort of, um, got off on the wrong foot." I felt a pang. Jesse and I had wanted children. We'd wanted them right away. It hadn't happened.

"Ben—" I paused. "I really have to tell you something." I pulled the note out of the pocket. "Kricket, the real Katherine Patterson, was at my house. She was living on my boat."

"What—"

I told him the whole story—well, not exactly the whole story. I told him everything except the Jesse part. I don't know why I kept not telling him the Jesse part. I just didn't. I told him Kricket had a gun, but not the part about the registration. I told him that a "second" computer at my house had been stolen, but not that that it belonged to Jesse. I told him about the wooden bowl and apples, but not that

Jesse had made them. I told him about all the stuff strewn everywhere on my boat. I told him the missing phone story and how fishy that was, and how I was sure that Kricket had my phone. "So, that's why I couldn't call or text or why you couldn't reach me."

I handed him the note which he read carefully and slowly, then he looked at me. "Why would she leave your car for you when she could get farther by car?"

"I have no idea. She seemed really scared. That's all I know. Maybe she figured she'd have to ditch the car eventually, so why not now?"

"She would have to get off your island by ferry, right?"

"She wasn't on the ferry. I asked. The tide was coming in when she left. She could have made it across on foot if she hurried. Maybe that's why she left the car…"

He pulled his phone out of his pocket and stood. "Wait here, Em, please. Don't go anywhere."

While he was gone, I covered my face with my hands. Peter dead? It made no sense. A few moments later, Ben was back. "We're going to check the highways. If she's on foot, she won't get far. She's on the run and she has a gun. That's not a good combination. Would you mind, right now Em, going to Patterson's with me?"

I looked at him. "The Pattersons?"

"They're still at the hotel. They plan to stay there until their daughter is found. They will have a recent picture of Kricket, and this might help confirm if the girl who was at your house was really Kricket. Also, we haven't been able to locate Roy Patterson since Peter died. I'm hoping his wife will know where he is."

We went in his car to one of the swankiest hotels in Portland, and even though I knew I would be cold, out of deference to the place, I left the stained lobster coat in Ben's car. On the elevator to the top floor, I was very quiet. The closer we got to their room, the more nervous I became. What do I say to a mother whose daughter I had lost not once, but twice?

Elaine Patterson answered our knock almost immediately. "You found Katherine? Is she okay? You have her? Where is she?"

Ben said, "Captain Ridge may have seen her."

She put a thin, shaky hand to the side of her neck. The skin of her face was papery, veiny, and her hair stuck up on one side of her head as if she'd recently been napping. She wore loose gray track pants and an oversized faded-purple sweatshirt. There were rings on her fingers and thick bracelets on both wrists that looked curiously out of place with her pajama wear. As we entered the suite she looked behind us in all directions down the hall, as if looking for someone.

As soon as I entered the lavish suite, I didn't want to be here. My throat was dry, my stomach hurt and all I kept thinking about was Peter. Through a weepy haze that reminded me too much of what it was like after Jesse died, I heard Ben ask if Elaine knew where her husband was. She said she didn't keep tabs on him.

I thought I heard her say, "I heard about that young chap who died on the boat. So much trouble, all of this. Just so much bother."

I looked at her suddenly. *Bother?* My friend's death was a *bother* to her? I did not trust myself to say anything, so I didn't.

When we were in the main living area of the suite, she said, "I could call down and have some coffee brought up. Or tea, if you'd like. Juice? Wine? Beer? Anything?"

Ben said, no, thank you and we sat down in armchairs across from her. Her hands were clasped in her lap, and she kept twining and untwining her bony, jeweled fingers. The nails had been bitten to the quick. "You have news of my daughter?" she asked. "What is it?"

Ben told her that Kricket had been on my boat, and that I'd had a conversation with her, but that she'd disappeared. He asked if she had any recent pictures of her daughter.

She rose and was back quickly with a tablet. I followed Ben's lead, and we sat on either side of Elaine on the large couch while she scrolled through photos. There was Kricket on a ski slope, bundled up in an ice-blue ski outfit, a huge, white-teeth smile on her tanned face. There was a formal picture of an unsmiling Kricket in a gown. It looked like she meant it to look dramatic. It didn't. It merely looked sad. There were school photos, going back to grade school. There was a tanned Kricket at an outdoor café with friends, beer mugs on the table in front of them. There were more pictures, but I didn't need them. This was definitely the girl who'd aimed a gun at me on my boat.

I nodded to Ben. Elaine turned to me, "How could you let her go?"

I was about to say something when Ben interrupted. "Your daughter had a gun. Do you have any idea where she was able to get a gun?"

"How should I know?"

"Is your husband missing any guns?"

"My husband doesn't own guns."

I sat quietly as another thought assailed my brain. I really needed to tell Ben about Jesse. It was unfair of me not to. He needed to know the whole story, not just the bits and pieces I had offered. However Jesse had betrayed me, Ben needed to know about the cat picture and his missing computer. Was I impeding this investigation? I made a resolution to tell Ben everything as soon as we were out in the car.

Ben showed her the note, ensconced in a small plastic bag and she verified that it was Kricket's handwriting.

"That is like her," Elaine said. "So concerned about others, but never herself." The statement was said not with pride, but almost derision. I could hear the highway sounds down below, that's how quiet it was. I looked at her profile.

"Mrs. Patterson," Ben began, "the girl who took your daughter's place on the boat had a photo on her phone of a dark-haired girl, maybe six or seven. We've since found that girl. She was part of a group of undocumented children and babies who came to this country from Eastern Europe. Does this make any sense to you? Do you have any idea what this might be all about?"

Her face went from sad to stolid. "No. Why would I? That girl was obviously an interloper. I have no idea what you're talking about."

Ben kept looking at her in his most gentle way. Even I could tell she was lying.

"Mrs. Patterson?" he said. "Anything you can tell us will only help us find her now. We are trying to figure out if there was any kind of connection between the girls. Did Katherine ever talk about children, about adoptions, human trafficking, that sort of thing."

"Oh," Elaine looked toward the large penthouse window when she said. "You mean her nanny work?" She spat out the word nanny.

"Nanny work?"

"Can you imagine? A child of privilege like her, and she wants to work for someone as their nanny. Or in a day care. That was her second big idea. Run a day care."

Ben's look was earnest. "Was she interested, perhaps, in helping couples adopt from other countries?"

She shook her head and without answering the question directly she said, "It was a phase." She paused, sighed and looked down at the tablet in her lap, which still displayed a high school class picture of her daughter. "Roy is always more lenient with her than I am. He would give her whatever she wanted. I thought this trip would do her good, get her mind off these crazy career plans. Roy disagreed."

Ben said, "On *Blue Peace* you mentioned a young man she was associated with. But you never told us his name. Are you ready to share that information with us now?"

She stared at Ben with an intensity I hadn't seen in her before. "That would be Captain Tom Mallen, our usual captain." She ground out his name.

I, all of a sudden, became very still.

"I couldn't tell you then. Roy was standing right there. He would have gotten more furious than he already was. Roy still thinks the sun rises and falls with that man. But I know what he's really like. He hurt Kricket badly and she just wouldn't snap out of it."

"How did he hurt her?" Ben asked.

"They were together," she said. "The two of them. It didn't last. He broke her heart and after he dropped her, she changed. She became a different person."

"How so?"

"Acting out. Staying out late, partying, some nights not coming home at all. She and I had several out-and-out screaming matches about the whole thing. I made the decision that she would go on the boat. Her father was opposed to it. I insisted. But, of course, with a different captain. That was a given. Tom is not a good person. He is not a good influence on anyone."

I found myself studying the pattern in the carpet while she talked.

"Her father was opposed to her going out on the boat?" Ben asked.

She nodded. "He wanted her home. He said the boat was no place for her. I insisted. Our mistake—my mistake, really—was in trusting her to drive up there to get onto that boat. That was Roy's idea. He even hired a car for her."

She had arrived in a cab. I had told Ben this at the police station when we were first brought in. He raised his eyebrows. I'm sure he noticed the discrepancy, but didn't say anything.

She looked away from us. "Detective, it's Tom you should direct your attention to. There's something you need to know about him. After they broke up he began to stalk her, coming around the house at all hours. Sitting in the garden under her window. He even made death threats against her. I wanted her to get a restraining order against that man, I wanted to go to the police. Roy, of course, would not agree to it."

Chapter 24

Tom was stalking Kricket? Kricket and Tom were lovers? Tom was making death threats against her. It was too bizarre to contemplate.

Ben and I didn't talk much in his car on the way back to the police station. It wasn't because I didn't want to—I was working in my mind the best way to tell him all about Jesse—but because he received a phone call that took all of his time, from getting into the car until he dropped me at my own car in the parking lot of the police station. I heard the words "roadblocks" and "armed" and "approach with caution," and "Yes, we have alerted the Coast Guard," and, "good, good, you found Patterson. Bring him in. I'll be right there."

I leaned my head against the headrest, trying to quell my headache. It was late afternoon by the time we got back to my car. Ben frowned and told me that something serious had come up and that he'd get in touch with me as soon as he could. I told him fine, that I would be driving home and would soon be with friends.

"Good," he said. "Good, good."

He seemed in a hurry to leave. It was only after we parted that I remembered that I didn't have my phone. There would be no way for him to "get in touch" with me.

What I really wanted was to talk with Tom, find out if any of these allegations against him were true. I didn't have my phone, that much was true, but if I got to a computer I could email him. I remembered vaguely in a part of my brain that there was a way you could check your text messages from a computer. I drove to an internet café, paid my money and after wracking my brain for passwords—which I store, conveniently, on my phone—I was able, finally, to get online. I shot Tom a quick email saying that my phone was stolen and I was in town at an internet café—could he get back to me? Otherwise, I was on my way home.

He must've been right on top of his computer because he answered right away.

Can we meet? You probably heard about Peter then, if you're in town.

Outside the café window, fog was moving in, as Sandberg had described, on "little cat feet." It carried with it a quiet heaviness.

He suggested a pub on the waterfront. At the doorway of the place, I scanned the crowd. It was busy with happy-hour revelers filling up on cheap beers and nachos. Several TV screens were mounted high on walls, sound muted, while brightly colored teams ran up and down a field. Finally, I saw him. Tom was sitting in the booth closest to the kitchen and farthest from the door. He raised his hand when he saw me. I hurried past clots of people at tables and booths, hoping nobody would recognize me. I slid in across from him.

"Hey," he said softly. There was a sad smile on his face.

"Hey, yourself."

A tall Guinness was already waiting for me, along with a plate of Irish nachos, the kind made with potatoes and mountains of cheese. How did he know these were my favorite? I was suddenly struck by something—this was the sort of thing Jesse would do. We would arrange to meet, and Jesse would have Irish nachos and a cold Guinness waiting for me. I felt a lump in my throat and a weird kind of déjà vu. And yet, I couldn't erase what Elaine had said about this man.

He said, "You don't know how good it is to see you walk through that door. This has been one hell of a day."

"I totally agree."

"Thought you might be hungry," he said, pushing the plate closer to me. His wink took me off guard. "I know these are your favorites."

"I don't think I can eat anything." I studied him. "How did you know these are my favorites?"

"I know a lot about you." he said. "I've made it my business to know a lot about you."

I felt a warmness in my face that I hoped he didn't notice. I said, "Ben told me what happened."

His smile faded. "Bad. Really bad."

"What was Peter doing on *Blue Peace* in the first place? I just don't understand that. I don't understand any of this."

He looked down at the cheesy plate as if composing himself. "Em, I'm so sorry." He picked up his beer, then put it down. "I know you were close."

"We were."

"Scott and I, we'd just gone out for a few more provisions, and I got back to the boat before Scott did. And there he was…" His finger was tracing the foam on the rim of his beer glass. "At first I had this weird thought. What's Peter doing sleeping on the floor of the cabin? And then I saw the blood. There was, um, there was so much blood." His voice broke and he looked away from me. I could have sworn there were tears in his eyes.

"I, uh…" He coughed, put his hand to his mouth, kept it there, leaned his head into the back of the booth. It was relatively quiet in our little corner of the restaurant.

"Why would he be on the boat in the first place?" I asked. "That's the part I don't understand. First of all, Peter gets all this money, then he goes off and no one knows where he is. He doesn't go home, and then he comes back and ends up dead on *Blue Peace*. It just doesn't make sense."

"Don't try to make sense of something that doesn't make sense," he said.

I picked up my beer, took a sip, put it down. If I was driving home later, I wouldn't drink much of this, not with the state I was in. I told this to Tom, who apologized, said he just wasn't thinking and called over our waitress who came back with an iced tea for me.

"The thing is," I said after a long drink of my tea, "I just came from talking with Elaine Patterson, and she said—"

"What?" He leaned forward suddenly. "You were there? At the Pattersons' hotel? Why did you go there?"

"We needed to see pictures of Kricket. I went with Ben."

He stared at me. "What for?"

I shut my eyes briefly. "I have a story to tell you, Tom. Kricket, the real one, paid me a visit—"

"What!" His eyes were wide. I thought his beer was going to spill.

I told him that Kricket had been living on my boat, that she stole my car and I was pretty sure my cell phone too. "Also," I said, "I learned some things about her—and you—"

His expression was grim. "Do tell. This should be good. I'm waiting."

"That once upon a time you and Kricket were lovers. And that when you broke up you started stalking her. Made death threats, even."

His hands stilled around his beer mug. His expression was flat, emotionless. Yet there was a suppressed energy about him, as if he was doing everything he could to will himself to remain calm. "Em, you don't know the whole story. I've crewed for that family a long time…"

"Enlighten me. I'm all ears."

He ran a hand over his face before he said anything. "That's what Kricket would like to believe, that I'm stalking her. That's what Elaine believes, but it's not true. Roy knows the truth. Kricket and me, well, our time together was short-lived, and it's not something I'm very proud of. In fact..." He brushed a hand across his chin before he went on. "...if I could go back and erase that time, I would. At the time I thought she was cute and funny. I didn't realize how emotionally disturbed she was. After we, um, parted ways, she became obsessed with me. She claims I'm stalking her? It was more like the other way around. She would call me sometimes fifty times a day. Emails, texts."

"Really?"

"That girl has emotional problems, very serious ones, Em. I believe she's mentally ill. Roy wants to get help for her, but the mother and daughter are in denial."

"Do the police know this?"

"I would imagine Roy filled them in."

I sighed, looked at the nachos which I was sure I wouldn't be able to eat. Maybe what he was telling me was true. What kind of a girl steals a gun and then takes off and lives on a small boat? Her actions certainly made her seem mentally ill.

"What about Scott?" A sudden loud burst of conversation at a table a little ways away from us jarred me for a moment. "Kricket told me she and Scott aren't together. She called him a jerk. Yet at Joan and Art's he seemed to indicate that they'd been in conversation all through this."

"Frankly, I don't know. They have one of these on-again off-again things. I assumed they were on-again, but maybe according to her they were off-again. They live together until one of them gets mad and storms out—" He stopped mid-sentence and gave me a half smile—"and let me tell you, Kricket and Scott make for one tumultuous relationship."

"I can only imagine."

"You saw how hotheaded Scott is. I don't think he's good for her. In fact, one of her major breakdowns occurred after the first time he left her. That's when we got together. Kind of a rebound thing. I know her. She sounds close to having a breakdown now. This has happened before. I have a theory..." He leaned toward me. Our faces were almost touching across the table. He whispered to me, "I believe Kricket is behind everything that has happened aboard *Blue Peace*. That girl was poisoned? I'll bet my boots that Kricket had something to do with it. I also have a theory that Kricket is the famous anonymous source that fed the newspaper all that false information about you."

I was aghast. "Why would she do that?"

"You have no idea what she's capable of."

"And Peter? She would have something to do with that, too?"

He nodded. "I wouldn't put it past her."

"How does she know my husband?"

"That, I have absolutely no idea. She's very resourceful. When she discovered you were the captain she would have looked you up and learned all about you."

"But why? I'm so in the dark about this."

"I don't know, either." He paused, reached into his pocket. "Oh, I almost forgot. You mentioned in your email that she stole your phone?"

"Yes."

"Here's one you can use." He slid it across the table at me. It was the same brand of smart phone as mine but not as new.

"Really? you have spare cell phones lying around?"

"This one, yes. It's set up with a local number, but no long distance or data plan, or even text messages, but it does get Wifi, so you can probably get texts that way." He gave me a bit of a half-smile that reminded me in that instant of Jesse. I hated to be reminded of Jesse that way.

"Oh wow. Thanks," I said.

"It should do until you can get a new phone there."

I fiddled with a few of the settings until I had logged into the Pub's free Wifi. I opened a web browser. Then it was a fairly straightforward matter of clicking into my service provider and clicking on my messages. Two text messages, I noticed.

The first was from Amanda, wife of Bryce, Jesse's former partner. I'd forgotten all about emailing her.

We should meet. It's been long enough. Maybe there's been enough water under the bridge. I'm out tonight. Call me in the morning. Don't call tonight.

The second was an email from Dr. Meyer.

Call me at your earliest convenience. I have some information that I think you might find extremely interesting. Extremely.

Declan

"Problems?" Tom asked.

"Nothing I can't handle." I stared down at that message before beginning rather tentatively, "Tom? Did you ever have a chance to meet my husband, Jesse?"

He kept his eyes steady on me when he said, "I'm sorry to say that although I heard many good things about him, I was never privileged to make his acquaintance."

Chapter 25

"Let's go for a walk." Tom leaned across the table after we'd eaten a scant third of the nachos. "I think we both need to get out of this place. As I said before, it's been one hell of a day. Fresh air would do us both some good."

"I've got to get Jeff and Valerie's boat back to their dock," I protested. "I need someone to drive my car." I described my predicament to him.

Tom took my hand. "Don't worry about that. We'll take care of that. There's still time tonight to do the car boat switch."

"Thank you."

Still holding my hand he said, "I can't believe that girl is on the loose. It must be such a shock for Roy. He's been through a lot with that daughter of his."

His fingers tightened on mine. My hand was cold. His was warm. I liked this, I thought. But was I ready for this?

We were on the waterfront path when he stopped, turned to me, took both my hands in his and said, "Why don't you stay with me tonight? At my condo? It's getting late. We can take care of your car and boat situation tomorrow, first thing."

I simply stared at him. What was he asking me, this man who reminded me of Jesse and yet didn't? I stumbled for words, "I don't, um...I don't know."

"Nothing untoward." He gave me a half smile. "If that's what you're thinking. I've got a foldout couch in my living room. I just don't think you should be alone tonight, not after what happened to Peter and with an emotionally disturbed young woman on the loose."

"I need to get home to my dog," I said averting my gaze.

"Ah, your dog."

I tried to decipher his tone when he said that. Was he making fun of me? There was so much about him that was hard to read.

We walked again. It had turned into a beautiful early evening, clear and crisp, stars and a half moon. Seeking to change the subject, I asked him how his boat was coming along. Was Scott managing to get the engine done?

"He's working on it."

"You know him well?"

"I told you, he's a hothead."

"You've said that, yeah. But he was going to be your crew on *Blue Peace,* right?"

"Under great protestations by me. I wanted you."

"Then why take him?"

"Because he's the best mechanic there is."

Really. I hadn't heard that. Minutes later, Tom and I were at the place on the wharf above where *Blue Peace* was tied. It was hard not to miss the yellow crime scene tape this time, and police cars and lights. Ahead of us were a few news vans. We stopped short before we got to them. All I wanted to do was flee. It was Tom who seemed rooted to the spot, watching it all.

Ben was down on the wharf, talking to some officers. He didn't see us, hidden the way we were in the semi-darkness. Maybe that's what the phone call in the car was all about—him having to run off to this.

Tears pooled in my eyes as I stood there. I don't know how it happened, but a moment later I was in Tom's arms and I was crying. Peter, gone? How could this be? Tom's hands were in my hair then, and he was telling me that everything was going to be okay.

"Why?" I kept shaking my head. "Why would someone do that?"

He quietly said, "It's crazy and sad and doesn't make any sense, and it's okay to cry. Just cry, Em. Just cry."

"Peter was one of the good guys."

"I know."

"He shouldn't have died."

"I know."

"I don't understand any of this."

"I know." He kept stroking my hair and holding me close while I cried. Then, I don't know how it happened, but he was kissing me, and I fell into his kiss.

After we broke away, despite his eyes, which looked warmly into my own, something felt off. Something I couldn't name. It was me, I decided. This was the first man I'd kissed since Jesse, and I expected it to feel, somehow, different. It didn't.

His arm remained around the small of my back, and he said, "We have company."

Ben was walking up the hill toward us. I tried to gently move away from Tom's embrace, but he held me even more tightly, protectively. It was almost as if he wanted to make sure that Ben saw that we were together. Which was exactly the opposite of what I wanted.

"Em," Ben said.

"Ben," I said.

"Tom," Ben said.

"Ben," Tom said.

"Been trying to reach you," Ben said to Tom.

I felt the briefest of quivers of his hand on my back and then Tom said quite calmly, "Horrible business."

"I was speaking with Roy Patterson earlier," Ben said.

"And?"

"Patterson said he never authorized you and Scott to take *Blue Peace* to Bermuda and the Bahamas."

Tom broke away from me. "That's an outright lie."

"Roy Patterson said that he did not want his boat to continue on the trip. He said he never authorized this trip."

"Patterson himself called me." Tom was shaking his head, looking utterly confused. "The man is deluded. I've worked for him before. The whole family is crazy." He grabbed his cell phone. "I can probably even find his email. Here, give me a minute." Tom rapidly scrolled through his phone, I asked Ben, "Did you find Kricket yet?"

He did not look at me when he said, "Not yet."

"Have they identified the girl yet?"

"Not that either."

I opened my mouth to say something more, but before I could, a couple of forensics officers clad completely in white approached us.

"Detective?" the officer said, "We found something."

Chapter 26

Even though Ben put up his hand to caution us to keep back, Tom and I followed Ben down the hill. Tom even ducked under the crime scene tape the way Ben did, almost daring Ben to stop him and ignoring the uniformed officer who yelled, "Hey."

Tom climbed right aboard *Blue Peace* with me close behind. I wasn't sure I wanted to be there, but a moment later I was in the cockpit and looking down into the cabin.

It was then that I noticed the smell. I know what dead fish smells like. I've had the unfortunate experience once of sailing too close to a huge floating and decomposing Minke whale. It was like the stench was living particles in the air. Later, I felt like washing down my entire boat with Lysol. I've watched enough episodes of *CSI* to know that decomposing bodies smell, although I've never had the privilege.

This wasn't that smell. This was a smell I recognized.

This is the sour, meaty smell you get when you forget to empty your holding tank in hundred degree weather. This is the smell you get when your holding tank has a leak and is draining into the bilge. Regular household sewage smells different than boat sewage, because boat sewage is combined with the sickly, sweet smell of the chemicals you throw into the tank precisely so that it won't smell. I've worked on enough heads in my life to know this smell.

I looked down through the companionway, expecting to see a chalk mark outlining where Peter's body had been. Instead, the interior of *Blue Peace* was torn apart. The teak and holly sole on the port side of the boat had been ripped up, revealing the murky bilge water. As well, the settee cushions had been removed, the lockers under the cushions had been pried open and the holding tank had been, it looked like, sawed in half.

Next to it on a tarp was a brownish, sodden duffel bag. It was partially open and brimming with rubber-banded hundred-dollar bills in all their brown sludgy glory.

I could only stare.

"What the—" Tom was right behind me.

An officer, someone I knew vaguely from sailing, said to me, "That was inside the holding tank."

"That's kind of a feat," I said. "Holding tanks are sealed units."

"This one looked like it was two pieces that were carefully glued together," he said.

I remember Joan complaining of a faint head smell. This must've been the reason.

Even on a boat the size of *Blue Peace*, there's not a lot of room down inside once you add a whole squad of police officers and their paraphernalia. Several forensic officers in head-to-toe white outfits and gloves had to scrunch against the sides of the boat as they walked past.

Ahead of me, a couple of cops were dismantling the bulkhead between the main cabin and the head with a crowbar. I flinched at the sight of all that beautiful teak being splintered and ruined.

"We found something else, too," one of the officers said to Ben.

Reaching in between the two boards that made up the bulkhead, the officer removed what looked like a long, plastic mailing tube. "This," he said.

We all looked on as one officer photographed it, while another opened the end of the tube carefully with a sharp-edged knife. With a gloved hand, he pulled out a rolled-up piece of canvas. He laid it on the forward berth and unfolded it. It was the lighthouse painting that had been on one of the postcards that Ben had found underneath the bed mattress.

Ben yelled, "Get Patterson again. Now. Find him. Now!"

I heard a cell phone ring behind me. I turned in time to see Tom hop up into the cockpit to answer it.

Ben seemed to notice me for the first time. "You shouldn't be here. Who let you down here?"

"I thought you might need my help."

"Em"—his voice was hard—"please leave."

I turned around, thinking that Tom was right behind me. He wasn't. I ducked back under the crime scene tape and headed up the knoll, but didn't see Tom. I stood on the path, waiting. He didn't seem to be around.

I walked back down toward the wharf, then back up to the walkway, but didn't see him. I pulled the unfamiliar cellphone out of my pocket and called his number. No answer. I put it back in my pocket and sat down at a picnic table above the water and hugged myself in Jeff's jacket. Five minutes later, I tried him again. Again, nothing. I walked back up to the café with Wifi and stood outside and checked my text messages.

Nothing.

I headed back to the pub we'd been in. He wasn't there. I went back down to the wharf. No Tom. I leaned against a tree and wondered where he was. An hour later, I began to be afraid.

Chapter 27

I kept calling him, but it rang and rang without even going to voice mail. I drove up and down the main street and back again. I drove down by the wharf and parked there. I wondered what to do. I drove over to the building that Tom said was his condo and parked next to it. I called him again. There was no open Wifi so I was basically out of luck for texts or emails. I got out of my car.

His was a new condo, and I could see that the builder had spared no expense. With its multileveled decks and manicured walkways, it was just about as luxurious as the hotel that the Pattersons were staying in. I managed to find the path that led to the front door, said hello to several people who were exiting, found which apartment was Tom's and rang his bell. No answer. I leaned on it again. Nothing.

I sat down in one of the chairs in the lobby and tried to figure out what to do. A few people came and went and looked at me huddled small in the smelly lobstering jacket. I ignored them and wondered if I should call Ben, but Ben was dealing with all that crap down at *Blue Peace*. Crap, being the operative word.

Out in front of the condo was a private wharf for residents. I wondered if Tom might be down at his boat. Maybe that's why he left so suddenly—more trouble with Scott. I walked down the shrub-lined pathway to the wide, wooden dock. Several steps onto the dock, I could go no further unless I had a key for the lockbox on the metal gate. "Boat Owners and Guests Only," read the sign. I looked around me. The tide was fully high now. There would be no way I could wade out and climb onto the dock, even if I could get away with doing that without anyone seeing me and immediately calling security.

That old wooden boat at the very end of the southernmost dock had to be his. I peered at it. Next to it was a lobster boat. This was probably the boat Scott was living on while he worked on Tom's.

From this distance, Tom's boat looked open. Was he down there? I craned my neck, but it was too dark, and even with the light standards on the dock, I couldn't see as well as I wanted to.

Then my salvation came. Walking toward me up the dock were a couple carrying a few canvas boat bags. I stood beside the door, digging in the bottom of my bag as if looking for my keys. When they opened the metal lockbox, I said, "Thanks," as I sidled in. "This saves me the trouble. Darn keys always get stuck right at the bottom."

"Know the feeling," the woman said.

"Have a nice evening," the man said.

"Thanks. You, too."

If they wondered about my smelly jacket, they didn't say anything. I quickly made my way down the dock past million-dollar yachts and ginormous powerboats to the very end, where Tom's rather old and stodgy wooden boat was tied. As I got closer, I realized that the hatch boards weren't off his boat after all. In fact, when I got there, his boat was locked up tight. Even so, I knocked on the side of it.

"Tom? Hey, Tom. You in there?"

No answer.

Next to it, however, the powerboat was wide open. Was Scott there? Maybe he would know where Tom was. I knocked on the side of the boat. "Scott?"

Nothing. A dock light standard, situated in the right place, afforded me a clear look into the opened cabin. "Scott?"

I could tell by the array of blankets on the berth and clothing on hooks that Scott was definitely staying on board.

I shouldn't have. I know I shouldn't have—It goes against the sailor's code, to go on someone else's boat without permission, especially when they're not there—but I climbed aboard Scott's boat anyway. I knocked again at the entryway and called his name. I looked through the companionway.

And then I saw it.

Underneath a small pile of magazines on a shelf next to the berth was Jesse's computer. I would need to see the top of it to be absolutely sure, however. Tentatively, I made my way into the cabin and moved the magazines, looking for the Sail America stickers that Jesse had used to decorate the outside of his computer. They were there.

I was so stunned that for a moment I just stared. I was even afraid to touch it. What was Jesse's computer doing in Scott's boat? Scott had actually come into my house and rummaged around my office closet until he found it? What could Scott possibly want with Jesse's computer?

It made no sense. I barely knew Scott. I was certain that Jesse hadn't known Scott. I put the computer firmly under my arm and climbed out of the boat.

"Hey!" came a voice from behind me.

I attempted to hide the computer in the folds of the yellow jacket and turned.

The voice belonged to a heavyset man in a flowered Hawaiian shirt who was sitting in the back of his sailboat, a bottle of beer in one hand. "You looking for Scott?"

"Yes."

"Just saw them," he said.

"Them?"

"You just missed 'em. Scott and Tom. You hear what happened over there?" He indicated with his beer toward the public wharf and *Blue Peace*. "Maybe that's what had them so riled up, Tom being the captain and all."

"Yeah."

"A few minutes ago, Tom came running down here, and the next thing I know they're taking off—Scott screaming his head off. Like I said, you just missed 'em."

"Thanks for telling me," I muttered.

I walked quickly back down the dock toward the lockbox. Too late, I realized that not only did you need a key to get in, it was one of those uber-security places where you also needed a key to get out.

Now what do I do? Go back and borrow Hawaiian shirt's key?

I looked down below the dock. The tide was high, and the water would be deep and cold and swirling. I had Jesse's computer. Which I had stolen. No, not stolen. Retrieved. I pulled Tom's phone out of my pocket. No Wifi down here either. Back in my pocket it went.

The chain link fence stuck out a good three feet on either side of the dock. It was built that way so you couldn't do what I was thinking of doing and that was hooking my feet into the chain links and sidling myself around it. Instead, I walked back down the wharf to Mr. Hawaiian Shirt. The lid to his engine was open, and he was down below with lights blazing on his work.

"You stuck?" he asked when he saw me.

"Forgot my stupid keys. I was supposed to meet Tom here. I've been texting him and texting him." I showed him my non-functioning phone.

"Yeah, I guess something came up, the way those two took off.

Here, wait a minute. I can let you out. You want a beer?"

I sighed and said I would love to, but Tom and I had apparently gotten our signals crossed. I thought I was supposed to meet him here, but obviously not. Could he be so kind as to let me through the gate?

"No problem. Give me a minute to climb out of this mess."

He walked me to the door, unlocked it and let me through. If he noticed I was carrying a computer, he didn't say anything. I thanked him profusely and profoundly. He said he hoped I found Tom, and I said, me, too.

I headed up to where there was Wifi, and the first thing that came up when I got online was an email from Tom. Three words.

Something came up.

After that, I called the only safe person I could think of to call. Joan.

Chapter 28

"Why would Scott drive all the way out to the end of Chalk Spit, walk into my house, *into my house*, Joan, and to my office and go into the closet, find the computer case, open it up and take it? Oh, and not take the power supply or Jesse's wedding ring. And now why this stupid message from Tom? *Something came up.* Why would he just leave like that without letting me know where he is? What was so important with him and Scott?"

I was driving too fast, and Joan was mostly shaking her head or shrugging or making sounds of sympathy at appropriate times.

Earlier when I'd called her, Joan had said she would be happy to do the car/boat swap. She could probably hear the panic in my voice.

When I'd shown up at her door, she'd taken one look at my stricken face and given me a long hug, and Joan isn't a hugger. Everything tumbled out of my mouth then. Kricket living on my boat, then disappearing, Peter's murder—which she already knew about—the painting found on *Blue Peace*, the duffle bag of money, my computer on Scott's boat and Tom running off with Scott when he'd promised to drive me home.

While waiting for Joan to grab a jacket, I had managed a cursory look through my husband's computer. I'd been on it before, just after he died. At that time, though, all I had been looking for were emails that needed answering. Now, I had so many questions, too many questions. When I was finally home on this strange and awful night at the end of this strange and awful day, I would study absolutely everything on his machine.

I would read through all his emails, carefully examine his Web history and go through all his files until I learned a) if he was having an affair, b) who it was with, c) how this related to what was happening now, and d) what was on this laptop that would make Scott come all the way out to my house and steal it?

I was mad, angry, hurt and scared all at once. I had told Joan a lot, but not about my growing feelings for Tom. She and I are close friends. We share a lot, but I'm the type of person who keeps things close to my chest. I've never been one of those women who has a close female friend who she gigglingly shares everything with. That's only in movies. This is life.

"Why would he leave?" I asked again as I took the exit toward Chalk Spit and home.

"Maybe he had a reason," Joan said quietly. It was dark, and striated clouds undulated in front of us like tree branches. It was like we were driving through a horror movie.

"Well, obviously he had a *reason*, or a reason that he thought was a reason..."

As we waited for the ferry, I added to the story. I told her about meeting Elaine Patterson, about Kricket's emotional problems and her obsession with Tom, about how Kricket said she hated Scott now. I just kept going on and on, like I couldn't stop.

At one point, Joan said, "Tom and Kricket..." Her voice trailed off. I looked over at her but she said nothing more.

By the time Joan had heard my entire story, plus another rant about Tom, we were off the ferry and at the turnoff where the *Valerie J* was tied at the fishing dock.

"I'll meet you at my house," I said, getting out of the car, "And then I'll drive you back to Portland right away."

"That's a long haul," she said.

"I don't mind. Gives me more time to think."

I clambered down the still-wet grassy bank to the dock, computer under my arm. I didn't even trust leaving it in the back seat of my own car. The *Valerie J* started first crank and was painfully loud in the still night. I arrived at Jeff and Valerie's dock way before Joan did, as I knew I would. I tied up the lobster boat, hung the yellow rubber coat back up and put the key under the rub rail by the ledge. It was dark when I climbed the path to my house. The only light on the whole point came from one room in EJ's house, his ham radio/woodworking studio. I could picture him in there, bent over one of his miniature boxes, eyes bright, a tiny glue gun in his hand, or headset on as he sent dots and dashes to someone in Belgium or Belize.

Usually I welcome the darkness. I'm not normally afraid of it. I love moonless sailing, when it's just me and the vast dark sky, but now the utterness of it made me feel vulnerable. Was Kricket, emotionally fragile Kricket, out there somewhere? Was she lurking behind a tree?

Was she on the island? I thought about Peter and was filled with such sadness again.

I headed over to EJ's to pick up Rusty and to thank him.

"Come on in." EJ was smiling widely. "Rusty and I have been fine. Do you have time now to come in and look at some of Jesse's handiwork? I was just going through some of his things."

"Oh, EJ, I would love to, but it's late and Joan is driving in with my car." I told EJ about Peter, and he looked sadly at me and said, "Oh, my. Oh, dear. What a tragic shame. I haven't had the radio on all day. Well, I guess I have, but to music not news. Oh, dear Emmie, he was a close friend?"

I nodded, felt teary-eyed all over again. "One of my sailing kids."

"Oh, Emmie, I'm so sorry."

I nodded, didn't know what to say.

He said, "Earlier you said someone stole your car? A girl?"

"I got it back."

"Well, that's good then. Oh, wait. Before you go back home—" He turned.

I shifted my weight from foot to foot. "EJ...I...I have to hurry..."

He held one hand up and retreated to his kitchen. He returned with a plate heaped with roast beef slices and topped with a sheet of waxed paper. "Here, you take this home with you. I bet you haven't eaten much lately, have you?"

"Thank you, EJ." I took the plate. "You're sweet. And you're right, I haven't eaten much lately."

"Oh, wait, here's something else." He went back into his kitchen then came back with a small china pitcher of cream. "I know you like cream in your coffee and you probably haven't been to the grocers yet, either, have you? Here, you take this."

"That's so nice of you."

"And promise me, promise me you'll come back to look at Jesse's woodworking."

"I will."

I balanced the pitcher of cream on top of the meat and quickly headed home. By the time I'd stuck the meat in the fridge, headlights were visible through the back window. I ran outside and hopped in the car. Joan had already scooted over into the passenger seat.

"I so appreciate you doing this," I said. "I had no idea how I was going to get both the car and the boat back home. This is so helpful."

"I'm sort of glad Tom crapped out on you," she said. "It's given us a chance to talk."

"A chance for me to talk anyway. I've done most of the talking."

"Em, a lot has happened to you. I don't mind listening."

"I'm starting to worry about Tom."

"Don't." She said it quickly and turned her head away from me. I looked at her sharply. "Tom can take care of himself," she said.

"Joan?" I prodded.

"Ever since Tom showed up that morning, I've wanted to talk to you about something," she said.

I glanced over at her.

"I thought about this on the drive here, whether I should tell you. Or wait until after I talk to Detective Dunlinson."

"Talk to Ben about what?"

"You need to know something," she said.

Gravel crunched under my car tires. I waited.

"I think I recognized the girl," Joan said. "The one who died. The one who was pretending to be Kricket."

My fingers tightened on the steering wheel.

She went on. "As soon as she came aboard, she looked familiar to me and I felt immediately that she wasn't Kricket Patterson. But since she had the correct passport, and you seemed to approve her, I figured maybe I had it wrong. I tried a few times to approach her while we were underway, but she always deflected my questions, or seemed to be so interested in learning about navigation. I think now that she was just misleading me. And then in the past couple of days, I remembered where I'd seen her. Especially that morning when Tom and Scott came over. It has to do with them."

I nearly drove off the road. "Tom and Scott? Why didn't you say something when I was going on and on about them earlier?"

She shrugged. "I didn't know if I should, or if I should talk to Ben Dunlinson first."

"You should have talked to me right away. I was the captain, Joan."

"Oh, Em."

I clamped my teeth together.

We were at the ferry now, and I stopped the car and turned it off, while we waited for the ferry to get back to us. It wouldn't be long. "What are you going to tell Ben?" I asked.

She sighed. "You know how you meet so many people on boats it's hard to remember one marina or anchorage from the next, or even what season it is, let alone month or year?"

I looked at her. She was fingering her right earring, a small anchor she always wore.

"It was in Bermuda," she said. "Art and I had taken our boat over there. This was a few years or so ago. I could look up the exact date in the log, especially if I go to the police with this information. We were out for a walk and saw her up on the deck of the yacht the Pattersons had then. It wasn't *Blue Peace*. It was a huge powerboat. The girl was there along with Kricket and Scott. Those three. I'm sure it was Scott. The three of them sunbathing on the foredeck of the boat."

I looked over at her. Her hands were now folded on her lap, her long fingers entwined.

"Kricket told me she didn't know the girl," I responded. "But Tom said that Kricket and Scott were a couple once…"

"Well, they obviously were a couple then by the way they were acting." She put a hand to her earring again. "When she came onto the boat and I felt I knew her from some place, I decided I was going to befriend her. She seemed kind of lost, didn't you think?"

"I'm not sure."

"I felt like she needed a friend. Turns out I was right."

The ferry had docked. One car came off. I drove on, trying to make sense of what she was saying. "You said Tom had something to do with this?"

"I'm not sure." She looked past me and into the far distance. "I saw him in town later. In Bermuda. So he was there, although I didn't see him on the boat with the three others. He was on the street, and it was obvious by his actions that he didn't want to be seen. He's from Maine, and I'm from Maine, and people from Maine usually chat each other up when they see each other in foreign countries. I'm fairly sure he recognized me, but when he saw me he put his head down and turned and dove across the street."

I stared at her, not knowing what to make of what she was telling me, of any of this.

She bit her lower lip. "Em, I would watch my heart with Tom." Her voice was gentle now. "He doesn't have the most stellar reputation with women. He's a bit of a charmer." She cleared her throat. "Em, he's an opportunist. Have you seen his new condo?"

"Not inside, no.

"Well, I have. Not Tom's particular condo, but Art knows someone who lives in that building. They're gorgeous places. Decks, beautiful views, high ceilings and of course that private wharf. You know what those properties go for these days?"

"What are you getting at?"

"I'm just wondering where Tom gets his money, is all."

In all my years of knowing her, I have never known Joan to be catty. "I do know what those properties go for," I said, "but how do we know where people get their money? He could have inherited it. Look at the place I live in, Joan. Right on the water. But it was in Jesse's family for generations. I could never afford a place like the one I live in, unless it came to me in a will. And look at your house, Joan. So perhaps Tom came by it honestly."

She folded her hands on her lap and looked out her window, frowning. We were on the ferry now on this pitch-black night, and the water around us churned, dark and oily. After a little while, she said, "I don't trust him, that's all. I don't understand his relationship with Scott."

"Scott's working on Tom's boat."

"I know some boat owners who won't even allow Scott on their boats, much less as crew."

"Really? Why?"

"Sticky fingers. Of course, no one's been able to prove anything ever, and Tom sticks up for him. He always sticks up for him."

"Scott was the one who stole my computer," I mused.

"See? My point exactly."

Once we were on the road heading into Portland, I said, "Joan? You knew Jesse real well, right?"

She turned to face me. "Of course. We knew him before you did, Em. We met him when we sailed up to Grand Manan that time. If you recall, I think it was Art who introduced the two of you. Why do you ask?"

I shrugged, tried to appear nonchalant. "Did he ever have, um, really short hair? Like almost a military shaved-head thing going on?"

She laughed and then quickly stopped. "As a matter of fact, he did. It was not an attractive look for him. Made him look too tough or something."

"When was this?"

She must've heard something in my voice, because she turned to look at me. "Several years before you and he were together. Em? Why are you asking?"

"I saw a picture of him."

"Oh?" Was there too much of a rise of her tone at the end of her sentence?

"Joan," I said, without looking at her. "What do you know about Jesse when he had short hair?"

"What do you mean?"

"Joan, if you know anything about Jesse that I don't, you need to tell me."

"What could I possibly know about Jesse that you don't? Why are you asking this question?"

I sighed. "Just before he died... There were some things that didn't add up just before he died."

"What things?" She was fully facing me now.

I shrugged. How do I voice what I was feeling? I hemmed and hawed and cleared my throat until she turned to me and said, "He would never have intentionally hurt you. Never."

Intentionally hurt me? The road was dark, and I steered carefully to avoid a snarled piece of road kill. What did she mean by that? I asked her.

She sighed. "Ben came to Art and me. He wanted to know about Jesse. Apparently, his phone number was on a card found on the boat. Is that why you're asking about him?"

Of course Joan would know about this. Of course this would be part of the investigation. Ben was pursuing all avenues. What had I expected, that Jesse's name would be kept out of the questioning entirely?

"What did you tell him?" I kept my voice even.

"Em—" She turned to face me. "There was some talk at the time—"

"Talk about what?" I snapped.

"It was just before Jesse died. I refused to even listen to it, because I knew the real Jesse, but you know how gossipy and political the sailing community can be."

"What did the gossipy and political sailing community say about Jesse?"

"That he was involved in something. I didn't get what. I really didn't listen, Em. I refused to."

Involved with something or someone? "Tell me," I demanded.

"It was a long time ago."

"It was less than two years ago. That's not a long time." I decided to come right out with it. "So you knew Jesse was having an affair and you didn't tell me. How could you not?"

"What—"

"His affair, Joan. If you want to know all the sordid details of my marriage, I suspected him of having an affair."

She shook her head. "Em, I didn't believe those rumors. Neither Art nor I did. I didn't then and I don't now, no matter what Scott seems to think he'll find on the computer. Your husband wouldn't have cheated on you. We knew the real Jesse."

So had I, I thought. But maybe I hadn't. "So, you think Scott may have taken Jesse's computer to find some dirt on it. Why?"

Very quietly, she said, "Did you ever think that *you* might be the target of all of this? That you're the reason all of this is happening? Maybe someone wants to blackmail you. I'd be careful, Em. Someone may be using this old stuff with Jesse to get to you."

"Blackmail?" I snorted. "I'd be happy to give whoever it is access to my bank account. It has a negative balance, thank you very much. If someone wants to take it off my hands, I'd be grateful."

"Oh, Em."

"I know. Sucks to be me."

By the time we got to her house, we were both quiet. Before she got out, she put a hand on my shoulder and said, "I love you, Em. Both Art and I think the world of you. You're the sweetest person I know. I always want the best for you. Please remember that."

I moved away from her. I didn't want Joan to hug me. I didn't want anyone to hug me on this night.

I was driving away before she even made it to her door. Some strong and in-control boat captain I am, I cried all the way back home. I had trusted Jesse, and he had failed me. Joan said he would never cheat on me, but what if he had? I wasn't altogether sure I could trust Tom, and Peter was dead, and my own career was in a shambles. Oh yes, and I had no money. My parents and sisters were right. Jesse had been nothing but a boat bum who'd slept around. I should go out to Ohio and work in Katie's husband's company.

Excuse me while I pull over and throw up.

I tried to remember any time that Scott and Jesse had even been together. I could not. I barely knew him. But something had me wondering as I pulled into the space beside my house. I needed to figure this out. I needed to figure out the connection between Scott and Jesse. And what about Rob? Did he figure into this whole thing, too? If it took me all night looking through every friggin' file on Jesse's computer, I would do it.

I unlocked my house, greeted my waiting dog and got Jesse's espresso machine going. This night called for a double.

Chapter 29

While Jesse's computer was firing up, I used a Wifi connection and returned Dr. Meyer's call, apologizing for calling so late. No worries, he said. He told me that the explosion that had destroyed *Rosalena* might have been deliberately set. He was continuing to research this. He'd been able to secure some of the police photos taken at the time, and did I want copies of them?

"Of course," I said.

"I find the whole thing rather curious," he added. "I think there is a bit more to this story than meets the eye. I think you'll find the photos very enlightening."

He told me his personal notes on the case were still missing, and he found this strange as well. He was always so fastidious about his things. Knowing him the little that I did, I believed him. He said he had contacted the local police—the county squad, not Ben—about reopening the case, and they had told him unequivocally that the case was closed.

My thoughts spun. "Even if the state medical examiner says it should be reopened?"

"I don't have a lot of sway. I know this is a matter for the sheriff's department that deals with Chalk Spit and the waters up around there, but I'm tempted to take this right to Detective Dunlinson in Portland. Although, I suspect that could elicit a turf war. Being so new to Maine, Detective Dunlinson doesn't need this."

Before we rung off, I thanked him for continuing with this. So many things were running through my mind as I opened Jesse's files. Since I had been through most of Jesse's emails after he died, I decided to first look through some of the files on his laptop. Jesse had given them names like Keel Concepts New, Old Designs, Correspondence and Em. Yes, Jesse had named a file after me. I had looked at this after he died, but the designs in it had told me nothing then, and besides, at the time I was too sad to make sense of anything.

I saw on the computer that the file Em had been opened as recently as a week ago. That would have been when I was aboard *Blue Peace*. That must have been when Scott had stolen the computer from my office. I remembered that Dot and Isabelle had told me that a handsome young man had been looking at the house for sale. Could Scott be described as a "handsome young man"? To two old women, maybe.

I opened screen after screen of drawings, examining each one as I chomped on pieces of EJ's roast beef. The sailboat in the drawing I was looking at now had a long keel and a mast that was slightly forward of it. I had no idea how this would sail. I just sail the boats, I don't design them. That had been Jesse's job. I went over drawing after drawing, trying to figure out what, if anything, I was looking for. One of the pictures was a mockup of a sailboat, and the name on it was Em. That gave me a pang. He had named a boat after me? Had this been the boat he'd wanted to borrow yet more money to fund for production?

Then I wondered. I'd heard of people stealing designs, and I knew how protective Jesse had been of his. Was *that* what this was all about? Might it not have been an affair after all?

On the last page of the Em file there was a small smudge mark on the bottom of the page. Some sort of logo for the new boat? Using the zoom function I made the page bigger and bigger until I could see that the image was a line of text. I zoomed in even further, until the text was readable yet highly pixilated:

The key for this is at a place only Em will know about.
What?

Jesse had left a clue. He'd known something was about to go south, and he'd left me a clue—a key. Hidden only where I would know? Kricket had talked about someone looking for a key. My boat had been torn apart. Tom had said someone had searched through his boat. Early on, Bryce had come to me looking for Jesse's keys.

I got up and paced around my kitchen. A key for what? Was it a real key? Maybe it was some sort of figurative key?

I dug around in my office junk drawer until I found an old flash drive. I copied the entire folder that contained the file. And then I copied as much of the rest of his computer as would fit.

I decided to make myself another cup of espresso. Before I did, I looked at the machine. This fancy espresso machine from Italy had been my husband's pride and joy.

The key for this is at a place only Em will know about.

I took the water reservoir out of the machine. I dumped it out and looked at the bottom. I took all of the moving parts out and looked carefully at each one. Keys were small things. Keys could hide anywhere.

I picked up the bottom reservoir tray, rinsed it. No key.

I put the machine back together and set it up to make my espresso. While my little espresso brewed, I decided to read through Jesse's email, all of it, all accounts and all folders. It would take me awhile, but what else was I doing?

It was business correspondence—things to do with his boat-building. It made me so sad to read them. From my own computer as a trial, I sent an email to Jesse's account. It bounced back, proving that the account was indeed inactive.

Long after I had finished my coffee, I was hyper, alternating between reading email and pacing around, talking to myself, while Rusty eyed me from the couch. Finally, I found something in a folder called Old Work. The first email was from Bryce to my husband, with the subject line Expansion, and contained only three words:

What about Mallen?

Jesse's answer back read,

If you want to go with him, go ahead, but count me out.

This correspondence was a week before his death. Tom had told me that he didn't know my husband. I had never heard Jesse speak of Tom Mallen, but apparently there had been no love lost between the two.

I checked all of Jesse's mailboxes, and there was one I almost missed because it was buried in his Sent folder. It was one line from Jesse to Tom Mallen at the same email address I had for Tom,

I want out of everything.

Jesse

Chapter 30

I kept reading through the files on Jesse's computer while Rusty snored. A few times, his legs twitched and he flinched. I wondered if, like me, he was bothered by dreams.

It was now nearly midnight. I'd long since put the meat away and washed up the plate. I poured myself a glass of wine, hoping the alcohol would counteract the caffeine. It would probably just make me more wired.

Had Tom wanted to work with my husband on this new Em design? Why hadn't Jesse told me about this? Why hadn't Tom mentioned it? Nearly one-thirty, and I had more questions than answers. Because, of course, Tom had lied to me about not knowing my husband.

In the night, Rusty curled up with me in bed. This is rare for him. Since his hips have gotten bad, he mostly stays in his well-worn stuffed cloth bed on the floor in my bedroom. Tonight, he managed to climb up onto a chair and then into the bed with me. Maybe he knew I needed extra comfort.

I had another Jesse dream, but it wasn't a sailing one. He was standing way out on Pistol Rock in the middle of the channel. The tide was coming in, but not the way the tide normally does, slowly, inch by inch, rising steadily and swirling gently around rocks as it does so. Instead, there was a huge rogue wave out in the bay. I could see it, massive and rolling in, closer, closer. I kept yelling at my husband to climb down and hurry to the shore. But, Jesse was looking the other way, and I could not get him to turn toward my voice. I could not yell over the bell buoy out in the bay, ringing out its loud and insistent warning at regular intervals.

The bell buoy kept ringing. And when I awoke, I realized it was the sound of the phone on the bedside table.

I scrambled to answer it. *Jesse!* Then, more awake, I thought, maybe it was Tom. Or even Ben. But no. It was a text message.

I blinked down at the caller ID. Amanda. I got to it quickly. She was in Camden, and if I wanted to talk with her, I could meet her on the town dock at two that afternoon.

Fine, I texted back. *I'll be there.*

She ended by writing, *It's time we talked.*

I looked at the time on the phone. I had a few hours before I would have to get driving. Given my late night, I probably should have tried sleeping some more. I got up instead. My computer and Jesse's computer were still side by side and open on my kitchen table. I hit both return keys to wake them up. The file open on my laptop screen showed a search engine. I had gone to bed after giving up trying to find the black cat on Jesse's laptop. Jesse's computer was opened to the page with the enlarged words, *The key for this is at a place only Em will know about.*

There is a kind of secret compartment drawer in this big, old table of mine. There are drawers that pull out from either side, but in the middle, there is one that is accessible only if you pull out one of the drawers completely. In the old days, this was probably meant to hold a gun or two.

Why hadn't I thought of this yesterday? *A place only Em will know.* I pulled the outer drawer all the way out and laid it on the table next to the computers. With a growing sense of excitement, I reached way underneath the table, undid the hook and tugged out the secret drawer.

Empty. Except for a half inch of dust and a couple of old kitchen knives. No key lurking underneath them. I wiped the dust out with a tissue from my pocket and put Jesse's computer into the flat, shallow drawer and secured it back under the table.

I spooned some more beef and some of the tuna casserole that Dot and Isabelle had given me onto a plate and heated it up in the microwave, frowning at my unconventional breakfast. I really needed to get some groceries. I sat down in front of my laptop and went online. One more thing—I wanted to satisfy my curiosity about Ben. If Tom was lying about Jesse, maybe he was lying about Ben, too. Tom had said that news of the demise of Ben's police career was easy to find.

I looked. Sadly, it was. I easily found news articles from several media sources in Montana. Two years ago during the arrest of two drug dealers, Ben had shot and killed an innocent bystander. From what I could glean from the articles, he'd gotten faulty information. So the blame was not entirely his. It took a toll on him, however, and he had gone out on stress leave.

I stopped for a long time on a picture of Ben and his wife. His *wife?* Her name was Melanie, and she was short, way shorter than he was, which would make her shorter than I am. Blond hair, thick, cascading and curly, the kind of hair I always wanted. She was round-faced and pretty, with a gap between her two front teeth. She looked like the sort of girl who would giggle a lot. The article mentioned a son, yet there was no picture of a son nor a name. That's all I could find. Ben was married. He had a son. Were his wife and son here in Maine?

On our long trip together on *Blue Peace*, Ben had shared a lot about Montana, the little fly-fishing stream that ran behind his house, his canoe with 9 HP outboard, the small waterfall upstream from where he lived, how the beavers built dams and lodges that always wrecked the trout ponds. But nothing about a wife. Or son. I kept looking at his face in the grainy low-resolution online photo. We all have our secrets, I thought, you, me, Tom, Jesse.

Rusty and I went for a walk, but instead of walking down by the beach, which is our usual haunt, I decided we would head up into the woods.

When Jesse was a boy, he knew these woods like the back of his hand, he told me. For most of every summer, he and his family came to this place from their home on Grand Manan. On our many walks, he had shown me "secret hiding places," such as caves in the rocks and old sheds that seemed to serve no purpose out in these woods except to house monsters and boogeymen and entertain an inquisitive and imaginative young boy.

The path underneath my feet was spongy and wet, but the air was warm. I easily found Jesse's "shack." A former hunting cabin, it now was a big, falling-down, log shed full of wood scraps and the occasional cooking pot or implement. I went inside and stood in the damp, smelly place and even with a high powered flashlight, I didn't know where to even begin looking. A small key could be anywhere.

On the ground next to the wall was an empty bag of Oreo cookies. I picked it up. It looked fairly new. Had Kricket been here? Was she here even now? I looked all through the bag. No key.

Rusty and I made our way to a few more of Jesse's places, but neither Kricket nor the key were anywhere that I could see, not on ledges, or under boards, or behind stones. I was stumped, and it was time to head to Camden if I wanted to meet Amanda.

Later, on the city dock in Camden, I wandered up and down it until I found Amanda down in the engine compartment of a small sailboat.

"Uh," she said when she saw me. She was not smiling.

"Hey, Amanda, you get a new boat?"

She looked at me. "Hell, no. I wouldn't take this piece-o'-crap boat if you paid me. Nope. Doing a survey. Some schmuck wants to buy this thing. Be my guest, is what I say. Guy's asking way too much. I'll tell him that, too. I'll write it right in the survey."

She told me she was up to her ears in work, and if she and I were going to talk, I would have to accompany her on sea trials right now. If I wanted to offer an opinion or two on this monstrosity of a boat, I was welcome to as well.

"I didn't know you were a surveyor," I said.

"Gotta make a living somehow," she said climbing out and onto the deck.

I climbed aboard. When we were younger, and drawn to the sea, we crewed on boats, hitchhiked up and down the coast, spent winters in the Caribbean, got sunburned, got jobs polishing decks, crewing, cleaning, waitressing in marinas. But then there comes a time when you sort of grow up and have to make a living. I had wanted to make mine captaining. Hers, it seemed, was surveying.

"And it'll be quiet out there. Private," she said.

She started the engine, and I undid the bow line and brought it aboard. We motored easily past the docks in the inner harbor. She had a clipboard and pencil and was writing notes while I took the tiller.

When we were out in the mooring field, I said, "Enough water under the bridge. What did you mean when you told me that?"

"Shh." She bent her head toward the engine. "Something's not right. Stupid gas engines, they ought to be outlawed. This old thing, I'm surprised it started. Surprised they even wanted sea trials. You get a boat this old, just buy it if it's cheap enough. If the engine doesn't work, if the thing leaks like a sponge, well, then for the price you paid, you can always fix it. Or take it out into the ocean, open all the sea cocks and let it sink."

I said, "But sometimes these old gas engines run forever. I was on delivery of a Pearson 35 all the way from Bermuda to the Bahamas with an Atomic 4."

"Yeah right."

I leaned back and looked at the surroundings. Amanda hadn't changed, still as abrupt as ever.

She engaged the autopilot and was opening the engine compartment again. She is younger than I am by a few years and extremely fit. Her big thing was triathlons, and I wondered how many she had done since last we were together. So, I asked her.

She sniffed. "You come all the way to Camden to ask me about triathlons?"

Right. I forgot. Amanda doesn't do small talk. I watched as she fiddled with the engine. She had cut her dark brown hair shaggy and short, and she wore it under a Marblehead Race ball cap. Her outfit was complete with black bicycle shorts and a red tank top with a button-down plaid shirt over it, the sleeves rolled up. On her feet were a pair of beat-up deck shoes. I decided I would just sit here and wait until she was ready to speak to me. A fly crawled across my knee. I swatted at it.

After a few minutes of fiddling she came up into the cockpit and said, "Okay, now we can talk."

"I have a whole bunch of questions. For starters, why did you leave so suddenly after Jesse died? I would really like to know that. I emailed you lots of times, you know."

"And you want to know that now? You come all the way to ask me this *now*?"

I said, "Yes. That, among other things. But now is good. I have other questions, too, but that's first."

She took the tiller and disengaged the autopilot. A couple, drinks in hand and seated on the back of a large, moored sailboat, waved to us cheerily as we motored past. I waved back. That's what people on boats do, wave to each other, engage in small talk. Amanda didn't wave. We eased past Curtis Island.

We were out in open water now, heading southeast past The Graves. It was choppy and windy, a perfect day for a sail, but her job was checking the engine. I was sure that before the day ended, she'd try all the sails.

"Bryce and I are divorced," she said. "Did you know that? He screwed around on me once too often."

I remembered this about Amanda. If she didn't like the subject matter, she simply started talking about something else. "How would I know that when you never answered any of my emails?" I retorted.

"You hear that? That knocking in the engine? I'm thinking not good."

"I'm sorry about you and Bryce," I said.

"Don't be. Guy was a class-A jerk. Know what I did? Threw all his stuff on the front lawn. You only see that in movies, but I really did it. You shoulda seen his face."

"Well, good for you, then."

Two wet-suited guys in a heeled Hobie cat were screaming up the bay. The air was cold out here, the breeze brisk. This was a good day for sailboats. A schooner was off to our port.

I said, "My initial question was about Jesse's email. That's why I emailed you in the first place. I was trying to get into his old account from my computer, and I couldn't. It wasn't accepting his password, but now I have his computer and emails."

"So, what do you need me for then? Surely you know by now Jesse was no saint."

"That's what I'm learning."

"It was why Bryce and I finally split. I couldn't condone what either of them was doing."

I stared at her, swallowing. A swatch of hair blew in front of my eyes, and I pushed it away. They had both been having affairs? Some kind of old boys' network of affairs?

She stared at me dumbly. "You were in the dark entirely, weren't you?"

"Amanda, who was Jesse having an affair with? Everyone seems to know this but me. I've suspected it, but who was it? I need to know."

She took her hand off the tiller and stared at me. "What?"

"Was it Kricket Patterson? Or the girl who fell off the boat who nobody knows? Do you know who she was?"

"Jesse having an affair? Are you out of your frickin' mind?"

My lips felt dry. I reached into my pocket for my lip balm, which I always carry with me. Ahead of us, way out on the water, the sky was darkening. I was sick of rain. I was sick of this weather. I was sick of everything.

She went on. "Okay, crazy girl, Jesse was not having an affair. He adored you. He would have done anything for you. I was jealous of you, if truth be told. Jesse was a good man."

I stared at her. After a while I said, "If it wasn't an affair, then what the hell was going on?"

"Jesse and Bryce stole some art."

I heard the words, but they hit my brain and then bounced off again. Stole some *art*? "Jesse was never interested in art."

"You don't have to be interested in art to steal art. You do it for the money. And they needed money. For that Em design. Named after you, if you must know. Not named after me, I might add…"

I was incredulous.

The two on the Hobie cat came within inches of our stern. "Hey, Amanda!" one of them called. Amanda gave a weak wave. When they were well past, Amanda said, "You had no clue, did you?"

I shook my head. We had turned starboard and were passing The Graves again.

"I think the Famous Captain Tom Mallen was in on it, too," Amanda said.

"Yeah and Tom told me he never met Jesse."

"And you believe him? When did he tell you that?"

I shoved hair behind an ear. "He came to Joan's the morning after the accident on *Blue Peace*. I stayed with Joan for a few days after it happened."

"And you didn't just happen to wonder why he just so happened to come to see you that morning?" She shook her head. "That was no accident. He's still looking for that frigged painting."

"They found it. The painting was on *Blue Peace*," I said. "The police found it. With a duffle bag of money, too."

She nodded. "Saw that. It was on the news."

"So, Jesse, Bryce and Tom put it there? But that makes no sense. Jesse's been gone almost two years. That painting has not been on *Blue Peace* for that long. I don't think Roy Patterson has even owned the boat that long. Why is all this happening now?"

She shrugged. "I'm only saying what I know."

"Where's Bryce now?" I asked.

She shrugged. "Who knows? Who cares? On a boat somewhere. Last thing I heard, way down in South America. If you want to disappear, there are plenty of places you can go on a boat. To my way of thinking, it's the best way to stay off the grid. In this day and age, maybe the only way to stay off the grid. Okay, help me with the mainsail. I want to check out these babies."

While she went up on deck to raise it, I aimed the boat into the wind. Paintings? That explained a lot of things. Maybe the cat picture had been a photo of one of the paintings they stole or planned to steal. And, Jesse writing to Tom that he "wanted out?" Obviously, he had had a change of heart and hadn't wanted to steal any more art.

Once we got the boat on an even fifteen-degree heel, I told Amanda about the "wanting out" email.

She said, "Oh, man, look up at that sail. What a piece of crap. Totally blown out. Look at those streamers. You wouldn't be able to get those straight if you climbed up and glue-gunned them in place." She paused for a moment, then said, "As for what Jesse meant, I don't know. All I know is that Bryce told me Jesse stole a painting of a cat and then locked it up somewhere and stashed the key. Then the accident happened, so no one knew where he locked up the painting."

"Is that why Bryce called and wanted the keys back? The ones I couldn't find?"

"Probably."

I nodded. "Okay, now it's time for you to tell me why you didn't answer my e-mails after Jesse died? Why you left all of a sudden..."

"And here's my answer. I couldn't stand what Bryce and Jesse were doing, what they were doing to you. I didn't want you in the middle of it. You had enough on your plate..."

"But if you knew about the art then, you should have gone to the police. Or, at the very least you should have said something to me."

"I didn't know about the art then. I just know that Bryce seemed way more concerned with getting those damned keys back than about his dead friend. It was only later that I learned about the art."

As we tried out sail after sail, I kept thinking. It was all beginning to make a crazy kind of sense. Bryce and Jesse, wanting to fund the new design called Em, had decided to take matters into their own hands when they couldn't get a bank loan. They conspired to steal artwork that they could then have somehow fenced for the cash they needed. Had they stolen Roy Patterson's art? Was that why they had enlisted Patterson's captain, Tom?

Amanda interrupted my thoughts. "Maybe that 'wanting out' email is what ended up getting Jesse killed."

Chapter 31

My thoughts were in turmoil the following morning as I gathered soap, bucket, rags and garbage bags to take down to *Wanderer*. To get my mind off everything, I would clean up my boat this morning. Maybe, just maybe, Jesse had stashed the key or the cat painting aboard *Wanderer*. I knew all the secret places on my boat. And the thought was there, too, that I was too late, that whoever it was who had wrecked my boat had found those items already.

All the previous evening, I had mulled over what Amanda had told me. Art theft? That was so out of character for my husband as to be laughable. Unless it had some sort of nautical theme, Jesse didn't even like art. I had to remind myself, though, that this was not about art. This was about money.

I'd gone through my husband's computer again last night, pondering every message, even trying to make sense of boat plans, as if that would tell me something. Had Jesse really been murdered? The police had told me over and over that it was an accident. But the boat that had run into him had been destroyed in an explosion—a purposely set explosion, according to Dr. Meyer. Why? To cover up the evidence? This was becoming more and more likely.

I searched and searched online sources about the explosion. All I found was a very small news item about a fire on a private wharf near Winter Harbor. There was a tiny photo next to the article that simply showed a lot of flames. The more I zoomed in and blew it up, the more grainy and unclear it became. It told me nothing. I put it back to its normal resolution, backed away and looked at it again. I squinted. It looked like there were a couple of figures in the corner, but they could be anything from firefighters to curious neighbors. Was this even significant?

My head hurt from the thinking.

On the night Jesse died, he had walked out of our house around midnight. The police hadn't come until after three-thirty. Had he been kayaking that whole time or had he gone someplace else first?

I found a bucket, threw a container of spray cleaner into it and half a container of dish soap. On a shelf behind my washer were some rags. I lifted the lid on my washing machine. Yep. I'd put these clothes in here three days ago and got them washing. I switched the now-almost-dry clothes from the washer to the dryer, realizing that I really, really needed to get my act together.

Maybe I was partly right about the whole thing. Maybe it had begun with an affair that had led to something criminally deeper. Jesse and Kricket. Jesse and the dead girl. Jesse and someone else. No matter how hard I thought, I couldn't make anything fit.

As I scrounged around my mudroom for more cleaning supplies, I remembered that the painting had been stashed in the bulkhead of *Blue Peace* and the money in the holding tank. I'd check the bulkhead on *Wanderer* for screwdriver marks. I knew my boat so well. I'd be able to tell in an instant if someone had messed with anything. I'd also check the holding tank.

I had trouble finding big garbage bags, started cursing and stomping around when it looked as though I had none left. Kept looking. Finally, I found half a grungy box wedged between my clothes dryer and the wall. I pulled them out and angrily threw them onto the pile of stuff I was taking down to *Wanderer*. I cursed myself some more for not buying a box last time I was in the city. You'd think I could make decent grocery lists like normal people, instead of walking up and down the aisles like a dolt.

As I walked out my back door, EJ called over to me, "Hello, Em!"

He was on his wraparound porch, bent over his huge metal outdoor pot in which he could plunge an entire turkey to deep fry it. And the frying medium? He uses goose fat that he gets from a farmer.

I waved back.

"Getting a turkey ready." He pointed at his pot. "Family's on the way."

"Have fun then."

EJ, a widower for more than thirty years, has three sons, two daughters, and many more grandchildren and great-grandchildren, so many that I can never keep track. I sometimes wonder if he can. So when I see little boys down at the water's edge in front of my house squatting over tide pools to collect all manner of aquatic life specimens, I know they belong to EJ. Sometimes I think—*That was Jesse a long time ago.*

"I'll bring over some turkey later," he called. "White meat or dark?"

"Both," I said, but then waved it away. "But keep it for your family."

"I've got two birds here," he said. "Plenty of meat."

Between EJ and the sisters two doors down, I was well kept with food, which was a good thing. Because lately all I was eating was what they gave me. I thanked him and headed down toward my boat.

Isabelle was on her sun-deck with a cup of coffee, and Dot was in the garden filling up a wheelbarrow with dry weeds. They called me over and told me in great detail about Syb's hip replacement and how they finally found a home care nurse who was "up to snuff," according to Syb and Mary and Gladdy, the oldest of the sisters. I nodded as they talked and talked. When they asked me how things at my end were going, I merely shrugged. I didn't tell them that Kricket had been sleeping on my boat. I didn't tell them Jesse was an art thief who might have hidden a stolen painting. I just said I was trying to put behind me what had happened on *Blue Peace* and so was headed down to do a bit of spring-cleaning on my boat. I smiled cheerfully.

"So, the police are done with you then?"

"Maybe. Maybe not. I have no clue."

Isabelle said. "You just need to put that whole nasty business behind you."

I agreed and waved good-bye.

The sun was out, spring was here, the day was warm. Rain, though, would have better matched my mood. I lifted out the hatch boards and laid them on the seat in the cockpit. Inside was even messier than I remembered. The floor was entirely covered with debris, food, radio parts, wires. The sugar on the floor would be sticky and require heavy doses of spray cleaner or my bare feet would be glomming onto it for months.

I stood for a while at the bottom of my companionway and surveyed my surroundings. Rusty, who'd come along with me, found himself a comfy place to sleep on the starboard settee. I decided to begin at the bow of the boat and work back. I climbed up into the v-berth, trying to convince myself that all this cleaning was therapeutic. Up in the forepeak under some grimy lengths of plastic tubing, I found a pair of sandals that I thought had been lost forever. I looked them over and decided to get rid of them since they smelled and were moldy from years in the salt-wet. I threw them into a big black bag that I designated for garbage. I added the moldy plastic tubing to the garbage, some rags and bits of this and that. My forepeak completely empty, I sprayed it heavily with disinfectant and then doused it with a bucket of fresh water from a hose on the deck. It would all flow into the bilge, which I would clean later. That done, I gathered up sheets and blankets that needed a good washing and put them into a second garbage bag.

The painting was not in the forepeak. Nor the key. I checked everywhere. Keys are small, but my boat is not that big. I know just about every place that a little key could hide.

Next was the head. I cleaned it entirely. A thought came to me that Jesse had flushed the little key into my holding tank, in which case it would be stuck to the bottom of the tank. Yum! I'd save that tasty task for later. I cleaned all of the cupboards in the head. I found nothing amiss. No painting. No key. I threw away a ragged, moldy toothbrush and a few other odds and ends, hair elastics and Q-tips.

In the main cabin, I took the cushion off the settee under which resides my holding tank and shone my high-powered light into the translucent and mostly empty tank. I couldn't see any sort of a key at the bottom. Could it be in the plastic hoses somewhere? Maybe. I got out tools and rubber gloves and one at a time, I undid the hose clamps and checked each hose with my light. No key.

I looked at both bulkheads, but could find nothing amiss. Time passed. My shoulders grew achy. I wished I had my own phone. At least then I could listen to some music.

I found packages of Ramen in the main cabin that I'm sure were three years old. I found a coagulated Tetra Pak of milk that had somehow opened and was all over the bottom of one of the storage boxes under a seat. How long had that little gift been there? I went at it with a rag and a bucket and ended up chucking the works, including the rag, into the garbage bag.

The floor was next. I swept and sprayed and scrubbed it with wet rags. I cleaned out cupboards, put things away, went through blankets and tarps. The galley was last. I have a two-burner propane stove, and I looked all through it. I checked the hosing. No key. I went through my pots and pans and cleaned under my cupboard where I store them. Nothing.

I opened up the door of my seldom-used cooler. I say "seldom used" because the thing is very inefficient. I'm so used to just bringing along a little Igloo packed with ice that I forget about this thing. One of my projects is to remove this completely, which would give me more dry shelf space.

There was something on the top shelf. I looked at it curiously. I bent down for a better look, and my hand flew to my mouth. My missing wooden bowl.

I pulled it out, gasped and dropped it on my cabin sole. Instead of the carved apples, there were five fresh mushrooms, each inside a colorful tiny foil cup, arranged decoratively on the plate, like something you'd serve as hors d'oeuvres at a fancy dinner party. One rolled off the plate when it fell onto the floor.

I backed away in horror.

Chapter 32

For several seconds, I stared at them. I sat down on the settee next to my sleeping dog and forced myself to breathe normally while I kept my eye on the offending fungus. Had Kricket or Scott or someone else left these mushrooms for me as some kind of warning to back off? Or, worse, was someone trying to frame me for the murder of that girl? Was this what the girl had eaten, a fancy little mushroom like this on a plate?

I don't quite know how long I sat there, but I was still shivering and shaking when Rusty and I finally made our way back up to my porch. I was glad none of my neighbors were outside to greet me. I don't think I could have held it together.

A squad car was parked next to my house. Ben got out and came toward me. He was frowning.

"Ben!" I said.

"I have something to tell you, Em."

I went toward him. "Ben, I...I was just going to call you..." I could not stop shaking. "Something happened..." I pointed down toward my boat.

Ben said, "Em, I have important news. We know who the girl on the boat is. Her parents have come forward and identified her."

I stopped. This trumped my mushrooms. "What?"

"Her name is Roxanne Wishert. Name ring any bells?"

"Roxanne Wishert." I rolled the name on my tongue. "No, it doesn't."

"Her parents recognized her picture on the news. They'd been away and only just got back. They were surprised to learn that she'd told her boss she was taking some time off due to a family emergency."

I felt immediately sad. The girl was no longer a nameless person who'd gone overboard. She had friends and a family who would miss her.

He continued, "She'd been working in Boston, interestingly enough, at the office of a private investigator."

"She was a private detective?" My eyes were wide.

He said no. "She worked for one, office work. Apparently, Kricket and Roxanne knew each other. They went to the same college there. Joan Bush also confirmed it. She came to see me."

I nodded. "I know about that," I said. "She told me, too."

There were dark circles under his eyes. He kept rubbing his face with his hand. I got the idea he was just as tired as I felt. It also looked like he hadn't shaved in a while.

"Tom and Scott both deny what Joan told us about them being in Bermuda when the girls were there," he said. "We're requesting boat logs from the Pattersons. Perhaps later today we'll know more."

"Boat logs can be manipulated." I looked away as I asked, "Have you found Rob Stikles yet?"

"No, and here's something interesting, we checked with the passport office, and a Rob Stikles from Burlington, Vermont, reported his passport missing."

I frowned a bit and looked down at my hands. I had failed to spot not one, but two fraudulent passports.

He said, "We're going under the assumption that the passport was handpicked and then stolen. Someone wanted to get on that boat with that girl."

I looked down at my boat. "Ben, I have something you should see. Mushrooms. Down at my boat."

"Mushrooms?" He raised his eyebrows.

"On my boat."

The two of us made our way back down to the dock. At the entryway to *Wanderer's* cabin, I pointed to the foil wrapped pieces on the floor.

"I was cleaning my boat and found this little offering in my cooler, on a plate that was stolen from my house. I'm assuming they're the poisonous kind and the same variety that killed the girl. I think someone might be trying to frame me and I don't know why."

I followed him as he went down into the cabin of my boat. Pulling out a pair of latex gloves, he bent down and picked one up by the edge. "Looks that way," he said. "I'm no mushroom expert. I'll get these to Dr. Meyer."

He asked me if I had any clean plastic bags. I found a couple in a cupboard in my galley and handed them to him. Using the edge of one he picked up the mushroom that had fallen onto the floor, and plunked the plate and the mushrooms into a second bag.

We climbed out of the cabin and into the cockpit, where I sat down on the seat. "I think I should tell you something." I sighed. "I need to tell you a whole bunch of somethings. There's a lot you should know. A lot, actually…" I looked down at my hands. "…A lot that I have kept from you, actually."

He sat down across from me in the sunshine. He wasn't smiling. I wished he was smiling. His blue shirt was the kind that had a button-down collar, and one of the buttons was missing. Don't ask me why I noticed this. I kept looking at the missing button. For some reason it seemed out of character for him. Looking at the missing button made me think of his wife. Whoever she was, wherever she was.

Holding my shaking hands between my knees and staring at where his button should have been and not at his face, I told him what Amanda had told me, about Jesse and Bryce stealing art. I told him about Jesse sending the email indicating he wanted out and then maybe hiding the painting and a key.

His first words to me were, "And you didn't think this was important enough to tell me prior to this? Or did you think it was fun letting me run around the universe trying to figure out why your husband's phone number was on the back of an art postcard?"

His reprimand stung and stung hard. In fact, it totally flummoxed me.

"I'm sorry," I said. "I'm so sorry. It's just…"

He said, "I'd like to take Jesse's laptop with me."

"It's up at the house."

We walked up, him determined and me nervous. Rusty ambled ahead of us. When we neared my front porch, he said, "The team on *Blue Peace* also found a few other goodies."

"Really?"

"There was a large quantity of unopened bottles of hard liquor stored under the engine."

I stopped in the path. "But I would have seen something like that. I checked that engine."

"The bottles were carefully placed under a bunch of oil-absorbent pads. You might not have noticed them."

I tried to picture that. I had fully acquainted myself with the engine room. How had I missed bottles of liquor stored in there? Was I really that inept? Maybe I deserved everything I was going to get.

Inside the kitchen, I quietly pulled out the secret compartment drawer and handed over my husband's computer. Before he left, he pulled out a small manila envelope from an inside pocket. "This is for you," he said.

"What is it?"

"It's from the medical examiner. He said you would know what it is."

"You haven't looked at it?"

"It's private correspondence."

I raised my eyebrows.

Just before he left, he turned to me and said, "Captain Ridge, this whole thing is nothing to fool around with. We're in the process of uncovering the layers of what's going on. If you come across more information about your husband, for example, call me right away. Don't try figuring things out for yourself. I know that relationships can hurt, especially in a marriage. I know that more than anyone, but you can't withhold any of this, you hear? And if you stumble across something like the mushrooms again, promise me that you will call me right away."

"I was just going to call you about the mushrooms, Ben." I was beginning to sound like a petulant child.

"Just promise."

"I don't have a phone, remember. I have this weird borrowed one and I can make calls but I don't know the number to get incoming ones."

"But you can email, right? Or call from a neighbor's."

"Right."

He said, "I'm afraid you might go off on wild-goose chases when you might not understand fully what you're getting yourself into. This is dangerous territory."

"I was just cleaning my boat," I said. "And after all, Kricket came to see *me*. And the mushrooms were on *my* boat. I'm front and center in this, Ben." I kept using his first name.

"This thing is bigger than you."

I glared at him. "I know that. Of course, I know that. and I'm sorry—"

"Em, I'm worried about you. That's all it is."

"Thank you. Do you still need help with local culture?"

"Yes, culture. Leave the crime-solving to me."

After Ben left with the mushrooms and Jesse's computer, I sat down on the couch with the envelope in my lap and thought about what he said—especially the veiled things he said about his marriage. I found myself feeling sorry for him in that instant. We all have our ghosts. We all wrestle with demons.

From the envelope, I pulled out two five-by-seven, grainy, black-and-white photocopies of photos. A small yellow sticky was attached to the top picture.

Thought you might like to see these. Don't think there's much in them that tells us anything, however. Notes are still missing. Can't understand it.

Declan

The first was a shot of *Rosalena* ablaze. I found a magnifying glass from my office that I use for reading small symbols on charts and carefully looked over the photo. I couldn't find anything out of the ordinary.

I put that photo aside and looked at the second one. This was the same picture I had seen online, only this one was bigger. With my magnifying glass I could make out the boatyard. The smudges I'd seen all along the side were people standing and watching.

I studied each individual. One of them was a young man who clutched something in front of him. A package? A grocery bag? No. A duffle bag of some sort. That small line in the lower left was a strap. I took in a breath. The only man I'd ever seen who held his pack like that was the man who'd passed himself off on *Blue Peace* as Rob Stikles. I could not make out his face, could not be sure. And yet—

Behind him, and barely visible, was another man. I could see only the top of his head and one muscular shoulder. I looked this way and that. Was this—Scott? They were there and watching the *Rosalena*, the boat that killed my husband, burn?

I made a list in my mind of things I knew for sure:

1. Rob pays Peter to come aboard *Blue Peace*.
2. He and Roxanne Wishert—who'd also wanted to come aboard the boat—are friendly, almost as if they know each other.
3. The girl is looking for something. Perhaps they'd been tipped off that someone had hidden money and a painting aboard the vessel. Or the mysterious key.
4. The girl dies of mushroom poisoning.
5. The faux Rob disappears.
6. 6.Peter is murdered.

A cold shudder went through me. I went into my kitchen and

opened my laptop to the online news reports of my husband's death.

Then I knew.

That was why Rob had seemed so familiar to me on *Blue Peace*.

Rob had been one of the boys who had run over Jesse! And was the other one, perhaps—Scott?

I remembered something else, too, the odd thing that Peter had screamed at Rob. "Go back to your farm."

Farm? Where does one grow mushrooms? By any chance are they called farms?

I thought about the one TV news picture I had seen at the time—a young man, face covered, hunched forward and leaving the court room. Rob! It had to be. Was that why Rob had seemed so familiar to me?

Chapter 33

I needed groceries. Even though I didn't want to leave the safety of my house, I knew I should be eating something other than beef and two-days-old tuna casserole which had been heated up three times already. The chips on the top had crumpled to mush two microwavings ago.

Since I didn't feel like driving all the way into Portland I decided on a closer destination. Where the ferry disembarks on the other side is a small general store. It doesn't have much, some staples and gas. In the summer, it's a thriving farmers' market, but that isn't yet. That would be my destination, and I would have plenty of time to get a few things and get home before the tide came in.

I drove across the tidal road and to the general store. As soon as I was inside filling my basket I realized it was a mistake. I didn't feel like talking much to Dorothy, who with her husband, Dave, runs the place. I answered questions as best I could. Yes, it truly was horrible what had happened on *Blue Peace*. And, no, we don't get that kind of thing happening out here much. Yes, horrible, horrible. I gathered up eggs, cheese, bacon, toilet paper and, for good measure, a bag of chips. Two bags. They were on sale two for one.

As I dug in my bag for cash at the checkout, Dorothy asked, "That guy ever find you?"

"What guy?"

"Handsome sort of fellow. Built like a steamroller. Came in here yesterday wanting to know if I'd seen you, like if you were back home yet."

"Oh, that would be the cop," I said, although I would never call Ben Dunlinson a steamroller. "You sure he looked like a steamroller?"

"Cop?" She gave me back some change.

"Blue shirt? Tan jacket? About yay high?" I motioned with my hand. "Light brown, medium-length hair?"

"Nope, that wouldn't be him. This guy had really short hair.

Light. I really don't remember what he was wearing."

My eyes went wide. Scott! It had to be. Who else did I know who could be described as "built like a steamroller?"

Back home and back to Wifi land, I texted Ben,

I think Scott was asking about me here on Chalk Spit. Please tell me what to do.

For the next hour I waffled. Do I pack up and go to Portland and stay with Joan and Art, or do I stay here and wait it out? I kept staring at Tom's phone willing Ben to get back to me. I decided I might be safe here. EJ's big family was coming today. I'd be safe here with all those people around, right? They were all only staying one night, he told me. In the afternoon I watched EJ's family arrive in their mini-van. I watched little ones run down to the water's edge, while the wonderful aroma of deep fried turkeys pervaded the neighborhood.

The next afternoon, I sat at my kitchen table and decided that instead of looking all through Jesse's files, which were nicely copied onto my own laptop, I would answer emails. Various sailing friends from all over the world had emailed me. Hey, we heard what happened? Anything we can do? I answered them all.

I wrote a long reply to a four-day-old one from my sister in which I really tried to be nice. When I saw EJ's family pull away in their van in the afternoon, I closed up shop and Rusty and I wandered over next door. Today might be a good day to look at some of Jesse's woodworking. Anything to keep my mind off wondering if Ben was any closer to figuring it all out.

EJ was drinking tea and sitting on a rocking chair on his porch. I called to him.

"Emmie!" he said rising. "Glad you came. Everyone just left and I've mounds of food I'll never eat."

Translated—his family had brought lots of vegetables and left them for him to eat. EJ doesn't like vegetables.

"Come inside," he motioned.

"Wow," I said when we entered his kitchen and I surveyed the bowls and plates full of green beans, salad, cooked beets, beet salad, mounds of kale, kale chips, even.

"Yes, and there's a broccoli salad going begging in the fridge. You'll take these all home, of course. My family seems to think I'm not eating enough green things."

"Your family is right."

He pulled out a roll of waxed paper and began tearing off sheets to cover the plates and bowls for me.

He began to tell me the story that I had heard so many times that I could recite it myself. "When I was a boy, I never liked to eat my vegetables. My mother made me. If I didn't eat my greens, there was the strap to contend with. I decided then and there that when I got to be an adult, I would never eat vegetables again. I never have."

And I said what I always said to him at times like this, "Well, you must have a different kind of constitution than normal people, then."

He went on, "And when Jesse would come over here when he was little, I never made him eat vegetables, either."

I smiled again. I knew this, too. "Speaking of Jesse," I said. "Do you have time to show me some of the stuff he made?"

"Of course. That would be a lovely way to spend the afternoon."

I thought so, too.

"But first let's enjoy our tea."

"Fine with me."

EJ's is a comfortable home, with pine board walls and numerous wood stoves—I think there are four throughout. Like so many times before, I imagined my husband as a little boy coming over here and this man telling him he didn't have to eat his veggies and showing him everything there was to know about how to work in wood.

For a while, EJ and I sat and drank tea and talked. He told me about his great-grand kids and what they were up to, and I gave him the bare bones version of what was happening with me.

He began talking about Jesse then, about how he was as a boy and how Gladys, EJ's late wife, used to say over and over, "Now that boy has talent. We'll be hearing more from that boy."

It always made me weepy and happy when he said these things. After tea, which was good and hot and sweet, I followed EJ into his work studio, where all of his projects were laid out. "Jesse loved to whittle, you know," he said.

"I know."

"People don't whittle so much anymore. Not like they did when I was a boy. When I was a tadpole, every boy had a knife. The sharper the better. It was a rite of passage. You turned twelve, you got a knife. And all of us would sit on the porch steps and whittle. It's a dying art form, I'm afraid. But I'm pleased that I was able to teach it to Jesse. Did you know that I was the one who gave Jesse his first knife?"

"Yes." Even though EJ had told me this a hundred times, I never tired of hearing the story.

"I was going through some of his things and I found something that he was working on quite recently. I forgot about it, actually, until a few days ago. It was a little box, Em," he said, "with a beautifully whittled top which fits perfectly."

I nodded.

"When I saw it, I remembered. It was going to be a surprise, a special present for you. He never had a chance to finish it."

EJ laid the small tissue paper wrapped box on the table in front of me. My heart stopped. I began carefully peeling off the layers. When the last piece of tissue was removed, I lifted out the smallest most exquisite box I think I have ever seen. The tiny box was a perfect square and made of teak. It was carved with an intricate design which looked like the leaves of a maple tree, but it was the lid which was a masterpiece. It was a design of many branches of a tree, and when the lid was on the box, the branches extended themselves down the sides and onto the bottom with their gnarled, twisted forms. I turned the box over and the branches met at the bottom, and formed the shape of a perfect heart.

"Jesse made this?" I asked.

"Yes."

"It's beautiful."

"It is."

"When did he work on it?" He never talked about making this. Yet another mystery about the man who was my husband.

"Shortly before he died. You should open it. He used to tell me that he always wished he could afford a proper engagement ring for you."

I shook the box slightly. There was something inside. I sat down at EJ's table, and took off the snug fitting lid.

"Is it a ring?" EJ asked.

I shook the contents out into my trembling fingers.

"No," I said.

Chapter 34

"It's a key," he said. "But for what?"

"I don't know."

It was an old key—antique brass with a long base and stubby T at the end. I couldn't imagine what it unlocked. Maybe an old chest. A chest big enough to fit a painting of a cat?

EJ went and got his magnifying glass. "May I see it?" he asked.

I handed it to him. He examined every inch of it. "Well, I'll be." He turned it over. "Well, well." He paused. "Well, well."

"EJ?"

"I know what this is for."

I stared at him without speaking.

"An old shed. My, my. I haven't been there for years. Don't even know if it's still standing."

I thought about the sheds and caves of Jesse's childhood. "You have a shed here on the island?" I asked. "In the woods? One of Jesse's old sheds?"

He shook his head. "No. No. It's on an out island. Been in my family for generations, used back when our clan were all fishermen. Don't even know the state of it now. Since I don't have a boat anymore, I can't get to it. Jesse knew about it, though. I think from time to time he went there when he was a boy. Can't imagine how he came to have the key to it."

"Where is it?"

A few minutes later, he returned with a very old navigational chart, the edges of which were softened by the passage of years. We went to the big kitchen table, and he laid it out, pressing it flat with his gnarled fingers.

There are many islands along the coast of Maine that are basically rock outcroppings, and many contain the remnants of old fishing sheds. If they have wharfs on them at all, they have usually been broken up by storms and full-moon tides.

When EJ pointed out his island, I knew exactly where it was—four nautical miles eastward into the bay, give or take, part of a rocky outcropping. I'd sailed past it many times, but never too close, because of the shallows and rocks and swirling currents beside it. I couldn't imagine someone putting a boat shed there.

"Can we go there?" I asked.

"You want to go there?"

"EJ, are you up for it? You could show me where the shed is. Can we go now?"

"My dear Emmie, I haven't been in a boat for years. Don't know if these old knees could make the trip."

I looked at him crestfallen.

"But on a nice day, you could go. Once you get on the island, the shed's the only building there. Can't miss it."

"I'll go now. I'll take a fast boat, Jeff and Valerie's."

"Don't go today. The weather channel's saying a bad storm is coming in early evening."

"It's still early. I can be there and back in no time."

"Make sure you take a dinghy. I don't know the state of the dock there. You won't be able to get too close to shore, anyway. Bad currents. And mind those dark clouds, Emmie."

Four miles. That was all. It would take me no time at all to get there.

At home I found an old bicycle fanny pack and added a few tools. I didn't know what I would need on the island, but I wanted to be prepared. It was early afternoon when Rusty and I hurried down to the dock to board the *Valerie J*.

I sent Ben a quick email. *I may have found something. I'll call you when I get back. I won't be too long.*

When I got down to the dock, however, the *Valerie J* was gone. I glanced up at Jeff and Valerie's. Their car was beside their house. I ran up to their house. No answer to my insistent knocks. Were they all out on the boat? Probably. I looked around. I didn't even see their son's fast inflatable. Okay, I had no choice. I'd simply have to sail there on *Wanderer*. Thinking about it, that might not be such a bad idea anyway. If anyone was watching—meaning Scott—he wouldn't immediately believe that I'd found the magic key and was on a mission. They might simply think I was out for a casual afternoon sail.

I considered the weather. Those dark clouds EJ was warning me about? They were too far away to worry about for hours and hours.

My faithful dog wagged his tail at the prospect of a sail. I helped him aboard.

It was windy in the bay, and I decided to sail off the dock rather than motor. That's me, always up for a challenge. Plus, today I was running on adrenalin. I fastened my little Jesse-built wooden dinghy to the stern of *Wanderer*, raised the mainsail, untied the dock lines, and cast off. I thought about my promise to Ben about not getting involved any longer, but it wasn't my fault he wasn't answering his phone or his email.

I tacked around a few lobster pots on my way out into the bay. Instead of being annoyed that I couldn't get to the island faster, I ended up being glad for the sail. Sailing always gives me time to think. On a fast boat, it's about the destination. On a sailboat, it's all about the journey.

Rusty ambled down below. That's what my dog does. He heads right down into the cabin, finds himself a comfortable place on the quarter berth and goes to sleep. I don't mind. Better down there than up here and underfoot. He's not as surefooted as he used to be.

An hour later—yes, it took a full hour—EJ's island was in sight. The winds were heavier now and getting stronger. In the distance to the south, the sky was pretty black, but on my little spot on the ocean, the sun shone down in straight lines. Right now, the wind was great, near perfect, but winds that precede storms usually are. My favorite sailing is strong winds on a flat sea, something you only get prior to a storm. Once the wind has whipped up the water, sailing is not as smooth, still doable and fun, but not like sailing on ice. Like now.

The winds were increasing, so I climbed up on deck and pulled the mainsail partway down to reef it. Sailing the rest of the way with a shortened main would not make a difference to the speed, but it would make the boat a bit easier to handle with a bit less heel.

Ten minutes later, I was heading north on a starboard tack at a twenty-degree heel and going seven knots, which was just about hull speed for this little boat of mine. Despite where I was going and the key in my pocket, it was still exhilarating. When I finally reached the island, the wind had increased. I climbed up on deck, extinguished the jib, opened the forward hatch and threw it down into the boat. With the main still reefed, I dropped the hook as close to the island as I dared, and then lowered the sail. I called down into the cabin and asked Rusty if he wanted to come, but my big dog barely raised an eyebrow. I decided to just let him sleep.

Because this was not the sort of place I would ever anchor long term, I found the longest line I could—my two-hundred-foot swim rope—and tied one end to a cleat on my stern and carried it with me in the dinghy. To be on the safe side, and one must always endeavor to be on the safe side when sailing, I'd tie *Wanderer* to a tree on shore. A line to a tree plus an anchor should secure it.

I got into my dinghy and rowed against the wind to shore. You might call me a purist. I don't like to run the engine unless I absolutely have to. I don't even own an outboard motor for this sleek wooden dinghy of mine.

I made several passes along the shore, trying to find the best place to beach the little boat. I rowed toward a place where four or five thick rotting boards marked the spot where a dock used to be. Maybe through those weeds was as good a place as any. Weeds meant there might not be too many rocks.

The small island was well-treed and offered some protection from the wind, for which I was glad. Boat lines in hand, I climbed out of my dinghy, got my feet royally wet in the process, and tied both lines to a tree.

I stood for several seconds on the land, getting my bearings. The island was oblong and about half the size of a football field. One end of the island led out to an exposed and rocky point. The wind was already whipping the water around the rocks. When I looked up I could glimpse a bit of a cabin through the trees.

I glanced back at where *Wanderer* seesawed back and forth in the growing chop. My better judgement was urging me to get back on *Wanderer* and sail her home, but I had come this far. It wouldn't take me too long to unlock the cabin and see what was inside, would it? I didn't see Rusty. He'd stay down below in this for sure. He's become a bit of a chicken in his dotage. Good dog.

I found my way onto an overgrown trail and headed up the rise toward the structure. I wondered how many ocean kayakers had found refuge in this place. A few, I suspected. But yet, because this island is so exposed to winds from every direction, and swirling tides, I couldn't see it becoming a popular destination.

The cabin itself was old and sagging and covered in moss. The main door was bolted shut with a modern padlock. The key I'd found didn't have a hope of fitting. Nevertheless, I tried it, felt my spirits crumple. Maybe this wasn't the right place after all. Maybe the key was for something else entirely. A chest? A chest that was inside the locked cabin?

I looked around and found a pretty hefty log. Maybe if I used it as a battering ram, I could get in. This seems easy in movies. All it did was give me a bruised shoulder.

I gave up and walked around to the back of the cabin. The few small windows were high on the wall and grimed with age. If I couldn't find another way in, maybe I could break one of them and climb in.

A massive pile of tumbledown rotten firewood leaned against the entire back wall of the cabin. Weeds grew up between the logs, many of which crumbled as I kicked at them. Was there some sort of a door behind all that wood? I thought I could see the top lintel of one, but maybe that was a window. If I could move some of this wood, maybe I'd find the door with the lock this key would fit.

One by one, I began removing the firewood. I do this at home, chop and lug wood, so I certainly was no stranger to hard work.

Yes, there was a door there, albeit a narrow, short one, an inside firewood retrieval door. I continued to kick at logs, pick them up, shove them aside, only vaguely aware that a small droplet of sweat was making its way down my back. Was it that warm? I stopped, wiped my brow with a hand. It wasn't sweat. It was an itch. I reached my back as well as I could and then got on with my log moving. When the itching continued, I went and scratched my back against a tree.

As I got back to work, my arms were itching, my thighs, too. I swiped at them absently while I continued picking up and heaving old logs. There was still so much piled-up firewood that I needed to move. Plus, the sky was threatening with rain any minute. What kind of a crazy person was I to come all the way out here? I pulled Tom's cell phone out of my pocket. I expected Wifi out here? Yeah, right.

I picked up a log and about a hundred spiders scurried over my hands, seeking safety. It was then I realized the source of my itchy back and arms. I backed away, horrified, yelping, cursing out loud. Swatting at my face, my hair. They were everywhere.

I threw off my jacket. The lining of it was crawling with spiders. What I really should have done was tear down to the water and submerge myself. Seawater is one of the best antidotes for insect bites. Ocean water in May is far too cold, however. I tore off my sweatshirt, fanny pack, T-shirt and was down to my underwear in the cool May woods. They were all over me, crawling up my legs, on my stomach, my neck. I stripped down even further, glad I was alone on this little part of the planet. Groaning, yelping, I wiped the offending insects from every part of my body while I did the spider dance. Once I was satisfied that I had gotten them all, I shook out my underwear, hard while I shivered in the increasing wind. Before putting my clothes back on, I made sure there were no little culprits hiding in any of the seams. I already had several welts on my inner thighs, arms and stomach. Ugh!

I looked at the pile of logs. The old and rotting wood was completely infested with spiders. And yet, I still wanted, still *needed* to get inside that place.

I ventured into the woods a bit, looking for some kind of sturdy stick. To make sure I didn't pick one up that was spider-infested, I used my knife to tear a green stick from a growing tree. I used this to move away the rest of the spider logs from the back of the cabin without touching them.

The door, when the last piece of log was finally removed, was maybe a foot and a half wide and four feet high, which made me feel like I was in Hobbit land. The antique key fit perfectly into the very old keyhole lock.

I had to crouch sideways to get inside, and while I did so, I thanked the stars above that my girth wasn't such that it prohibited me from getting through.

It was dark and cool inside and smelled of mildew and decayed wood. A tumbledown pot-bellied stove leaned precariously against one wall. Its rusted feet, decorative at one point in their history, barely held the thing up. Behind the stove and high on the wall were shelves that held a few blackened and rusted pots and other implements which looked like they hadn't been used in a hundred years.

"Jesse," I said into the stillness, "what do you want me to find here?" My voice echoed strangely in the perfectly square room. I walked around, looked at every wall.

A rickety, dust-covered card table leaned against the wall opposite the stove. It was so old, that the moment I touched it, it collapsed onto the floor. The sound of it hitting the wood startled me. A couple of broken oars leaned up against one wall, along with sticks and some old fireplace implements, some rusted shackles and a couple of very grungy lobster floats. On the opposite wall was what used to be a sink, the fixtures of which had long ago rusted out and been removed. That was the trouble with a salt water environment, it was hard on everything—cars, boat engines, hair, plants, metal. Underneath the sink were pieces of fabric which I could tell probably once belonged to a kapok life jacket. I didn't want to touch anything and was glad I'd brought my green stick in with me.

I poked around a bit trying to figure out what it was Jesse wanted me to find.

I walked around the room, my hands on the walls this time. I noticed that three of the cabin walls were unfinished, the vertical beams visible. The fourth looked as if someone had decided to finish it with pine beams nailed horizontally, yet haphazardly. I went to that wall and attempted to shine my little flashlight down through the cracks. I could see nothing.

I dug out a screwdriver from my fanny pack and was able to pry one of the boards loose. Then another. And another, scratching spider bites on various places on my body as I did so. Outside the wind was picking up. I needed to get out of here and back before it got too bad.

There was something behind the boards. A flat package or piece of cardboard. I knew instantly what this was. A gust of wind hit the building with such force that I stopped and looked out of a small, grimy window. Rain had started. I glanced down to where *Wanderer* was anchored and tied. It appeared okay, and since I didn't see Rusty, I knew he would still be inside, sleeping. Nevertheless, I needed to hurry. That was not the place you wanted to anchor in a storm for any length of time.

I went back to the wall and continued prying off boards. A few more boards, and I was able to see the package in its entirety. One more and I was able to free the thing from the wall. I laid the flat, newspaper-wrapped package on the table and carefully tore the paper off.

I had to control my breathing as the cat painting emerged.

"Oh, Jesse," I said. "What did you do?"

I glanced at the masthead on the newspaper which encased it. It was dated a few weeks before Jesse died.

I looked outside. The rain was more intense, the wind picking up. I really, really needed to get going. I also knew I wasn't going to be taking this picture with me, not through the rain. It was a valuable painting and I was sure the rain would damage it. I would come back. I'd head home, call Ben as soon as I could, and get the cavalry back.

I heard something clatter to the floor. I looked underneath the table and saw a flash drive had fallen out of the folds of the newspaper.

Chapter 35

It was raining heavily when I climbed into my dinghy to row out to *Wanderer*. The wind had backed and rowing there against the current and the rain, which blew at me sideways, was a feat. By the time I threw the lines aboard, I was drenched and breathing hard. I wondered if I should go down below and sit with my dog until the storm passed, or head out with only a reefed main and no jib.

I looked around me and realized that the waves were high and swirly in this area because of these rocky shoals and shallows. The way the boat was pitching and yawing in the growing storm did not leave me with confidence in the anchor. Yet if I weighed anchor to reset it, we could be blown onto the rocks within minutes. We were that close already. I really had no choice but to sail out.

Start the engine? I felt I would have more control with a sail in this wind, and with the hazards that I could only guess were underneath the water, I didn't want to get anything jammed around the prop. Better to sail. Always better to sail. That's my motto.

"Hey, Rusty," I said to my bored and still sleeping dog. "I think we're going to sail." My old, lazy dog barely raised an eyebrow from his comfy nest on the settee.

Once I made the decision to sail, I tried to comfort myself with the thought that I'd certainly sailed in worse. But it was usually way offshore, where the waves, though huge, are more predictable. Plus, there's way less to run into out there.

Once I was in my own bay, the winds would lessen. Maybe an hour or so of bad sailing and we'd be safe and home.

Topsides, I pulled my PFD buckles tighter, harnessed myself to the boat, lashed my tiller so it would stay in one place, then went up on deck and raised the still reefed mainsail. Crouching low and holding onto the lifelines, I crawled up to the bow and pulled up the anchor, all the time wondering about my sanity.

Then I was in the cockpit, and we were sailing. Sort of. Mostly we were heeled over, while I tried desperately to get us headed in the right direction. Down below, Rusty still lay there. I glanced down at him, a bit puzzled. The heeled boat had shifted his bulk, and underneath him on the settee was a patch of dark. What? He had wet the settee? My dog never, ever has "accidents." If I'm delayed, he'll wait all day and then some for me to get home and let him out.

Also, he didn't appear to be moving of his own accord. His body simply seemed to be swaying in rhythm with the boat. I felt a flash of alarm.

"Rusty? You okay, boy?"

I needed to go see what was wrong. We needed to heave-to, and that meant putting up a small front sail. Crouching low, I made it to the bow of the boat, unzipped the jib bag and reached for my smallest storm sail. Despite the rain and wind, I proceeded to hank it on. The boat was now heeling dangerously. As quickly as I could, I crouch-ran to the stern and into the cockpit, where I lashed the tiller to windward, sheeted the jib to windward and secured the mainsail to lee. The boat suddenly quieted and righted itself. This is what sailors do when stuck in storms far from shore. A hove-to boat will rest on the waves for hours. It'll push you way off course, but at least you won't get knocked down.

"Hey, boy!" I said as I went down. A sliver of fear moved down my spine. "Rusty?" I couldn't lose him! I couldn't lose the last bit of Jesse. Not now. Not like this. I checked the settee, yes, he had wet it. "Oh, poor old Rusty!" I said through the tears that were threatening. He's an old dog. I know there will come a time…

Visions of Jesse and Rusty running together, of Jesse throwing sticks and Rusty retrieving them brought tears to my eyes. I patted his head, put my face to his nose. He was still breathing. He was still warm. I felt his underside. His heart was still beating. I held his head in my lap, and he seemed to pick up a bit, opened one eye and whimpered plaintively.

The wind moved the boat again, and I looked behind me at an out-of-place piece of hose in my galley above my propane stove. One end was attached to the coach roof and led aft and outside to my propane tank, the other end was swinging to and fro with the bouncing movement of the hove-to boat.

What the—

I picked up my big dog and laid him on the floor—easier there with less chance of falling—and went over to my galley. The hose had been cleanly cut, its naked end moving with the motion of the boat. My hands trembled as I picked up the end of it and looked at it. It had been cut with a knife, and had not simply come free from the stove. I raced outside and opened the locker that houses my propane tank. I was stunned to see that the tank valve was turned to the ON position. I never leave it like that. I'm a very careful sailor. Lots of sailors and cruisers leave their tanks ON all the time. I do not.

Quickly, I turned it off. A lot of good that would do me, however. Ten pounds of propane had already been dumped into the bottom of my boat.

No wonder Rusty was drowsy. Probably the only thing keeping him alive was the fact that the hatch boards were open, allowing some airflow. I went back down below and, despite the rain, I opened up the top hatch. Maybe by now the propane had dissipated of its own accord. But propane sinks, and I couldn't take the chance.

I dragged my dog, as best I could, up the steps of the companionway and into the fresh air, albeit wet and cold fresh air. He needed air. And I didn't need to stay down there any longer than necessary, either.

Propane is a colorless, odorless fuel. It's heavier than oxygen, so it sinks. Even a tiny spark from a lighter could have exploded this boat like a bomb. I shuddered when I realized that if I had started my engine, the boat could have blown up! If there's one thing that brings the fear of God into my soul, it's a fire at sea. Storms, like this I can handle. Fires? Not so much.

Rusty, perking up a bit, raised both eyebrows instead of just one. I was crying tears of relief. A few more minutes, and he may have died.

I thought about something else. My propane detector alarm hadn't sounded. I told Rusty in no uncertain terms to "stay." Back down below, I received my second shock. My propane detector had been dismantled. As quickly as I could, I was back outside, sitting on the wet seat and breathing hard. I knew who had done this, of course—Scott. Who else? He stole my husband's computer, I had proof of that, Plus, he had probably fed Roxanne the mushrooms, and now the propane line. All because he wanted the painting?

I was drenched to the core and shivering—and still itching, too—but we couldn't stay here forever. I unlashed the tiller and changed the direction of the mainsail. There was nothing left for me to do but to get us home as best I could.

Climate change has done a lot of things to the sea, most of them not nice. One of them is changing weather patterns. I had noticed this. A few sailors had even talked of increasing numbers of rogue waves and waterspouts. The word tornado conjures images of carnage and death, while the word waterspout evokes pictures of teapots and country kitchens. But a waterspout is a tornado on the sea, and it's deadly.

Behind me I thought I saw the makings of one. I shifted the direction of the sail somewhat and prayed to my parents' God that we would get back home okay.

My poor old dog hates wind and storms and started skulking down below, whimpering slightly.

"Get up here right now!" I screamed at him over the wind.

His tail between his legs and probably wondering what the heck was wrong with me, he nevertheless crawled back up into the cockpit and curled down in a low spot. I sailed by rote, tacking back and forth, not looking behind me, but in front of me only. The rain lessened, and I thought, hoped, the storm was on the wane, and then just as quickly, the sky blackened and the rain came in sheets and the winds built back up.

I glanced at the clock on my bulkhead. The trip seemed endless, and I kept chanting to myself, *I've been in worse. I've been in worse. I've been in worse.*

Two hours of heavy sailing later, I reached the entrance to my bay. The wind was still strong, but sailing was a bit easier. Finally, I could see Jeff and Valerie's dock ahead of me in the mist.

Someone was waving frantically at me from the dock. Jeff? Valerie?

I went on deck and lowered the jib. I made for the dock with a reefed main only. As I got closer, I saw who it was.

Tom!

Chapter 36

Tom stood in the middle of the dock, waving his arms. "Hey!" he called when I got close enough to hear. "Throw me a line! You picked a hell of a time to go for a sail!"

"Tell me about it!" I screamed back.

I was still furious at him for leaving me in the lurch the other night, but at the same time so incredibly glad to see him, to see anyone. Even with no jib and a double-reefed main, I was heading directly into the dock and going a bit too fast for comfort. In my haste, in my nervousness, I overshot the dock by a few feet. I scrambled with the sail and yelled to him, "I'll throw you a line when I come around again!"

Despite what everyone had told me about him, and despite the fact that he owed me one huge explanation, he looked extraordinarily good to me standing there in the rain in the dark afternoon sky. And that made me angry. He wore a yellow rain jacket that looked so exceptionally clean, and his feet were bare in his boat shoes. His feet reminded me of Jesse's feet. I don't know why I noticed his feet.

"Okay," he hollered back over the wind, which was gusty and unpredictable this close to shore. "Wouldn't it be easier to turn on your engine?"

"Can't!"

"Ran out of fuel?"

"Something like that!" I called to him over the wind.

I tacked out and then back around. If I did this correctly, I should come along the side of the dock. I was so tired from sailing through this mess that I didn't know if I could do it again, but Tom was there and Tom was strong and despite what Tom may or may not be, he was an expert sailor.

I threw him a bow line, but an unexpected gust moved the front of the boat away from the dock.

"Hold on." I threw him a stern line. He caught it, put it quickly around a cleat, but the boat veered out and a moment later was perpendicular to the dock, the mainsail carrying it away.

"This isn't going to work," I yelled. "I'm going to veer right into those rocks. Let it go, and I'll come around again."

Five minutes later, I was back. Tom was ready this time, and when I threw him the bow line, he easily got it around a cleat and pulled me hard against the dock. I was able to back the boat in, jump off and tie the stern line to the cleat. After we had secured a few fenders between the boat and the dock, I clambered back up onto the deck, and doused the mainsail into the lazy jacks. Even though it was raining, I kept the top hatch up.

"Your hatch is open."

"I know."

"Aren't you going to close it?" he asked.

"No."

I got the sail ties from the cockpit and tied the mainsail down as tight as I could. I was tired, achy, wet, itchy and scared, mostly really scared. Tomorrow I'd put the sails away properly. Tomorrow I'd make sure the boat was cleared of propane. Tomorrow I'd deal with the severed propane line. Tomorrow I'd mop up the interior which would be sloshing with rainwater. Tomorrow I'd clean the dog pee off my settee.

A rather bedraggled Rusty managed to climb out of the boat and limp up toward the house. I didn't even have to help him, he was so eager to get home. I watched him go, glad that he was moving so well. I caught a sob in my throat when I thought of how close I'd come to losing him. My teeth were chattering when Tom finally came to me on the dock and put his arms around me. He held me close in the rain on that wet dock until I quit shaking.

"I don't know why you came or how you happen to be here," I said to him, "but I'm glad you're here. Even though…"

"Even though what?"

"We'll talk."

"Will you forgive me?" he asked. His face was so close to mine when he asked me, that my breath caught.

I backed away slightly. "Only if you have a very good explanation for lots of things. I have questions for you. Lots of questions."

He grinned widely. "And you'll get all the answers you want, but first you need to get warm and dry." He touched the side of my face. "What possessed you to go out sailing on a day like today anyway?"

"It wasn't this way when I left."

"And you didn't think to look at the weather?"

"Nope."

He raised one eyebrow and tried to put his arm around me as we walked up the path to my house through the rain. I kept pulling away.

"What's the matter?" We were on the porch now.

I turned to him. "You mean beside the fact that you left me in a lurch that night and haven't contacted me in three days, despite the fact that I've texted you and emailed you? You mean beside that? Okay, I'll tell you. Someone tried to kill me. My dog almost died."

Tom moved away from me slightly. "What?"

"That's why I couldn't use my engine. Someone cut my propane line. There's probably still propane in the bottom of my boat. My boat could have blown up."

A bedraggled-looking Rusty was sitting patiently next to the door, waiting to get inside and warm. Tom continued to stare without moving.

"Scott wants me dead, and I don't know why," I said.

He touched my arm, turned me toward him. "Em? What are you talking about?"

I pulled away, opened my door which was, of course, unlocked. That's part of my problem, I never lock my door. That's how easy it is for someone—Scott, Kricket, anyone—to casually walk into my home and take my wooden plate and Jesse's computer. I'm a wide-open target. In the future I will lock it, but obviously the horse was already out of this barn. I went inside. Tom followed insisting. "What did Scott do? Tell me what's going on. Em, you need to talk to me. What has he done now?"

I scratched at an itchy spot on my leg. "He cut the propane line in my boat." I made a snipping motion with my fingers. "I would be dead now if I'd started my engine."

"Why do you think it was Scott?"

"I know it was Scott," I said. "He stole my computer. He asked about me at the general store. But, I need to dry off and apply some antihistamine cream to a whole bunch of spider bites and then I'm going to have a cup of coffee after I've calmed down a bit from almost being dead and after you've properly told me why you ran off with Scott that night instead of driving me home like you promised, and why you haven't bothered to contact me for three days."

He was still standing in my doorway. He hadn't come inside.

"Em, you're not making sense."

"After they found those things on *Blue Peace* the other night, I turned and you were gone. So I went looking for you. Some guy on your wharf told me you and Scott had taken off running."

"You were down on my wharf?" His eyes flashed.

"Yes." Once inside my house, the gravity of what had just happened seemed to hit me all at once. I began trembling, and I couldn't stop. Tom came over and put his arms around me again. I felt like melting into them, but I pulled away in time and said, "I'm freezing. I'm wet. Let me go dry off first then you can tell me what the hell you're doing here now."

I grabbed a towel and in my bedroom, I changed into dry clothes. I was covered in bites and wondered if I should take a quick trip to the medical clinic. They'd probably just give me an antihistamine anyway, and I thought I had some in my bathroom. Because I sail offshore so much I keep a ton of first aid stuff for long boat trips. No food in my fridge but I can cauterize a wound with stuff you can only get in the military.

I brushed my hair and dried my face. When I was a bit more presentable, I emerged to find that my soaking wet dog had sought refuge on my couch. Tom was kneeling in front of my fireplace, arranging kindling over a crumpled mound of newspaper. He looked up at me. "Thought I'd get a fire going. It's not exactly warm in here."

"Yeah."

I went into the kitchen and reached up in my top cupboard for my French press. I was hoping I even remembered how to make coffee in it. When it's just me, I use Jesse's machine and either drink it in small espresso cups that he brought back from a sailing trip to Cuba, or add boiling water and cream and call it a latte. I filled up the kettle and plugged it in. Another gift from my Canadian husband. He insisted on a plug-in kettle rather than heating up his water on the stove or the microwave like Americans mostly do. *No matter what I do—even making coffee—Jesse is a part of me.*

I stood trying to collect my thoughts while I heard the sounds of the fire behind me. For the time it took for my kettle to boil and the coffee to be made, I kept my back to Tom. I could hear him in the living room talking to Rusty. In time, I brought two cups of coffee into the living room and put them down on my coffee table. I sat down next to my dog and Rusty nuzzled his wet fur into me. Tom sat down on the other side of my dog. I was glad Rusty was between us.

I looked at Tom for a long minute. He was wearing a clean white golf shirt, too clean, so clean it hurt my eyes. He looked too good. He always looked too good. Too perfect. I held my dog's wet head on my lap. That was it. He was too perfect. Something is wrong with a guy who's too perfect. There were times when he reminded me so much of Jesse, and times when he was the complete opposite.

"So, where did you go when you were supposed to drive me home?" I looked straight into his brown eyes when I asked him this. His face became grim. "Scott was having a bit of trouble. It was a matter that needed some attention."

"And you didn't think to call and tell me this?"

"I did. Didn't you get the text?"

"'Something came up.' That's all you wrote. And that was three days ago."

"Em…" His lips thinned. "There are things—things you don't understand…can't understand…"

"I need to call Ben," I said getting up. Ben needed to know that someone tried to sabotage my boat. He also needed to know about the cat painting on the island.

"Please," he said rising. He knelt down and took hold of both my hands. This time I didn't pull away. "If it was Scott, if he did, indeed take your computer, can you leave it with me? I'll get it back for you. I'll talk to him. I promise. You have my word."

There was such pleading in his eyes, such pain, that I blew out a breath.

"Never mind about the computer," I said. "I got it back."

"You have it?"

"Ben has it."

He shook his head slowly from side to side. "I am totally confused, Em…"

"It was on Scott's boat."

He shook his head. "You're losing me."

"I told you. Scott stole my computer. He had it on his boat. I went to his boat and took it back."

"You were on his boat?"

"When I was on your wharf I saw my computer there."

He rubbed his face and sighed deeply before he said, "Maybe I should head to Portland and see Ben. Maybe, it's time I quit giving Scott the benefit of the doubt."

I looked at him, waited.

"Maybe Scott needs to finally pay for what he continually does. That night I…" His voice broke. "I couldn't call you." He walked over to my front window. "I wanted to. I desperately wanted to. You have no idea how much. You have to believe me."

When he turned back, there was pain in his eyes. I picked up my coffee. Rusty whimpered a bit in his sleep.

"What happened?" I asked.

"I…uh…" He coughed, cleared his throat. "It's a long story."

"I'm not going anywhere."

The rain had stopped and ahead of us through the window and out on the bay, sun rays pierced through the trees and landed on the water like jewels. He said, "I've been cleaning up Scott's messes my whole life."

"And why would you be doing that?"

"Em…" His eyes were wet when he said, "He's my brother."

I'm sure my eyes were like saucers.

"That's why I left so suddenly the other night," he went on. "He called me, and I had some 'brother' garbage I had to deal with, as per usual. It even required me going out of town for a few days. I'm here now to apologize. And to try to get you to understand. He's been in trouble with the law before."

Stupidly, I said, "You have different last names."

"Stepbrother. Our mother wasn't the sharpest tool in the shed. You might say we had kind of a dysfunctional childhood. I don't know what he's done, but I'm afraid he's up to his ears and involved in this whole mess."

"You mean the whole mess with Peter and *Blue Peace*?"

He nodded miserably.

"Well Tom, I would say he's gone a bit too far now."

I told Tom about the plate of poisonous mushrooms Scott had left for me on my boat. I also reminded him that the girl had been killed by poisonous mushrooms. "I'm convinced he put them on my boat. Maybe to frame me, I have no idea. You knew her, right? Roxanne Wishert?"

"Who?" He seemed genuinely flustered.

"The girl who died on *Blue Peace*. They finally identified her. And you knew her? You were in Bermuda with her."

He backed away slightly, put up his hands. "I have no idea, none, as to what you're talking about."

"Oh Tom, don't be stupid. Joan and Art saw you." I sat down, took a sip of my coffee, added some of EJ's cream to it and stirred. Yes, they could be brothers, but there were still too many unanswered questions. "You and Roxanne and Kricket and Scott were in Bermuda."

He looked confused. "When was this?" He was still standing beside the window "I don't know anybody named Roxanne—what did you say her last name was?"

"Wishert. Joan couldn't remember the exact date, but it would have been a couple of years ago when you were in Bermuda. On one of Patterson's boats, a powerboat then. Ben's checking the logs."

"Uh…" He appeared to be thinking, then gave the teensiest bit of a smile. "Oh, yes, that would have been maybe two years ago. I remember that now. I'd flown over there looking for Scott to bring him home but never found him. I never was with him or Kricket or the girl on a boat. I flew home. I've always been my brother's protector. It's not been easy, with our mother, the ah…the way she was. It's why…it's why I've never even been able to even be in a normal relationship with a woman."

"Ah yes, your relationships with women…" I was thinking about something. "You and your brother both had a relationship with the boss's daughter?"

He frowned. "After she broke up with Scott the first time, she came to me. I'm not proud of that." He was so quiet that I had to strain to hear. "After our relationship fizzled she went back to Scott."

I moved my head from side to side. "Boy, family gatherings must be a hoot."

"Em…" He looked at me plaintively. "It's not funny. Kricket is emotionally disturbed, as evidenced by her stalking of me. And Scott, he has serious anger issues."

"One more thing…" I looked him square in the face. "Why did you tell me you never knew my husband? I found an email from him to you."

"What?" The change of subject seemed to catch him off guard.

"I was able to get into my husband's email account, and I found some correspondence between the two of you. He said he 'wanted out.' What did that mean? Why did you tell me you didn't know him?"

He came and sat down beside me on the couch, too close. "Em…"

I put my hands in my lap before he could take hold of them. Right now I didn't want him touching me.

215

"I believe I said I never had the privilege of getting to know your husband. Like meeting in person. I never said we never emailed. I never said that, Em." He looked sad. "What's with this third degree?"

I kept my hands in my lap and tried to think. Nothing was making sense.

He looked at me sadly. "Please trust me, Em. There are so many things about the Pattersons you don't know. And about Scott. This whole situation. And I'm just as much in the dark as you about this whole stolen painting thing. That's where I've...where I've been for the past few days. Trying to figure out the painting angle. And my brother, who's not talking. But I know the Pattersons. I know Kricket. And my brother..."

"I don't understand."

"And I don't understand most of it, either. You have to believe me."

I sighed. I didn't know what to think. This man in front of me, he seemed so genuine.

He said, "The reason I came to see you today. I've been working on the whole anonymous-source thing. I'd already come to the conclusion that it's Kricket who might be doing this, and now I'm thinking maybe it's Kricket and Scott together." His face was grim.

"But Scott doesn't know where Kricket is," I said. "Remember at Joan and Art's? He was calling her all day."

"I'm not so sure about that. That whole thing that morning might have been an act. I think they're in on this together. Maybe he was only pretending to call her. Maybe he made up the whole thing about being in contact with her the whole time. Maybe he knew Kricket wasn't on that boat. Maybe they planned the whole thing."

I thought about the scared Kricket who'd left me that note. "Why would Kricket and Scott do this to me? I don't even know them."

He paused. "What little I've been able to get from Scott is this—you have something they want. That's what he intimated, anyway. That's another reason I'm here. Maybe even to warn you. I got the impression from my brother that this has something to do with your late husband. Something they think your husband took from them? Does that make any sense to you at all? I haven't been able to get it all out of Scott. Maybe that's what Kricket was looking for on your boat. Hell, maybe they even thought I had it. Remember I told you that I felt someone had looked through my boat?"

I nodded. "I know what it is." I reached into my pocket and

placed the flash drive on the table.

"What's that?" he asked.

"I think it's what they were looking for and why Scott stole my computer. It was wrapped up with a stolen painting. Of the cat. I found it hidden on an island. That's where I just came from in this storm."

I told him about EJ's box. I told him about sailing out to the island and sailing home. He wanted to know where the island was. We went over to the window and I pointed in the general direction. He wanted to see what was on the flash drive, and I said I did, too. We decided we would look at it together before we drove it into Portland tonight and turned it over to Ben.

At the kitchen table I pulled my laptop toward me and paused. Something was off. I puzzled at the position of my computer. When I'd left it on the table, I thought I'd set it so that when I opened it up, the screen would be facing me as I sat down. Now, however, it was turned the other direction. A small thing, but it bothered me. With all the strange things I had seen around my house, this was just one more.

"Something wrong?" he asked me.

I shook my head. "Think I'm just tired." Had Scott been in here? I remembered what Dorothy at the store had told me about someone asking for me. Had he come here while I was on the island?

I turned my computer to face me, opened it up and plugged in the flash drive. There were two files on it, a graphic and a spreadsheet. I clicked on the graphic. I was not the least surprised to see the cat lithograph come alive on my screen.

"This is the painting I found on the island," I told him.

He leaned in to get a better look. "The one on the postcard Ben showed to us."

"The very one. I couldn't bring it with me because it was pouring rain, so I wrapped it up as best I could and relocked the shed door when I left."

"It was probably good you did that. Did you get a good look at it?"

"Enough of a look."

"If it was real and not a forgery, there would be an authenticating mark on the back."

"I didn't think about anything like that."

I clicked on the spreadsheet. The left column contained names of boats. I recognized most of them, all high-end yachts like *Blue Peace*, some sail, some power and most owned by the rich and the famous.

In the next column were the names of the owners. I knew most of these names. I saw Roy Patterson's name. The third column listed boat captains. These were all people I knew. Tom's name was there, next to *Blue Peace*. Crews were listed in the third column. Scott's name was there, along with friends of mine from around the world. My name was there, as well.

The next column was a list of random items that made no sense, things like: Painting El Gato, children, $50,000.

The next column listed dates, all prior to Jesse's death, and the furthest column to the right contained a series of numbers. Tom spent a lot of time looking at these numbers, running his finger down the screen.

He said, "I have an idea what this might be."

"Tell me."

"These boat owners are all art collectors. Maybe they had artwork stolen. Let's get this flash drive into Ben tonight." He was making fists with his hands. He seemed nervous, wired. He pushed himself away from the table and got up and went over to the big window again and stood with his back to me. "This is big." He seemed keyed up. "This is really big. You would not believe the number of private detectives Patterson has hired to try to retrieve his stolen art. I can't believe it's his own daughter. And Scott. My own brother."

I could see the tendons on the side of his neck, the fingers of his right hand forming fists.

"The two of them are a deadly pair," he said. "A dangerous pair."

"What does this spreadsheet mean?" I asked.

He pointed. "Those are the names of paintings. Those are the owners. Those are the paintings they'd either stolen or were planning to steal."

I tried to make sense of the spreadsheet. I couldn't understand his reasoning. Then, another question surfaced, if this was so important, why hadn't Jesse taken it to the police? Why had he hidden it the way he had with so many oblique clues? The only reason I could come up with was that Jesse bore some of the guilt and that he hadn't counted on dying when he had. Or—and I couldn't bear to think about this one—he was blackmailing them for money for his business.

"What about Roy?" I asked. "He told Ben he knew nothing about the painting the police found rolled up in the bulkhead on his boat. He said it wasn't his."

Tom's eyes flashed. "He's a liar. You've seen the family, how they interact. What do you think? That they have a happy marriage and have raised a well-adjusted daughter? I told you, I've worked for the family for a long time. Of course Patterson is going to deny the painting is his."

I went back to the spreadsheet while Tom began pacing. "Scott's name is here a lot," I said.

Tom spun around and faced me. I saw something flash in his eyes, something that frightened me, and then it was gone.

"Okay." I rose, removing the flash drive. "Let's take this to Portland. You can follow me in your car."

"Someone should stay here," he said. "You go, and I'll wait here at your house."

"Why?"

"In case Scott comes here. Or Kricket. Who knows their plans?"

"You think they're going to come here?"

"Yes. One of us should be here."

"Tom? Really?" I put my hand to my head.

"Em, you're tired, aren't you?"

"Exhausted. And these bites are driving me crazy."

"You need to take an antihistamine."

"Maybe."

"No maybes about it. And then you'll be in no shape to drive. Why don't we go tomorrow?"

"Ben needs this tonight."

"Okay then, here's an idea, why don't I take the flash drive to Ben tonight. I'll text or email you as soon as I speak with him."

Something about this whole conversation was making me feel oddly nervous. Did he really have my best interests at heart, or was he still protecting Scott?

"Trust me, Em. Just please trust me. I think I know what's going on here, and you shouldn't be involved."

"Funny, Ben told me the same thing."

"Well, listen to Ben, then. Ben and I will work this out together."

"Okay, but you text me the minute you talk to Ben."

He smiled. "Will do."

We walked to the door. His hands were on my face then, and he drew me toward him in a kiss. A part of me, a deep inside part of me, kept not feeling ready, kept feeling that this was too much, too fast.

I backed away, and I backed right into the wall. He moved in and kissed me again, harder, longer, and his eyes were dark, intense. There was something in his kiss that frightened me, and I couldn't define what it was.

I pushed him away as gently as I could. "Tom...I..."

"I care about you," he said. "A lot. Maybe a bit too much for my own good. When all of this is over..."

I felt my face go hot. I kept thinking of what Joan told me about his reputation. Did I really want a man like this in my life?

"Why don't I stay here with you tonight?" he said. "After you've had some rest, we can both head into the police tomorrow."

"No. No, I'm fine. It has to be taken care of tonight."

"You're probably right."

I nodded. I suddenly wanted him gone. I walked him outside to his car. I watched him drive all the way down the road until I couldn't see the back of his car anymore, wondering why I was filled with so much confusion every time I was with him.

I went back to my laptop where I had surreptitiously copied the entire contents of the flash drive onto my computer and put it in a folder named Groceries. I would study all of this, and if it took me all night, I would come up with all of the answers that Jesse wanted me to figure out.

Chapter 37

While the file opened up, I stood by the window and thought about Tom's kiss. I put my hand to my cheek and remembered the first time Jesse had kissed me. It was a memory I had carefully wrapped up in gold foil paper and stashed away in the part of my heart that I go to only very occasionally. I reached into that place now, took out the package and opened it up.

We kissed for the first time in the Chalk Spit boatyard following a really great and exhilarating evening sail. It had rained all day, a hot and muggy rain in a too-still day. By early evening, the rain moved on, and as is so often the case when the clear weather came, it brought a wind that kept increasing. We looked at the weather, looked at each other and decided to head out on *Wanderer*. It had been a wondrous sail. We sailed well together. He seemed to know what I was thinking at every turn, and I seemed to know what he was going to do. It was like we were a finely tuned sailing machine. We hardly had to speak, so attuned were we to the movements of each other and the boat. It's rare to find a sailing partner you can be one with.

After we got the boat tied up, we headed up through the boatyard and sat on a ledge of rocks overlooking the windy water. We talked and talked. After a while our conversation died, and he pulled me toward him and kissed me. We stayed in the middle of that kiss for a long, long time.

It wasn't like Tom's kiss. Jesse had seemed almost shy, which was odd and funny and strange, and later it made me smile to myself. When I'd gone home that night, I danced around the kitchen in my apartment.

Why wasn't I dancing now?

Please trust me.

Jesse had never said this to me. He hadn't had to. Why had Tom? Was it because he sensed that I didn't, couldn't, quite muster up enough trust? Maybe I needed to take those words out and examine them.

A deep part of me maybe knew why. I had trusted Jesse completely and implicitly, and he had betrayed me. Even if he didn't have an affair, he hadn't trusted me with his secrets. He should have told me what he was up to. We could have worked together to find some funding for his boat design instead of him turning to theft. I could have helped find another solution.

A small groan escaped my lips as I stood in my kitchen rinsing out coffee cups. If Jesse had trusted me, he might still be alive.

I made a quick call to Harvey at the boatyard. I told him that my propane line had been "accidentally severed," and I needed to purchase some new hose. I could install it myself if he could order it in for me.

"No need for that," he said. "I'm not busy. I can come tomorrow. You doing okay, Captain?"

"Yeah."

"That's good, then."

"If I'm not here, just help yourself to *Wanderer.*"

"Yeah, it's never locked, is it?"

"Right." I sighed. My life. After the phone call, I sat down at my kitchen table and looked at the files.

I got out the photos that Dr. Meyer had given me and with a magnifying glass I studied them again. I was ninety percent certain that the person in the foreground was the man who'd claimed to be Rob and about fifty percent sure that the guy behind him was Scott. I kept staring and managed to raise that percentage to seventy. Rob and Scott?

Had it been Scott and Rob and Kricket and Roxanne, together? The idea intrigued me. Maybe the four of them had stolen a painting and Jesse had caught wind of it, gotten it away from them and hidden it. I shuddered when I thought of my Jesse blackmailing anyone. But what other explanation was there? I remembered Kricket's statement.

Boy, there's a lot about your husband you don't know, isn't there?

Maybe there was. Maybe there was.

Yet, if the four of them had been friends at one time, they were close no longer. Kricket was running for her life, and Roxanne was dead, killed by poison mushrooms supplied by Scott.

How did Peter fit in? Wrong place, wrong time? Possibly.

I put the photos back in their envelope and looked at my laptop. The phone beeped, an unfamiliar sound. I really needed to get a new phone. A text from Tom.

I'm at Ben's now. He's taking this very seriously.

I texted back, *Good, keep me posted.*

The phone vibrated again, letting me know I'd gotten an email. I froze when I saw the name of the sender. Peter! I felt the blood leave my face.

I kept looking at it. How could I be getting a message from Peter? Had the whole thing been a mistake? No. I now noticed that the email had been sent the day before he was murdered, and I was just now receiving it. Barely breathing, I opened it up.

Can we meet? I have to talk to you about something. You wondered why Tom and especially Scott!! were at Art and Joan's that morning and why Rob took off. I know. I don't want to explain it in an email or a text. Sorry I was such an ass after the accident but it was because I really was an ass. I might go to that cop, Ben, but I don't think he'll believe me.

Peter

I read it over several times. I tried forwarding it on to Ben, but I couldn't figure out how to forward things from this phone. No problem. I'd log onto my laptop and send it from there. Trouble was when I got onto my laptop, the message from Peter wasn't there. I tried all of my mailboxes and my spam folder. Nothing. Talk about confusing. I may know a lot about boats and sailing, but as for computers and the internet, sometimes I feel like an idiot. I went back to the phone where I'd first seen his message and was surprised that it was nowhere on my phone now. Weird, weird and double weird.

I opened up the flash drive files. There were sixteen high-end yachts listed, along with their ports of registry. I recognized most of them. Some were registered in the United States, the United Kingdom, but most of the higher-end yachts were registered in off islands, such as the Grand Caymans. They did that to take advantage of the much cheaper taxes and registration fees. I made a list of the Caribbean Islands and their boats but saw no commonalities. They were, literally, all over the map.

So, maybe that wasn't the common ground. Next, I made a list of all the owners. These were often a bit more difficult to figure out online. The very rich have ways of hiding. I tried looking them up individually online, but my Internet was crawling slow tonight. Drat!

Because I have crewed on so many boats, I listen to the gossip. I know some of the inner-circle stuff that normal people don't know. I made a list of all of the owners and from my memory added any tidbits

I could remember about them, such as criminal arrests. I even wrote down what rumors I could remember.

Many of the very high-end yachts have full-time crew that never change. I made a list of all the captains and crew members. Many were friends of mine, or at least people I was acquainted with. I wrote down a list of their names, plus anything I could remember about them.

Then I went through the boats one at a time and wrote down any pertinent information I could remember. Three-quarters of the boats were for sale, but that's nothing new. Most high-end yachts are for sale. That's just a fact of the business. It told me nothing.

Next to the boats in the spreadsheet were dates. These made no sense to me, and of course, all the dates were from before Jesse died. Next to some of the dates were names, such as Virulent Sunset, Moonscape, Force. Names of paintings? Maybe.

I sat there, my brows screwed together, trying to figure things out until the sun set behind the clouds. "What is this, Jesse? Why did you steal a painting of a cat and then go and hide it?"

I thought about the liquor in the engine room of *Blue Peace* and the money in the holding tank. There had to be an explanation for every single bit of this.

Just before I finally turned in for the night, I managed to get online and check my phone messages. Dr. Declan Meyer had called me.

Using Tom's phone I called him back.

"Captain Ridge—"

"Yes?"

"Detective Dunlinson passed the mushrooms you found on to me. And your estimation is correct. They are the precise variety that killed Roxanne Wishert. There were, however, no fingerprints on either the wooden plate or the foil cups, which is not surprising. As we speak, we are still checking into known mushroom farms."

"Thanks for letting me know."

"This may interest you. They brought Scott Uphill in for questioning early today."

"Today?" I held my cell phone very tightly. Tom hadn't mentioned this. Might he not have known?

Today? He was there today?

"They let him go. They had nothing to charge him with."

I was quiet for a moment, thinking. Dorothy had seen someone who looked like Scott asking about me this morning, and my computer had been moved. If Scott hadn't done it, then who had it been? Rob? Scott's cohort in crime who had disappeared? Possibly.

The following morning, Dot and Isabelle put the final nail in the coffin of my suspicions.

I had taken my coffee out to my porch in time to see the two women on their daily jaunt along the sea front. It was high tide, so they were walking up close to my house. When they saw me, they waved and headed up toward me in the sunshine. "I'm going into town," I told them. I was going in to see Ben and also to finally get myself a new phone. This was getting ridiculous. They invited me in for a cup of coffee and I told them I didn't have time.

"Saw you sailing in yesterday," Dot said.

"You picked an awful day for that, that's for sure," Isabelle added.

"Rained like a sun of a gun," Dot said.

"Sure did," I said.

"Dot was there with the binoculars."

"We watched you."

"You did a good job bringing that boat in."

"We saw the young man you were with."

I nodded.

"He's a handsome young guy, that's for sure," Isabelle said.

"A looker," Dot said.

My lips felt tight with my fake smile.

"So," Dot said. "Is he going to buy the house next door then?"

"That would be nice," Isabelle said.

What?

Isabelle smiled broadly. "He's the young man we were telling you about, the one who was looking at that house."

"He even had a tour of it when you were away."

I felt my mouth go dry. "Are you both absolutely sure it was him? He has a brother who looks like him a bit, although a bit shorter."

"Well, maybe it was someone shorter. Would you say so, Isabelle?"

"No, I'm sure it was the guy you were with."

"And he was *here*?" I asked.

"Yes."

My brow furrowed. There was no time to waste. I raced to my car, started it, but then thought better of it. I could get to Portland and Ben faster by boat. And if I went by boat, I may as well make a quick stop on EJ's island. A theory was starting to fall into place. I couldn't quite put it into words yet, and if I tried to voice it, it would come out in a waterfall of intersecting ideas and concepts that made no sense. Yet, he needed to know. I made a decision then. I would head to the island on a fast boat, pack up the painting and then take it into Portland by water.

I was sure now, that Kricket, Roxanne, Scott and Rob were part of an art-theft ring. Yes, I was calling it a ring. One stolen painting is a stolen painting. Two stolen paintings is art theft. Three make it an art-theft ring. And there were three paintings involved here—the farm scene, the lighthouse scene and the cat. It might have had something to do with Patterson selling off his art—illegally, according to Tom. But what about Tom? I figured he was so busy running behind his brother and cleaning up his messes, that he ultimately became involved and got in over his head. That's what I wanted to believe, yet I knew it was more than that. Much more. I didn't call Ben. I no longer trusted this cell phone. I needed to see him by person and it would be quicker getting there by boat.

Somehow, Jesse had found out what they all were up to and tried to stop it. Maybe Jesse had gone to see Scott or Rob on the night he died and tried to reason with them. Maybe they had killed him and laid him out on his kayak and then ran him over with *Rosalena*. Maybe they knew *Rosalena* might have contained forensic evidence that would prove that, so they destroyed it. I found it difficult, though, to believe that four young people would be able to manipulate so major a crime scene. They must've had help with that from someone powerful. Roy? Or *Tom*? The newspaper had even had quotes about the boys being model students. Had all of that been fabricated? Maybe that was why Dr. Meyer hadn't been able to find the church they attended, or their addresses.

I thought about the numbers on the spreadsheet and wondered whether they corresponded to the authenticating marks on paintings that Tom had mentioned. I would find out.

Chapter 38

I clipped on my bike fanny pack of tools and zipped a warm jacket over the top of it. I stuffed two blankets and some garbage bags into a yellow wet bag, along with some cloth store grocery bags. I would pack up the painting and whatever else I could find there—because even as I cast about my house, another thought was materializing, a belief that this was more than merely about art. This could include the paintings, the duffle full of money, the liquor and even—God forbid—the children.

I glanced at my wall barometer, and outside I checked the direction of the wind. No problems if I was in the *Valerie J,* but it would be a brisk sail on *Wanderer.*

I race-walked a limping Rusty over to EJ's, and then I was down at the dock as quickly as I could get there. In addition to all the other hassles, my dog's limp was getting more pronounced. I wondered if this was an after effect of the propane. I would take him to the vet after all of this was over.

Drat! The *Valerie J* was out.

I left my gear on Jeff and Valerie's dock and ran up to their house. Their son, Liam, was on the porch, hunched over a tablet computer. I could hear the bleeps and music of whatever game he was playing.

"Hey," I said. "Your mom and dad around?"

"Dad's out on the boat," he said without looking up. "Mom's in town."

I nodded, wondering what I should do now.

"Um, Em?" He looked up. "Do you think I could take *Wanderer* out?"

"Sure. Sure. Wait a minute, Liam. No. Not today. Harvey might be over to fix a broken propane line."

"Okay."

I paused. "Oh, wait. Now it's my turn. Can I borrow your boat?" Liam has a twelve-foot, hard-bottom inflatable with a thirty-horsepower outboard. With that kind of power, I could make it to the island in no time. It was an open boat, but I would cover the painting with all the blankets I'd brought. As soon as I was off the island, I'd take everything to Portland.

"What do you want to borrow it for?" Already he was back into his game.

"I have to get somewhere fast."

"It's at the little dock."

"Thanks!" I called. "I won't be long, and you can take out my sailboat any time, just not today, okay?"

"Yep," he said without looking up.

What he called "The little dock" is a narrow, floating wooden dock directly in front of Valerie and Jeff's house. It's only use is for tying up small boats, dinghies, kayaks and the like. I ran down, stumbled across the uneven boards, some missing, got my feet wet in the high water, and hopped into the inflatable and got her going. I stopped at the big dock just long enough to grab my stuff.

In no time, I was speeding across the tops of waves, and soon the island was in sight. I returned to the place where I'd pulled in yesterday, beside the broken-down dock. I throttled down, aimed toward the beach. As I approached the shore, I pulled up the outboard so the prop wouldn't scrape against the rocks and shells. I climbed out, dragged the inflatable a few feet up onto the pebbly beach and tied it to a tree.

Running on adrenaline, almost out of breath and lugging along the blankets and bags, I clambered up the path to the cabin. At the top of the hill, I could see down to the other side of the island. Another inflatable was pulled up on the shore.

Someone else was on the island? I stopped.

I pulled out a pair of mini-binoculars from my fanny pack and looked for the registration number on the side. There wasn't one. Beachcombers? A couple of day-tripping tourists? Why did I think that was so not the case?

For a long time, I stood there at the top of the rise, not quite knowing what to do. I thought about running back down and heading into Portland. I didn't. I guess there was a part of me that had to know. Very quietly, crouching from tree cover to tree cover and trying to keep my running shoes from making any noise at all, I made my way to the cabin.

A few yards away, I could see that the door was wide open. Closer, I noted that the padlock had been pried open and lay sprung on the ground. I bent low, and taking one step at a time, I crept closer to the building. The few windows in the cabin were opaque, but I still crouched underneath them. I didn't want to take any chances.

I wanted to see what was going on in there. Where this sudden burst of confidence came from, I have no idea. Normally, I'm a bit of a scaredy-cat.

I heard voices. I crept slowly until I was behind the door where the inner edge of it met the wall. Ever so carefully, I peered into the room.

Kricket!

She was on the floor against the far wall. Her ankles were tied together, and her wrists were behind her back, presumably also tied. She saw me, and her eyes went wide. My heart was beating loud enough, I was sure, for everyone to hear. I quickly backed into the shadows. I stood there until my racing heart slowed a bit.

I dug out the phone again, hoping, hoping that somehow there would magically be Wifi, but of course there was nothing of the sort. I wrote a text to Ben's private number so it would get sent to him when I got within range of a Wifi signal again. Even though I didn't quite trust the phone, it was my only option. I fiddled with the phone for a minute or two before I crept back against the wall and squinted. I also took a few pictures for good measure.

I couldn't see who else was in the room with her, but I didn't have long to wait. It was the fake Rob's voice that yelled, "I'll kill you, and don't think I won't!" His voice was raspy and desperate and had a fearful edge to it. I couldn't see his face, but I guessed his eyes were bulgy and red. I caught a glimpse of a gun as he wildly waved it around.

From my vantage point, I could see that the gun was the one Kricket had had, the one she said belonged to Jesse.

The large cat painting was on the table, where I'd left it, but the paper had been entirely torn off. I also saw that the wall where it had been hidden had been further ripped apart. Boards were scattered this way and that across the cabin floor. I saw something then that made my blood run cold. Next to the Hobbit-sized door were two red jerry cans. I remembered that *Rosalena* had been destroyed by an explosion.

Rob was talking now. "I'm taking the painting, and I'm going to walk out of here. But before I go, I'm going to set this whole place on fire."

"You're going to kill me? What good'll that do? You don't think they'll put two and two together? That captain, Captain Ridge, she's already figured it out."

"Then she will have to die, too." His voice was very calm.

"You'll kill her like you killed everyone else."

His voice became very quiet when he said, "I never killed anyone. You know I didn't. I would never have killed Roxanne."

"You did so! It was your mushrooms that killed her."

"I never meant for that to happen." His voice was high-pitched. "That wasn't the plan. I just gave him the mushrooms. I didn't know what he was going to use them for. Me and Scott, we were in the dark about that."

My face went very hot and cold at the same time. Because I knew now. I knew for certain what had happened.

Kricket was talking now. "I just wanted him to quit stalking me, quit trying to get my family money through me. That's all. I just wanted something on him. He tells people I was stalking him. It's so not true, just like all the other lies that he tells about me. And Roxanne found out lots that I could use from the detective she works for. When I first saw that Captain Ridge, when I was on her boat, I lied to her. I lied to her about a lot of things. I couldn't tell her everything then—"

I listened carefully, realizing she was explaining all of this for my benefit.

"Shut up!" he yelled.

She didn't. "You guys killed Jesse Ridge, right? I figured that out. And he still didn't tell you where the flash drive was, did he? Even though you killed him, he never told you. You had to follow Captain Ridge around to find it."

Jesse! I put a shaky hand to my throat. I felt like I was going to throw up.

"I didn't kill that guy," Rob said. "He was already dead when we put him in his kayak."

"But you had to blow up the other boat."

"Quit talking so much."

"But you did blow up that boat. Why?"

"We had to. He told us we had to. He said it might end up being linked to the art."

"That's why you took the card with you, right? So, if you saw the right painting you would know."

"I said shut up. Quit talking."

I tried to keep my breathing under control. I tried to keep from screaming out. I pressed my ear against the crack between the door and the cabin.

I heard some more mumbling, then Kricket's plaintive voice. "Dom, we could go out on our own, you know. We could take the money. You and me. We could just do it. We don't have to listen to him."

So the fake Rob's name was really Dom.

"He thinks everyone double-crossed him," she said. "Including you, you know." She mumbled something more that I couldn't hear.

"No, you don't," Dom said. "You can't."

He leveled the gun on her. I held my breath, felt my heart stop.

She began screaming for help.

"No one can hear you. We're alone out here."

Kricket said, "How do you know no one will hear me? Maybe Captain Ridge will come back. She's the one who found this place to begin with, you know."

"She won't come back. I made sure of that."

"How?"

"The only way out here is on her sailboat, right? Well, we rigged it for another propane blast. Last time, it didn't work. This time there is no mistaking. As soon as the top hatch board is lifted from the boat, it triggers a bomb."

I couldn't help myself. My gasp was audible. *Harvey!* He was going to work on my boat today!

I had to get back and warn him. And what about Liam? I told him not to go out on my boat, but what if he did anyway? He was a fourteen-year-old boy. Fourteen-year-old kids don't always do what they're told.

And Kricket! I couldn't leave her. Dom would shoot her. I was sure of that. I cast about me for something, anything, that I could use as a weapon. I remembered that heavy switch I had cut to try to ram the door open when I was here before. I slunk around the side of the building until I found it.

Laying down all of my bags and blankets, I crept back to the door and stood in the shadows and waited for my chance.

The two were still arguing, Kricket begging Dom to let her go, and Dom still holding the gun on her. His back was to me. Thinking about all the action movies I'd ever seen in my life, I held the piece of wood in both hands over my head, and rushed toward him, yelling as loud as I could.

I lifted the log up to bring it right down on his head. I was off by about two seconds and two feet. He tripped me and I fell, right onto the log.

A sudden acute pain to my ankle and foot almost made me vomit onto the floor. I lay there for several seconds, trying to get my breath back and willing the pain to settle. It didn't. Dom still had the gun and he was aiming it right at me. Why he didn't shoot me right then and there I'll never know.

In the next minute, Dom was grabbing my shoulders and hauling me over to the wall beside Kricket. I pride myself on my strength, but for some reason, maybe it was the searing ankle pain, I couldn't break free. I yelled out in pain. I struggled. I reached for my ankle, but he was quicker, and in the next instant, he shoved the gun into his waist and cable-tied my wrists together in front of me.

"Let me go!" I screamed.

Several times I thought about kicking him, but with the pain in my ankle, it was all I could do to keep on my feet, or on one foot, as the case may be.

"What did you do to my boat?" I demanded.

"Shut up!"

"I know you killed Jesse, you piece of crap!"

"I said shut up."

"What did you do to my boat?"

"I said shut up or I'll kill you. I have a gun, remember? You're not the boss anymore."

"I never was the boss, you idiot. I was just the captain of the boat, the boat you were on because you paid off Peter. Did you kill him, too?"

"I never killed anybody."

He pointed to where Kricket was sitting. "Get over there. Against the wall."

Kricket was crying now. "I'm sorry. I'm sorry, Em. There was nothing I could do. I came out here with him because I thought I could talk some sense into him—"

"I said shut up!"

The pain was shooting daggers through my body while he kept the gun on me. At the last minute, I wrenched free from him and tried to make a run for it. He grabbed my legs, and I fell face down on the hard floor. I lay there, stunned for a moment, the phone out of my pocket and my glasses on the floor in front of me. Rob stepped on my glasses, grinding them into the wooden floor. He picked up my cell phone and put it in his pocket.

Hot tears threatened at my eyes. "What did I ever do to you?" I said.

"Same thing your husband did. You know too much. Same thing as Peter. Same thing as Kricket and her little detective friend. Get up!" he yelled at me.

"I can't," I said.

He shoved the gun into his belt, hoisted me up in his scrawny arms and hefted me over against the wall, about a yard from Kricket. He secured my ankles with cable ties, and I looked over at Kricket. She was quivering all over. I tried to reassure her with my eyes. Call it intuition, but I had a gut feeling that Rob wasn't going to kill us. He would have by now if he was going to.

"Why are you doing this?" I asked.

"He's doing it because he can." This came from Kricket. "Because he thinks he's such a big tough guy, and he's nothing but a little jerk."

I said, "You have to let me go. I have someone coming to work on my boat. He's got nothing to do with any of this."

He went to the opposite side of the room, lay the gun on the table—we were no threat to him now—and muttered something that sounded like "collateral damage." He pulled out his cell phone, then put it back in his pocket. "No phone reception on this whole friggin' island," he said.

He pulled out a second phone. This one I recognized by the green waterproof cover. Mine! "Hey!" I said. I looked at Kricket and she shrugged and looked down.

"You have to call someone?" I asked. "With my phone?"

"You being here changes things."

"And because you can't think for yourself, I suppose you have to figure out what your next order is."

"Shut up!" He put my phone back into his pocket.

I sighed and said, "Okay, you want cell reception? I'll tell you where some is. You know the rocky point? The one that goes to the mainland from the back of the island where you came in? There's a good signal at the end of the point, but you have to be on a boat to get it." It was such a stupid lie I was sure no sane person would believe it. It was around half-tide out there, high enough so that it looked safe but low enough so that it wasn't.

I said, "Go down there and make your stupid phone call. It's not like we're going anywhere."

He aimed the gun at us, said the word, "Pow," and then he pointed at Kricket. "But she's coming with me. And if what you say is a lie, I will come back and light this place on fire with both of you in it."

I said, "Leave Kricket here. Neither one of us is going anywhere."

He grabbed her roughly and dragged her to her feet. As much as I begged him to leave her while he went to make his call, he ignored me. He took a knife and undid her ankle bonds so she could walk. "No funny stuff," he said to her. "Remember, I've got the gun."

He put it into her back and out the door they went, her hands cable-tied behind her back. Through all of this, Dom hadn't noticed my fanny pack, which was scrunched under my jacket. In it I had a pair of wire cutters, my binoculars, a screwdriver, a small hammer and a small waterproof flashlight. My original plan in sending Dom off to get a cell connection had been to get us both out of here. I figured that the two of us working together might be able to free ourselves and get away.

As soon as they left the building, I began twisting my wrists to try to pull up my jacket and then maybe, maybe get into the fanny pack. Fortunately, and courtesy of Dom's ineptitude, my wrists were tied in front of me instead of behind me. I lay against the wall and managed to get my jacket up over my fanny pack. I twisted this way and that, and finally I was able to unzip it and dig inside with my fingers. I felt for the wire cutters, picked them up. I was home free—until I dropped them. I scooched over the floor, reached for them, trying the whole time, to ignore the searing pain in my ankle.

I heard the distant buzz of the departing boat. How long before they were back? Hopefully, Rob would keep going until he found his cell reception. I managed to find the wire cutters and, using both hands, arranged them in my fingers, and by some luck, I was able to undo my wrist bonds.

Leaning against the wall, I got up, flexed my fingers. Pain everywhere. I limp-hobbled out of the front door. What I needed now was to get on the inflatable and get out of here. I had steered Dom in a direction where he wouldn't see me on this side of the island. If I was lucky, he wouldn't realize he was dangerously close to a rock outcropping. I hoped that he would run aground and that his inflatable would puncture on the rocks. *Hang on, Kricket, I'm going for help!*

I limped down toward Liam's inflatable. It's amazing what

adrenaline can do. I undid the boat from the tree, pushed it off the rocks, hopped on, and got her going. I had to get back to Chalk Spit before Harvey or Liam opened up my boat. It wouldn't be long before Dom realized I was gone.

I heard it before I saw it. I wasn't alone. In the far distance behind me was a boat I recognized. Scott! And he was gaining on me!

Chapter 39

I set Liam's outboard to full throttle, but it was no match for the powerboat, and I knew it. Still, I sped over the tops of the waves as fast as the little boat would go, getting drenched with spray, my ankle complaining about every movement of the boat. He came toward me faster.

As I looked back at the oncoming boat, it all began to come clear, or at least not so murky. It has to do with being a sailor. It has to do with the routes we sailors use to go up and down the East Coast and to the Caribbean. I've sailed down the coast to the Caribbean more times than I can count. I've gone on the "outside" along the Southern states, and I've been down "through the ditch," which is what we call the Intracoastal Waterway.

I know what it's like out on the ocean. I know how easy it is to hide things, to throw things overboard in the middle of the night or as soon as you spot the Coast Guard. I know how easy it is to rendezvous with boats and exchange items, such as art, or money, or liquor, or drugs. Or children.

I know about pirates.

Amanda was right about one thing. Living on the sea is the easiest—perhaps the only—way to stay off the grid.

Jesse had discovered what these people were up to, and it had gotten him killed. Why hadn't he gone to the police as soon as he figured it out? I still couldn't answer that. That part didn't make sense to me. Yet—

Up ahead of me in the distance, I could see the lighthouse at the entrance to my bay. Would I be lucky enough to make it back before he caught me? Probably not. I heard a gunshot at the same time that I saw a tiny splash off to my starboard. I kept going. Oh no! The starboard pontoon was rapidly deflating. I reached for the PFD, put it on while I leaned low into the still-inflated pontoon on the other side. These inflatables are quite sturdy and have four or five inflatable tubes that hold them up over a Fiberglas floor. This boat had a lot of life left in it, despite the fact that a tube along the starboard side was almost nonexistent now.

Three more shots, and one of them hit the outboard. The little outboard on Liam's boat sputtered and died. Smoke poured out of it. In no time the lobster boat was right beside me. I flattened myself down on the wet floor. If I was going to be shot, there was nothing I could do. I glanced up, expecting to see Scott.

Tom?

I didn't have my glasses, but yes, it was Tom at the helm.

As my boat stopped dead in the water, I wondered how I should play this. If he felt I didn't suspect him, maybe, just maybe I could pull it off.

"Tom!" I called waving both hands. "It's me! Don't shoot! I'm not Rob! I know he's in a similar boat. But it's me here. And I hurt my ankle!"

He came alongside. I couldn't read his expression. Was that him trying to hide a smirk?

I threw him a line. "This is my neighbor's boat. We're going to have to tow it. Do you mind?"

I waited for him to say he was sorry for shooting at me. He merely took the line I handed him and secured it to a stern cleat. "Come on aboard." His voice was flat.

I tried to smile. "I might need some help getting on. I think I broke my ankle. It's the size of a balloon. I need to get to Portland and a hospital."

He made a sound that sounded like, "Tsk-tsk."

I didn't have a plan. All I had were a couple of tools in my fanny pack, zipped under my jacket. I tried to give him a look of eternal gratefulness. When he grabbed for my arm, I said, "This is the second time you've rescued me, Tom!"

I tried not to pull away or flinch when he touched me. "You're not going to believe what happened," I said. "I was out at the island again. The one I told you about? Rob was there. He must've seen me the first time and followed. He's gone. He took Kricket. But I guess you know that if you thought I was Rob." I rolled my eyes and said, "You're quite right about her being mentally unbalanced. Whew."

I was talking too much and too fast. Was I overdoing it? My breath quickened as I sat down on a seat outside in the stern. I should never have gotten on this boat. I should have done something, anything. Not this. How foolish I had been.

His hand stayed on my shoulder. He said, "You're not a very good liar, Emmeline."

"What?" I looked up at him innocently. "What are you talking about?"

"Don't be stupid, Em." He got up and stood behind the wheel.

My mouth was dry, and my tongue stuck to the roof of it. Through my fuzzy, no-glasses vision, I could see that he was turning the boat around and heading us out to sea.

"Tom?" I looked up at him from where I sat, hugging myself into my wet clothes and trying to find a comfortable position for my ankle. There wasn't one. "Where are we going? We should go into Portland. Ben's waiting. I called him. He knows I'm out here. He'll be here any minute with the Coast Guard."

"Still not a very good liar, Em. You forget what phone you had. I monitored all your calls and texts. I know you didn't call Ben. I also know when you went out to that island. The phone had a GPS tracker in it. Clever, wasn't I?"

My mouth clamped shut. There were so many puzzle pieces still not fitting together. I looked to the left of me at the receding land. I didn't want to die this way. I wanted to make peace with my sisters first. I wanted to tell my parents that I loved them.

"Do you want in? There's still room."

At first I wondered if I had heard him correctly. I looked up at him. "What?"

"You heard me. You want in?"

I said nothing, just kept looking at him.

"I'm picking up partners all over the place, captains, like yourself."

"I don't know what you're talking about."

"Don't act dumb, Em. You're smarter than that. I know you saw the paintings down below and the money. And the liquor. And the brats."

"The brats?"

"The kids and their keepers."

I stared at him, wondering how I ever thought him attractive. He looked like an evil thing to me now.

"I can always use a good partner. You'd be the first woman. That could come in handy."

I leveled my eyes at him. "Who are your partners?"

"Boat captains. If you want in, I know that we can smooth the waters for you, to use an apropos metaphor. You will be completely cleared of Wishert's death on *Blue Peace*. I can make sure of that. Just a little 'anonymous sourcing' to the press, and I'll have you cleared."

I said, "You did that."

"Had to. Seriously. I'm not kidding. Come in with us. The two of us, we make a good pair. I know you feel the connection between us."

I stared at his face not quite trusting myself to comment on that. To steer him away from that subject and to keep him talking I asked, "Are you and Scott really brothers?"

"Ah," he said, smiling into the wind. "Yes, sadly, we are really brothers."

"I need to use the head."

He raised his eyebrows.

I rose, leaned against the boat as I hobbled my way down into the cabin, favoring my good leg. Now what? I walked past the radio up on the small nav table. How fast could I reach over and call a Mayday? Not fast enough, not with Tom eyeing my every move. He was bigger, he was stronger and, with my bum ankle, a whole lot faster.

There was a port in the head, but not an opening one. It was a small head. There was no way out. What had I been thinking, anyway? I wondered what was behind the walls and the bulkhead, wires I could short out? These walls were solid. So far Tom, like Rob at the cabin, hadn't noticed the slim fanny pack under my shirt, next to my jacket. But what could I do in here? I wasn't so sure, and decided that my best strategy at this point might be simply conversation.

I went back outside and said to Tom, "Do you for one moment think I would be your partner after what you did to my husband?" I sat down in the chair and rubbed my ankle, which was twice the size of the other one.

"You won't be as stupid as your husband was," he said. "He wanted money for his big fancy boat design. Named after you, by the way. Bank wouldn't give it to him." He smirked at me. "He joined in with me. He jumped at the chance, Em. And then he got stupid."

I looked up at him, my hand still on my ankle. "I don't believe you."

"Believe it." He was laughing, and it wasn't a pleasant sound. He took the wheel with both hands. "Your husband was never opposed to a little smuggling. We are sailors, after all," he said. "Sailors have a long and proud history of smuggling. We smuggle anything—art, artifacts, money's a big one. Getting money down to the Caribbean, that's our main line of work. There is a never-ending stream of cold, hard cash heading down to Caribbean banks from up here. Surely you know that. Oh, and children. Babies."

"That's what got Kricket involved, isn't it? The children?"

"Little twerp. Yeah. We were together. She figured out what we were doing, so I had to cut her a deal, but when she found out we also trafficked in children, she balked. This was after your husband kicked the bucket, by the way."

I was shaking so hard I could barely get the words out. "I can't believe you smuggled babies. That is beyond the pale."

He grinned. "Yeah. You're right. Once was enough with babies. Even though the gig paid well, human cargo gets boats too damn messy."

"But they're children, little children."

"We're doing them a favor. What kind of a life do they have where they're from? We find nice adoptive parents for them."

"They need to be with their real parents."

"Now you sound like Kricket. This way, they get way better parents, and I get to live in a waterfront condo."

I stared at him. "You set up adoptions?"

"I don't set anything up. That's the sweet thing. My job is just transporting. Once the money gets to the Caribbean, once the children get to New England, once the art gets to whoever wants it, my job is done."

"What about Patterson? He doesn't mind you using his boat for this? He's part of this?"

"You really *are* stupid. Patterson doesn't know a thing. You think Paterson would allow this? No. The beauty of our business is that none of the people who hire us to deliver their boats know what we're actually using their boats for. They think we're just delivering their boats for them."

I looked at him. "People hire you as captains and then you go and use their boats for your smuggling operation? That's despicable."

He touched his head with his forefinger. "Smart. Think about it."

"But children," I kept protesting.

The engine was on, and we were chopping our way straight into the waves. I was feeling a little sick. I knew I had to keep him talking. "What about when the owners come on? What about surprise visits?"

"We get rid of the cargo, whatever it happens to be, way before we pull into a nice little yacht club. We rendezvous way out there." He pointed ahead of us toward the ocean.

I could only stare at him. I understood now the information on the flash drive. The spreadsheet included boats, routes, cargo and delivery schedules. I also understood why Roxanne was so interested in the nav equipment. Perhaps a rendezvous had been scheduled for *Blue Peace*. Perhaps the girls, who were friends, had gotten wind of it.

He said, "I have quite a little network all over the world. And I'm growing. This business venture of mine is getting bigger all the time. I could use a good female partner." He leered at me. "You and me. We could have a great time. A great time." He emphasized the word "great."

Maybe if I said yes to this outrageous offer I might find a way out. But no, the idea was so despicable that I didn't even think I could fake it. I tried to get into a comfortable position for my ankle and said, "How long have you been doing this?"

He grinned. "Three, four years. I started like every sailor does, smuggling the littlest bits of dope, some money, liquor, cigars from Cuba. It grew from there. Boats are so easy. The Coast Guard never comes aboard those big mothers."

"Why *Blue Peace*? Why me?"

"I was supposed to be on that delivery. That was a key delivery. The painting was supposed to go to some forger in Bermuda, the liquor and money to the Caribbean. Then at the last minute, Patterson wanted his daughter along and a woman captain. I recommended you, thinking maybe finally I could find where Jesse had hidden the key and the painting he was supposed to deliver and the flash drive with all the information. As insurance, I asked Dominic, that's the young man you know as Rob, to go along and have a look, too. And that turned Scott's knickers into a knot. He thought it should have been him."

"You thought I knew about Jesse's key?"

"It was a thought."

"But it's been eighteen months," I protested.

He nodded. "And we've been looking for that information since he died. That cat painting is very valuable. Because he was incriminated up to his eyeballs, he hid it instead of going to the police. My hothead brother and his low-life friend were supposed to find out where he hid the painting and instead they kill him. How's that for stupidity?"

"How did—" I cleared my throat. "How did Jesse get involved in the first place?" I couldn't imagine this. I really couldn't.

He looked straight at me, an unreadable expression on his face.

The boat bounced over the waves. "Jesse, Jesse, what can I tell you about your dear departed?" He opened his palms in a gesture of surrender. "He wanted money for his precious business and was happy enough bringing a case of rum up here from my buddy in Nassau for a little cash, but when I told him after the fourth delivery that the boxes contained cocaine, he got all holier-than-thou. Said he's going to the cops. I offered to cut him in on the action. Since he and Bryce were desperate for cash to fund their company, they did that for a while, but then your husband has a 'come-to-Jesus' moment and decides he can't do it anymore. Caused some strife between him and Bryce—who's still working for me, by the way. After he got the painting, Jessie started making noises again about going to the cops. Bryce and I, we tried to talk some sense into him, but he wouldn't go for it."

"Bryce," I said. Jesse's partner Bryce. Amanda's ex-husband.

"As we speak, he's off on a business trip to South America."

"What about Peter?" I kept asking questions while twining my fingers.

"Stupid kid figured it out. Threatened to go to the police. You should've seen him groveling on that boat. I hated getting his blood all over that beautiful teak. Such a shame. Have you seen the boat lately? All torn apart." He made a tsk-tsk sound with his mouth.

I closed my eyes. I couldn't bear this. "And Roxanne Wishert? You killed her, too? Why?"

"I had to apply a little charm to keep Kricket in line once she halfway guessed what I was doing. I had to know what she knew and what she was planning. She wasn't supposed to die. Dom's grandfather has a mushroom farm. He swore these magic mushrooms were like a truth serum. They'd knock her out and she'd tell us what she knew. Dom went aboard to chat her up. How did we know those stupid girls would trade places? And how did I know the mushrooms would kill her instead of make her talk? That was Dom's stupid fault."

"Why did the girls trade places?"

"Roxanne was a know-it-all. She worked for a PI, so she figured she can use her PI know-how to find the painting on the boat."

I looked down. "Instead, she was murdered. Why Dom? Why not Scott?"

"Kricket knew Scott. That part of what I told you was true. She and Scott had a tumultuous relationship. Dom was new. Dom had never met Kricket. All he was hired for was his mushrooms."

"And to kill my husband," I reminded him.

"Yeah, I guess there was that." I hated looking at his face right now. Finally, I said. "Why, Tom, why would you do all this?"

"Because we deserve it. I deserve it. Those rich guys who own the boats, they have it all, and we work harder than they ever do. And some of them treat us like dirt."

"It's what we chose," I reminded him.

His eyes flashed. "It's not what I chose!"

"Where are we going?"

"Emmeline, Emmeline, Emmeline, I had such high hopes for the two of us. I told you I made a study of you? That much is true. Every moment I spent with you has been about figuring out whether I could bring you on board. When I figured I'd never win you over I knew I had to kill you."

"It was you." I spat. "You cut my hose line!"

He put up his hands and grinned. "Guilty as charged."

"And the little bowl of mushrooms? That was a nice touch."

"I thought so."

While I stewed, he went to the stern and pulled in the inflatable and removed the oars.

I said, "You're the one who tore apart my boat looking for that flash drive, not Kricket."

"Yep. Right again."

"You searched my house, too."

I barely had time to react before he lifted me under my arms and threw me overboard onto the inflatable. I fell heavily on my ankle and groaned out in pain.

"You won't get away with this!" I yelled to him. "Ben knows I'm here. He knows exactly what you're doing!"

He laughed. "Ben does not know you're here. Don't lie. I've been monitoring the phone, remember?

He untied the stern line and let me go. The inflatable bucked on the waves as he cocked his fingers like a gun at me. I remembered that Scott had done the same gesture when he'd left the restaurant where Tom and I had been having dinner. Dinner! How could I have been fooled by this man?

Tom called to me over the wind, "Too bad you couldn't get your priorities straight, Em. We could have had a lot of fun together. I know you enjoyed kissing me."

Then he aimed his gun and shot at me. He turned his back and took off noisily to land, his wake a straight line behind him. He didn't look back.

That was his mistake. Maybe it was the rough water, maybe it was the angle of the gun, but somehow he missed the remaining inflated pontoons. Instead, the bullet hit the already shot outboard.

Helpless, I lay along the bottom of the boat, hugging the pontoon. He intended for me to die out here. Yet, I wasn't going to go without a fight. Tom was right about one thing, I am feisty!

Keeping myself low in the boat, and clinging to the side which wasn't deflated and sloshing over with cold sea water, I analyzed my situation. I still had my fanny pack with a screw driver and a pair of small side cutters. Underneath the seat of this little inflatable was an attached bag. Before my fingers were too cold, I managed to get the zipper open. There was a canvas tarp at the bottom. Good. Maybe that little thing will keep me warm. I pulled it out. I felt along the sides of the boat. Underneath the still inflated pontoon was a boat hook. Thrill upon thrills it was the expandable kind! Tom may have taken the oars, but he missed this little gem, hidden as it was. With cold and shaky fingers, I wedged it underneath me. My ankle was protesting loudly, but I didn't have time for that now. I had a job to do.

With cold, and wet fingers I untied the bow line from the front of the inflatable. I also managed to find a few pieces of odd line here and there in the bottom of the boat and in the bag under the seat. These I lined up on the floor in front of me.

I put the hook from the boat hook in a corner grommet of the tarp, and fastened it securely with a small piece of line. Then, using the grommets as they were available, or making small holes along the side of the tarp if I needed to, I entwined pieces of string and line to the boat hook. I did this down the length of the boat hook until the entire tarp was fastened to it. I got out the flashlight, turned it on and secured it to the top.

Then I set the entire thing upright, and tried as best I could to secure it to the bottom of this saggy boat. It might not get me sailing anywhere, but it would make me a bit more visible.

Then I leaned back against the most sheltered part of the pontoon and sang songs to myself and wondered what it felt like to die.

Eventually, I fell into a Jesse dream.

Chapter 40

It's sunny, pleasant and I am standing and holding firm to the tiller of a sailboat. I am relishing the absolute warmness. The mainsail is full of air, and the jib is powering the boat forward. It's a strong wind, something they call a "fresh breeze," which makes it just about perfect for a Caribbean afternoon. I can't stop smiling.

Jesse is here. We are sailing together. This time it isn't my old catboat, but it's the boat I have now, *Wanderer,* a boat that Jesse and I have sailed often. I am at the helm, and he is winching in the jib.

I look at him down at winch level, and I long to pull the ball cap from his head, touch his hair and pull him toward me. I want to see him laugh again, the way he used to. I decide to go down below to make some coffee for the two of us. Jesse always likes coffee on the boat. He, coffee snob that he is, says it tastes better out on the water. I always laugh when he says that. I laugh today. My Jesse. Such a coffee nut.

Down below, I decide to put together a plate of cheese and oysters, maybe even some wine instead of coffee. I call up to ask him. Do you want wine instead of coffee?

The boat lurches violently, and I lose my footing. The wine bottle shatters on the sole. Red everywhere. Like blood. The spilt plate of oysters are not oysters but are mushrooms.

Cold. Need a jacket. Can't find a jacket. Keep slipping in the blood. Something is strange. This cabin is not familiar to me. It is not the inside of *Wanderer.* There are no jackets down here, just blood on every wall. Splattered everywhere. Drops of it on the portholes, ribs of it snaking down the sides.

When I look out into the cockpit, I can't see Jesse.

Overboard?

Jesse! Jesse!

Em!

He is calling me. But I can't see where he is.

Jesse? Jesse! I call out to him. *I can't see you.*

Em! Captain Ridge! Wake up! Are you okay?

I open my eyes, try to figure out what I am looking at. I close them again when I can't make sense of things.

No! I am with Jesse again. We are sailing. I want to be with Jesse. I want to stay with Jesse.

Em! Someone calls to me again.

Hold on, Captain Ridge. Come back to us!

Something soft is around me. I smell damp wool in my nose. Can't breathe. A blanket. I am being carried, held by strong arms. *Jesse?*

I am inside some sort of structure that smells like diesel and fish. Again, I open my eyes. I am in the cabin of a lobster boat, and Ben is there, and he is looking down at me, his face very close to mine.

"You gave us quite a scare," he says. "As soon as we found Kricket and Rob, or should I say Dominic, we began looking for you. Dominic isn't talking and Kricket said you were tied up and on an island. We've been looking for you for a long time."

I look out the companionway and the sky is dusky dark. Night? I can make no sense of things and then I remember. A barely viable inflatable, a tarp raised as a sail on a boat hook. And being so thirsty. And cold. So cold. And then Jesse came and took me aboard his boat and we went sailing.

"Everyone was looking for you. We alerted all the fisherman. As soon as a lobsterman saw your blue tarp sail boat and called us, I knew it had to be you."

I am beginning to remember.

"Tom," I manage. "He...he..."

"We know what he did. We've apprehended Dominic Blake, who you would know as Rob Stikles, and Kricket Patterson. We've had our eye on Tom for a while."

"He was on Scott's boat."

"We'll find him. It's only a matter of time."

I look at Ben and wonder. Tom could be, even now, sailing off across to Nova Scotia and on up to Newfoundland and points beyond with a new name and a new passport.

"You have to—find him. He knows how to get away."

"We will. Right now our priority is to get you in and warm. And get that ankle of yours looked after."

But I am shaking my head. No. *He's gone. He's gone now.* I know him. *The easiest way to say off the grid.* "He's dangerous."

"We know." The boat is moving quickly through the heavy chop, the diesel engine noisy on this lobster boat.

I drift off again smelling lobster and the sea and salt and seaweed. *I dream of Jesse.*

Epilogue

I was in the hospital for three days. Many warm-water baths and heated blankets were needed to slowly raise my body temperature to acceptable human levels. For a long time, I simply could not stop shivering. I wondered if the shivering had as much to do with the ice that had settled in my soul as the cold in my body. My ankle was indeed broken. I have a lovely pink cast on it now, thanks to Isabelle who insisted on pink. I think I would have settled for black or white.

The doctor told me I'm lucky, considering how much stress I put on it after it was injured. In two weeks, I get a walking cast. Meanwhile, I hobble around on crutches.

Ben told me that when they found me I was clutching one pontoon for dear life. They had to pry my arms away from it while I screamed at them to let me go. I remember none of that. They said that the tarp and the light had been a beacon they could see. The doctors told me I was lucky to be alive after foundering out there for seven hours. Everyone kept telling me that, keeps telling me that now. If Tom's bullet had burst the pontoon, I would surely be dead by now. I was lucky, so lucky. Everyone said that, too.

Except I don't feel so lucky.

When I was ready to go home, Dot and Isabelle came and drove me to where I mostly sit on my couch now, my foot elevated while I read books or gaze out of my windows. I am trying not to read books about the sea.

My friends are determined that I get better. Dot and Isabelle come over regularly with casseroles while EJ brings thick steaks and chops and baked or mashed potatoes. Somehow I like EJ's offerings better. During the first week, Valerie was over every day with cooked lobster. Even Amanda came. She was as shocked as I was about her ex-husband's involvement in the smuggling ring. We decided we will keep in touch. I hope she means it this time.

What I spend my time thinking about is how close I came to dying on the water. Being out on the water is an unnatural act. We are not dolphins. We are land creatures. When we take to the sea in all manner of invented means and contraptions, no matter how safe we try to make them, we go to a place we are not meant to be. Some of us don't come back. I have known sailors, good sailors who have taken off on happy trips, and no one hears from them again. Sudden storms, rogue waves, these are the things we deal with.

I know more people than I care to number who have died at sea. Friends of mine. People I know. Young people. The sea doesn't care. The ocean bed is littered with our bodies.

It's been all over the news, of course, but I am trying not to pay attention. The Pattersons will be moving to California. The deeply grieving Wisherts will move on. We all do. Eventually. Even me.

My parents and both my sisters have called several times. I've been nice to them. I have this idea that they, in their own way, sort of like me, and my mother, in her own way, is even sort of proud of me. Maybe there will be a time when we will all be friends. I'm toying with the idea of going out to see them as soon as I'm ambulatory.

Kricket came to see me. She brought me a teddy bear with a sailboat on its T-shirt. She was sad and tearful and felt guilty about her friend Roxanne. I tried to tell her it wasn't her fault. But I know about guilt. It's what I feel about Peter. And even Jessie.

Kricket told me she was sorry about my phone, but she had to have some insurance that I wouldn't call Tom right away. That's how scared she was.

"Why didn't you tell me what you knew about Tom?" I asked her.

She was several seconds before answering. "Would you have believed me if I did?"

What she had told me about Jesse's gun was true. He was so frightened at the end of it all, that he had purchased one and used an old picture for the registration. He had taken it when he went out that night after our fight. He intended to confront Tom, and then go to the police. Unfortunately, Tom was able to wrest the gun from him, killed him and hired Scott and Dominic to make sure it looked like an accident out on the bay. Kricket was able to find the gun in Tom's condo and stole it. She hid it and the registration for two years.

Dr. Declan Meyer even came to see me, pulling up next to my house in a cherry red two-door convertible that seemed so out of character for him that I couldn't stop smiling. He called it his pride and joy.

"I had no idea you were into cars," I said.

He grinned.

He confirmed for me that yes, the specifics of my husband's death had been manipulated. I found it difficult to believe that Tom wielded so much power, but Dr. Meyer shook his head and said, "You would not believe what I see, sometimes."

Two weeks after Ben and the lobster fisherman rescued me from Liam's wrecked boat, Tom was found holed up in a cabin in New Hampshire. Ben came and told me this. I hated Tom for what he did to my husband. I hated Tom for what he tried to do to me.

I believe Jesse did try to do the right thing but had gotten in over his head with Tom. Yes, Tom was right. So many of us sailors are guilty of smuggling now and again. We'll take a couple of extra bottles of rum from Jamaica through Customs. We'll bring coffee and Cuban cigars home, wrapped up in plastic bags and hidden in our bilges.

But Jesse loved me. This is something I hang onto. This is something I know now. My husband always loved me. That knowledge makes me warm and secure.

Ben drives out to see me a lot, and I find I looked forward to his visits. We sit on my front porch, my leg up on a footstool and he tells me all about the smuggling operation that Tom Mallen had headed up, the tentacles of which are still being uncovered. It was worse than I had imagined.

Ben tells me all of this while Dot and Isabelle wash my dishes and vacuum my floors, and EJ fries me whole chickens on his porch in goose fat.

Ben is here today, and we are talking, careful to avoid personal things. We are always careful to avoid personal things. We are sitting on the ramshackle couch that is a part of my front porch in the summer, and drinking glasses of iced tea. It's warm today. Summer has truly come to Maine. He never asks me about my relationship with Tom, and I never tell him what I discovered about him online. I don't ask about a wife and child, I never do. That is his story, and his story alone to tell. Maybe he will tell me one day. Maybe he won't.

I know how hard it is to tell the stories of your life sometime. I have told mine here, and it hasn't been easy

Sometimes I wonder what it will take for me to move on from

Jesse. I wonder how long I will dream. I should tell Ben about the dreams. I don't. Not yet.

Ben takes my hand then, and we sit there and hold hands and watch the water until the sun sets behind us.

What can possibly go wrong in the Bermuda Triangle?

For the past two weeks, boat delivery Captain Em Ridge has been ferrying a well-known TV conspiracy theorist around the waters of the Bermuda Triangle. She is tired of his tales of reptilian governments, middle-earth civilizations, and of course, all his theories about the Bermuda Triangle. Em just wants to finish up this assignment, get paid, and head back to her home in Maine.

But a chance sighting finds them aboard a 'ghost' sailboat. The salon is set neatly for supper, wine in the glasses, pots on the stove, bread on the table and not a soul aboard. Worse, she knows this boat. When a black cat slinks noiselessly around her feet, Em's alarm hikes up to horror. Has someone purposely set this boat out here? Is it a warning? To her? Finding this boat plunges Em into a decades old mystery that threatens not only her, but her entire family.

The Bitter End is the second book in the highly acclaimed Em Ridge Mystery Series which began with Night Watch. The adventure continues for widowed boat captain, Em Ridge.

Turn the page to start reading Chapter One of *The Bitter End*, Book Two in the Em Ridge Mystery Series

THE BITTER END

An Em Ridge Mystery

Book Two

Chapter 1

The speck out on the horizon was still. Too still. And it definitely contained alien life. At least that was the loud conclusion of Dr. Papa Hoho as he gasped and panted his way up the ladder to the flybridge. His binoculars bounced around his neck, and all that wild red hair of his was caught up around his face like dandelion fluff. So far, the search for the Entrance to the Gates of Hell had not gone well. We had been out here on the body of water known as the Bermuda Triangle for twelve days now. For twelve days, we had seen nothing but ordinary boats doing ordinary things on this very ordinary body of water.

I could have told him it was ordinary. I've sailed these waters more times than I can count, and I've never encountered anything but ordinary. Nevertheless, he'd hired me to ferry him all around the Bermuda Triangle for two weeks in July, and I needed the job. I would have chosen another time, though. I would have picked a month that wasn't so hot. I would have gone for a month in which hurricanes didn't threaten every other week, but you take what you can get when you have a job like mine.

Papa—as he'd asked us to call him—plopped down in the plush, white leather chair beside me and pointed. "You see that boat or whatever that thing is over there? I been watching it. Hasn't moved a bit. We been out here searching for almost—what is it—two weeks? This could be it."

"The Gates of Hell?" I tried to keep the sarcasm out of my voice. For twelve long days, I had tried with varying degrees of success to keep the sarcasm out of my voice.

I'd been watching it, too. I'd even tried hailing it on the radio. Nothing yet. Either we were too far away or their radio was turned off.

"Head over in that direction, will ya? I got a good feeling about this one."

"Already on it," I said. Unlike Papa, I didn't have a good feeling about this one. As we moved ever closer, inside of me began to grow a fearful queasiness. I was watching the speck grow to be a boat, a sailboat to be precise—a sailboat with a torn mainsail hanging limply in the becalmed air. I tried the radio again. No reply.

Behind me, Liam, my young crew member, was leaning against a stanchion and watching it, too. Down on the bow, Jason, the photographer, was trying to set up his tripod. Papa grunted. The Hawaiian shirt he wore today featured a snarl of pink and orange flowers. He always wore these huge shirts unbuttoned, so we got to enjoy all his reddish chest hairs, the folds of fat on his belly, and the scabbing and peeling sunburn on his formerly white neck.

"Can't you get this thing to go any faster?" he said to me. "I want to get over there. See what that thing is."

"It's a boat."

"Yeah, I know it's a boat, but this could be it."

"Aliens?"

He pointed at me. "Don't make fun."

"You want to go faster? Maybe Jason should move all his equipment from the bow. Wouldn't want him losing that camera overboard."

Jason was a gangly twenty-something who wore jeans and t-shirts with the names of movie sets he'd worked on scrawled across the backs of them. Today's shirt was black. Most of them were black. Black. Let that sink in. Mid-July off the Miami coastline and he's wearing black tees and jeans. Made of jean material. Papa went back down and the two of them hefted the equipment to the stern. When they were safely off the bow, I pushed the throttles forward and could feel the power underneath me as we surged up on plane. The sudden wind felt good against my hot neck. I hailed the boat again on the radio. Again, no answer.

Liam came and sat beside me on the chair that Papa had vacated and said dryly, "I don't think there are aliens over there."

I looked over at him.

"But it could be the reptile people."

I laughed. We both did. We'd heard all these stories and more the past couple of weeks.

Liam is the fifteen-year-old son of Jeff and Valerie, my neighbors from two-doors-down. When Liam had overheard me tell his parents about my newest boat captaining job, his ears had perked up and he'd asked all sorts of questions. In the evening, he'd accosted me down on the dock in front of our houses. I'd been scrubbing out the propane compartment on my sailboat, Wanderer.

"Hey, Em, you need any crew for that thing you're doing?"

Before I had a chance to reply, he'd said, "It'll be in summer. I wouldn't have school then. I could go if you needed me. If I would be allowed. I could help out."

"Won't your mom and dad need you for the lobstering?"

"It wouldn't be that long, would it?"

"Two weeks. I'll talk to your parents, and then I'll have to talk to the TV people. How about I promise you that?"

"Cool."

I'm a boat captain. What I do is deliver boats. Mostly, I deliver luxury yachts owned by the rich and famous, from point A to point B. These wealthy people like the status symbol of owning big boats, but usually, they have no clue about boat ownership or operation, or actually being out on the water, so they hire people like me. Many of my captain friends have permanent jobs on high-end yachts and get to go all over the world. So far, in my budding career, all I've gotten are short hauls. Which is okay with me. Even though I love the ocean, love being out here, I would miss my big, old dog Rusty and my little cottage house at the very end of Chalk Spit Island near Portland, Maine.

Sometimes, I get hired to take people places by boat. That was the nature of this work. I'd gotten the call from Papa three months ago, shortly after Rusty and I had returned home from Florida. I'd found work in a marina down there for five months during the winter. It being Florida, I use the term "winter" loosely. I'd also managed to get a couple of jobs taking yachts across the Gulf Stream to the Bahamas. Always fun.

While in Florida, I'd put a lot of feelers out for work. I'd nailed up my sailing résumé at every marina I visited. I hadn't been home a week before the crazy, ginger-bearded man, who was now leaning over the port railing, called me.

"Do you know who I am?" had been the second thing he'd said to me, the first being, "I would like to hire you."

"Sorry, sir, I don't."

"Hmm." I Googled frantically. Had I ever worked for someone by that name?

"I host a highly acclaimed network television program."

"Oh." There it was, coming up on my computer screen now.

"Lots of viewers."

"I can see that." Conspiracy Theories FINALLY PROVED! was the name of the show. And yes, it did look to be quite popular.

"Do you know what the government is hiding from us?"

"No, sir, I don't." It was a weekly show. Eleven at night. Not prime time, but who cares in this streaming, TVOing world?

"Many things. Many, many things. You would be surprised."

"I'm sure I would be." Did he know what I did for a living? Hire me for what?

He was going on. "That's what I set out to prove. That and other things. I examine known conspiracy theories for their accuracy."

"Okay."

"I need to hire a boat captain."

"Really?"

"To take me all around the Bermuda Triangle. I've checked with the stars and rotation of the planets, and this summer, second week in July to be precise, is the perfect time out there."

Oh? "Oh." I could do that. It might be a hoot. "I know those waters well."

"Did you know that there's a theory that the Bermuda Triangle is the entrance to the Gates of Hell?"

I kept myself from snorting out loud. "No, sir, I did not know that."

When he told me what he intended to pay, I accepted on the spot. And that's how we happened to be out here on this July day, which was as still and as hot as a sauna on overdrive. I was beginning to believe his theory about the hot fires of the afterlife rising like steam from these waters.

Dr. Papa Hoho turned out to be as crazy as his name. For the past week and a half I'd learned we were governed by collusion of reptiles—you can tell by their eyes, he showed me pictures—and that an entire race of humanoids lived inside of our planet and that crop circles were alien prophecies of doom to come.

I never bothered with watching his show until I'd signed this contract. Then I binge watched nine episodes in a row, which left me feeling slightly queasy. Are there people out there who actually believe this?

"We won't make it to 2050," he had told me a few days ago while we'd been up here on the flybridge eating lunch. "They have something planned."

"Who?" I'd turned. "The government?"

"No, the aliens. Our days on this planet are numbered."

"Well, if I'm still here in 2050, I'll remember your words."

"The world will be gone by then. You mark my words. We can't last much longer."

"I suppose not."

All we'd done in twelve days was burn gas, lots of gas, thousands and thousands of dollars' worth of gas as we sped all over the calm waters in the heat. Each night, we'd head back to the marina in Miami where Papa put us all up in a five-star hotel. So far, we hadn't stayed out overnight on the boat, although he'd said that might be a possibility. I was getting the idea that he liked mingling with the tourists at the bars and luxuriating in his celebrity status. He would find being out on the boat at night far too lonely and strange.

Every morning at seven thirty, we'd be down eating our fifty-dollar breakfasts and then we'd head down to the boat. Thermos carafes of coffee, lunch, snacks, and drinks were delivered by the hotel staff and stowed in the appropriate fridges and coolers onboard Townie, the fifty-one-foot Sea Ray he'd chartered.

At first, it was fun, but after twelve days, I was becoming tired of this pompous man. I was getting anxious for this assignment to be over. I hated the way he brought his face too close to mine when he spoke, the way I felt I had to continually back up to be away from the line of spittle fire. I hated the way he continually made references to all the money he was making. I was bored with hearing about how many online followers he had, and how next year his TV show was going to be even bigger and better and be distributed to more networks than ever. Oh, yes, and that's not even to mention the constant talk about his seven-figure book advance. He dropped names of celebrities ad nauseam. I tried not to let him see how unimpressed I was. I needed—really needed—the money. Maybe I'd even be able to afford that new sail for Wanderer I'd been eyeing. Just two more days, I kept saying to myself. Just two more days.

And now, Papa was scrambling back up the ladder toward me and barking out commands. "Jason, get that camera up here, will ya?

We'll get some shots from up here. Hurry it up. Slow down the boat a little as we're coming in, will ya?"

We were closer to the disabled sailboat now, and through the binoculars, I focused in on the stern. The name across the back had been removed. Papa continued to snap out orders. "Get this shot! Get this coming in. Get my face on that shot. Come on. Hurry. We can't let this one go. This could be the mother-load. Film me now. I need a shot of me with that boat in the distance. Right now, Jason. Wait. My face is too sweaty."

He dumped a bottle of water on his hands and rubbed it over his head. "Get me a towel, dammit," he yelled to no one in particular.

Liam found a small cloth on the instrument panel and handed it to him.

"Greasy, sweaty face," he mumbled. "I can't be on TV with this greasy, sweaty face."

I said, "People will understand it's hot."

I was glad I was a bit upwind from Papa. His odiferousness got to be overwhelming in this heat, but at least he'd buttoned up his shirt.

"Hey," Papa said to me, "when we get a bit closer, slow down. I want to get pictures as we come up on it."

"Someone could be in trouble," I said. "I've been trying to reach them."

He shook his head. "I don't care. This is perfect. This is so perfect." And then, more to himself, he said, "I knew this would happen. I just had a feeling that today was going to be my lucky day." He grinned as he pranced around the flybridge, looking, for all the world, like an overgrown garden gnome. "Twelve has always been my lucky number. Did I ever tell you? And this is the twelfth day." He stopped. "I should check that numerology. Maybe I can figure that in somehow. Did you happen to watch the episode on numerology?"

When I showed no signs of answering his question or slowing down, Papa repeated, "I told you I want to come in dead slow. Now."

I ignored him. I held my hands tightly to the wheel. I stared straight ahead, my mouth dry.

"Captain Ridge. I said explicitly that you were to slow down as we came to the boat. Jason," he barked, "keep the camera going. I want to get some shots of us coming in on this boat."

I mustered up the courage to say, "No. I can't do that. There could be people hurt on that boat. This may be your TV show, but as captain, my first obligation is to whoever's aboard that vessel."

I was surprised he actually listened to me, but then I noticed the camera was up and running and aimed in my direction. He'd recorded what I'd said. Great. And then the camera was turned to Papa, and he was talking, talking and pointing. I had no idea what he was saying, and at this point, I didn't care.

"Jason," I said interrupting Papa's soliloquy. "You and Liam go on down. Get the fenders ready. Get him to show you what to do. We'll be alongside soon."

Papa answered for him. "Jason's busy with me up here."

I stood my ground. "He's needed down there. We have a boat possibly in danger, people possibly in peril, and we need everyone to help."

Papa turned quietly to Jason. "Peril. I like that word. You get all that recorded? Her tone? It'll make for good TV. Go on then." He pointed at me. "You better obey the mighty captain." He winked, and I turned my face away.

As we approached the boat, my hands shook. It was hot, tremendously so, but I felt a chill go through me as I looked down into the open cockpit of the silent boat. We were close enough that I could see two half-filled wine glasses set neatly on the snack table in the sunshine. Between them was what looked like a plate of crackers and cheese. And napkins folded into triangles. I kept my breathing steady as I idled in. I tried the radio again. No answer.

Down on the starboard side, Liam was telling Jason how high to tie the fenders while Papa tried to operate the camera by himself. When I maneuvered close enough to the sailboat, Liam expertly lassoed a line to one of the forward cleats. I pushed on the bow thrusters, and we sidled easily up to the boat. Liam hopped aboard the sailboat and tied her tautly, bow and stern.

"Hello? Hello?" I kept calling down to the boat. "Hello?"

By this time, Papa, himself, was holding the camera and yelling for Jason to get everything recorded. They needed the whole thing on camera, every bit of it, right from the start. That is if Jason wanted to keep this job after this, and it wasn't looking too promising if he continually disobeyed direct orders from his boss.

I ignored all of this and descended the rear steps to the stern of Townie and instructed Liam to stay at the helm of the powerboat.

As I boarded the sailboat, a skinny, black cat emerged from the sailboat's cabin, stared at me with her bright green eyes and meowed loudly.

I grabbed hold of the rails and swallowed over and over to keep from throwing up.

I knew this cat.

I knew this boat.

I'd been aboard this boat many, many times.

Available as both eBooks and Print.

About Linda

Linda Hall spent the early years of her writing career as a journalist and freelance writer. She also worked in the field of adult literacy and wrote curriculum materials for adults reading at basic reading levels. In 1990 Linda decided to do something she'd always dreamed of doing, she began working on her first novel. The book she wrote, *The Josiah Files* was published in 1992.

Since that time she's written seventeen more mystery and suspense novels and many short stories and essays.

Most of her novels have something to do with the sea. Linda grew up in New Jersey and her love of the ocean was born there. When she was a little girl Linda remembers sitting on the shore and watching the waves and contemplating what was beyond. She could do that for hours.

Linda has roots in two countries. In 1971, she married a Canadian who loves the water just as much as she does. They moved to Canada and have lived there ever since. One of the things they enjoy is sailing. In the summer they basically move aboard their 34' sailboat, aptly named - Mystery.

Both Linda's husband Rik and Linda have achieved the rank of Senior Navigator, the highest rank possible in CPS. The U.S. sister organization is the U.S.P.S. Linda's Senior Navigator diploma hangs proudly on her office wall. What this all means is that she knows how to use a sextant and can 'theoretically' find her way home by looking at the stars.

Rik and Linda have two grown children, seven grandchildren and a very spoiled cat.

Connect with Linda
Newsletter
   http://writerhall.com/newsletter
Website
   http://writerhall.com
Facebook
   http://www.facebook.com/writerhall
Twitter
   @writerhall
   #emridgemysteries

Other books by Linda Hall

Em Ridge Mystery Series
The Bitter End (Book Two)

Short Story Collection
Strange Faces

Whisper Lake Series - Harlequin Love Inspired Suspense
Storm Warning
On Thin Ice
Critical Impact

Shadows Series - Harlequin Love Inspired Suspense
Shadows in the Mirror
Shadows at the Window
Shadows on the River

Fog Point series
Dark Water
Black Ice

Teri Blake-Addison mysteries
Steal Away
Chat Room

Coast of Maine novels
Margaret's Peace
Island of Refuge
Katheryn's Secret
Sadie's Song

The Canadian Mountie Series
August Gamble
November Veil
April Operation

Made in the
USA
Lexington, KY